Sinbad
The Legacy

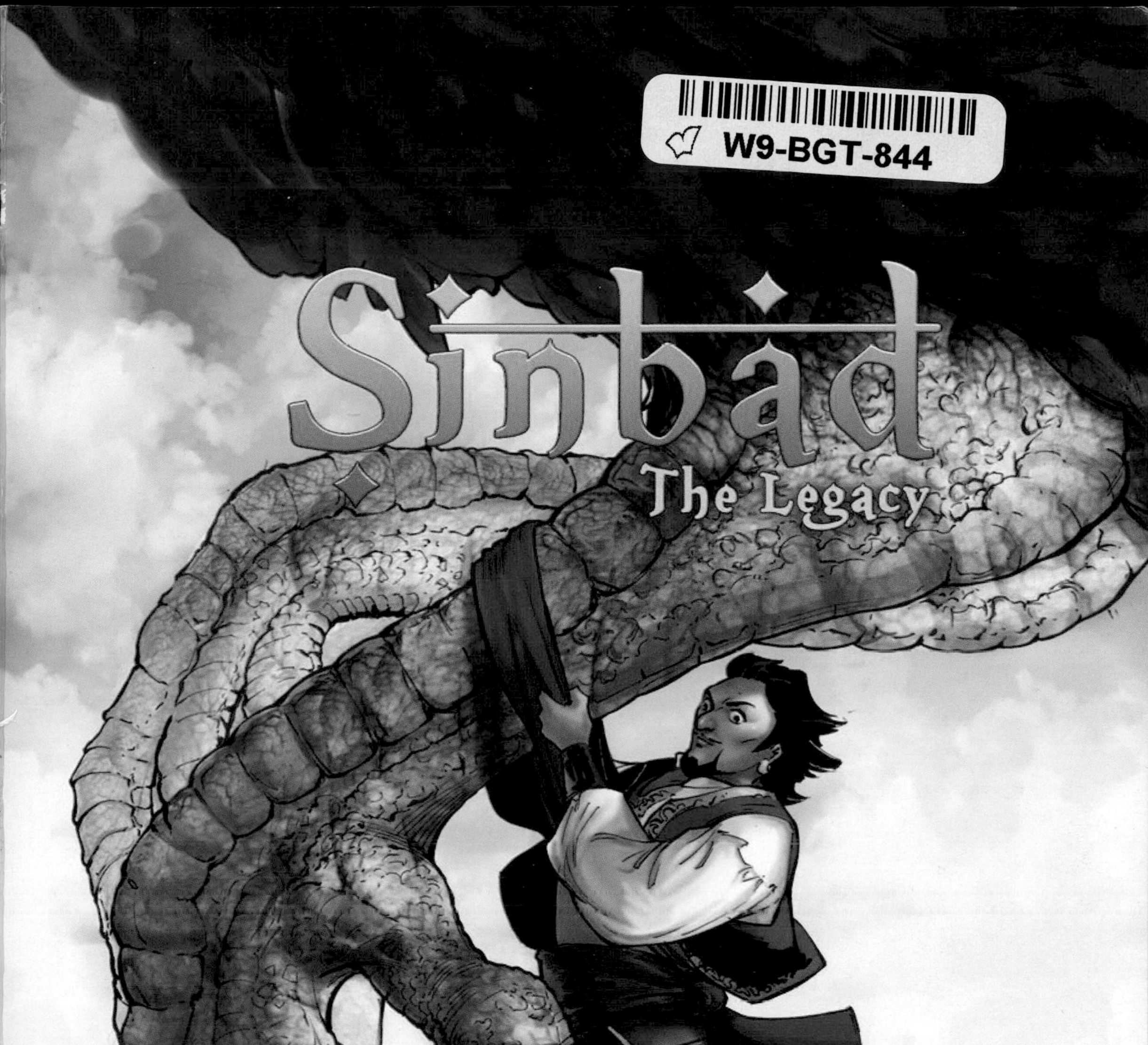

CAMPFIRE™

KALYANI NAVYUG MEDIA PVT LTD
NEW DELHI

Sinbad
The Legacy

Sitting around the Campfire, telling the story, were:

WORDSMITH **DAN JOHNSON**

ILLUSTRATOR **NARESH KUMAR**

COLORIST **AJO KURIAN**

LETTERER **LAXMI CHAND GUPTA**

EDITOR **SUKANYA MEHTA**

PRODUCTION CONTROLLER **VISHAL SHARMA**

COVER ART

ILLUSTRATION **NARESH KUMAR**

COLORISTS **PRADEEP SHERAWAT & JAYA KRISHNAN K. P.**

DESIGNER **JAYA KRISHNAN K. P.**

ART DIRECTOR **RAJESH NAGULAKONDA**

CAMPFIRE™

www.campfire.co.in

Published by Kalyani Navyug Media Pvt. Ltd.
101 C, Shiv House, Hari Nagar Ashram, New Delhi 110014, India

ISBN: 978-81-907515-5-1

Printed in India at Galaxy Offset (India) Pvt. Ltd.

Dan Johnson

Dan Johnson was born in Greensboro, NC, in the United States in 1970.

Johnson began contributing articles and news stories to local publications while attending Greensboro College. His first nationally published work came less than a year after he graduated, when he began contributing articles to *Scary Monsters Magazine*.

Since 1992, he has had articles published in *Alter Ego*, *Comic Book Market place*, *Con-Tour*, *Filmfax*, *Hogan's Alley*, *Monster Memories*, and *Monster News*. His work has also appeared in such online publications as *Monster Kid* and *Monster News Online*.

Johnson's first graphic novel, *Herc and Thor*, was published by Antarctic Press in 2006. In early 2007, Johnson joined the Campfire writing staff and has written several adaptations of classic novels for the company, including *Robinson Crusoe*, *Oliver Twist*, and *The Jungle Book*. *Sinbad* is his first original graphic novel for Campfire.

Besides writing for Campfire, Dan is also a regular contributor to the *Dennis the Menace* comic strip and *Back Issue*, a magazine devoted to the comics industry of the 1970's and 1980's.

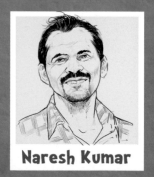

Naresh Kumar

A resident of New Delhi, India, Naresh brings an experienced hand to the drawing board. He describes himself as a seeker who is continuously trying to learn as much as he can, and his art is an expression of his curiosity about the world. His work features in a number of titles from Campfire, including *Robinson Crusoe*, *A Christmas Carol*, *The Adventures of Huckleberry Finn*, *Frankenstein*, *Perseus*, and *Kidnapped*.

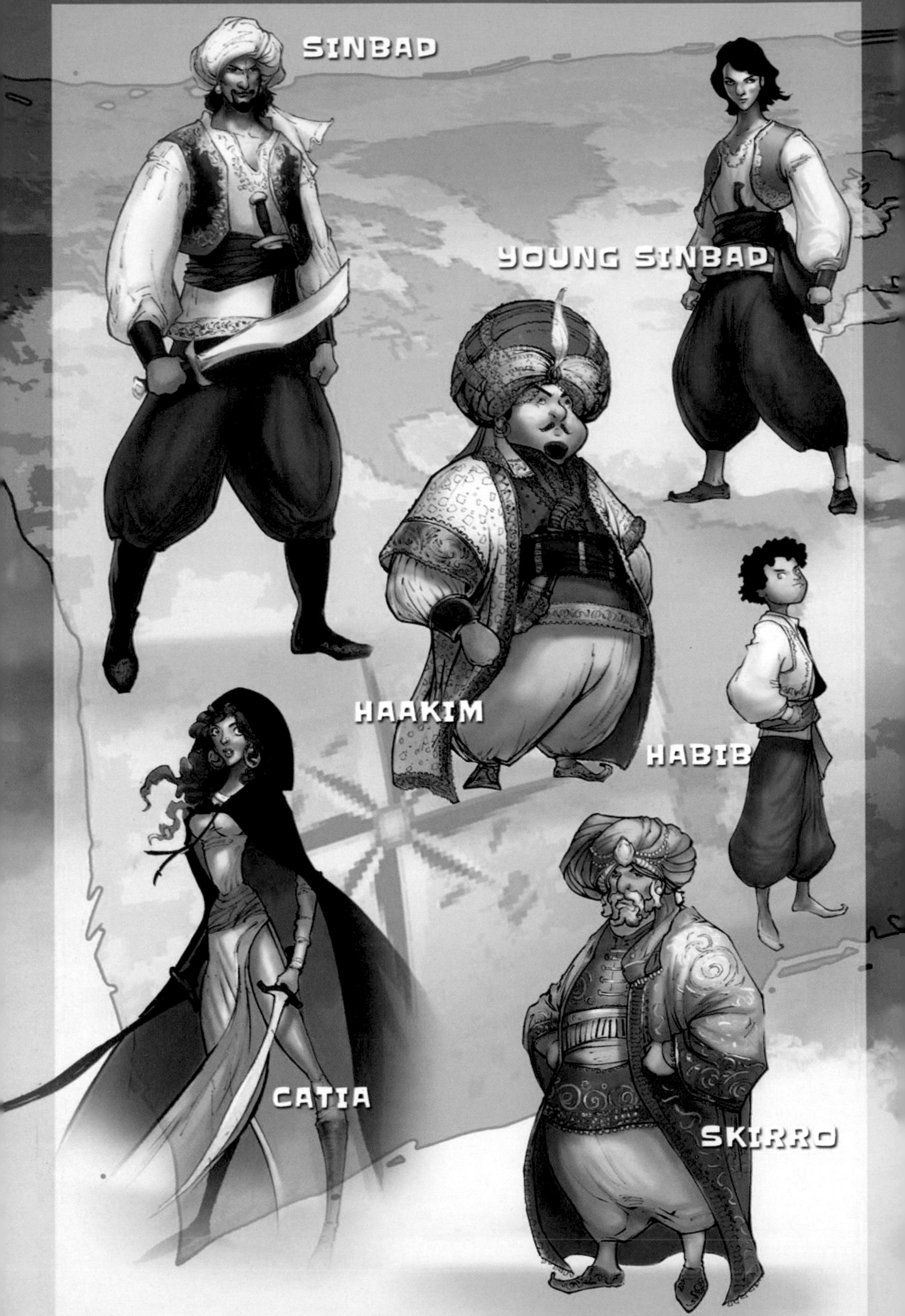
SINBAD
YOUNG SINBAD
HAAKIM
HABIB
CATIA
SKIRRO

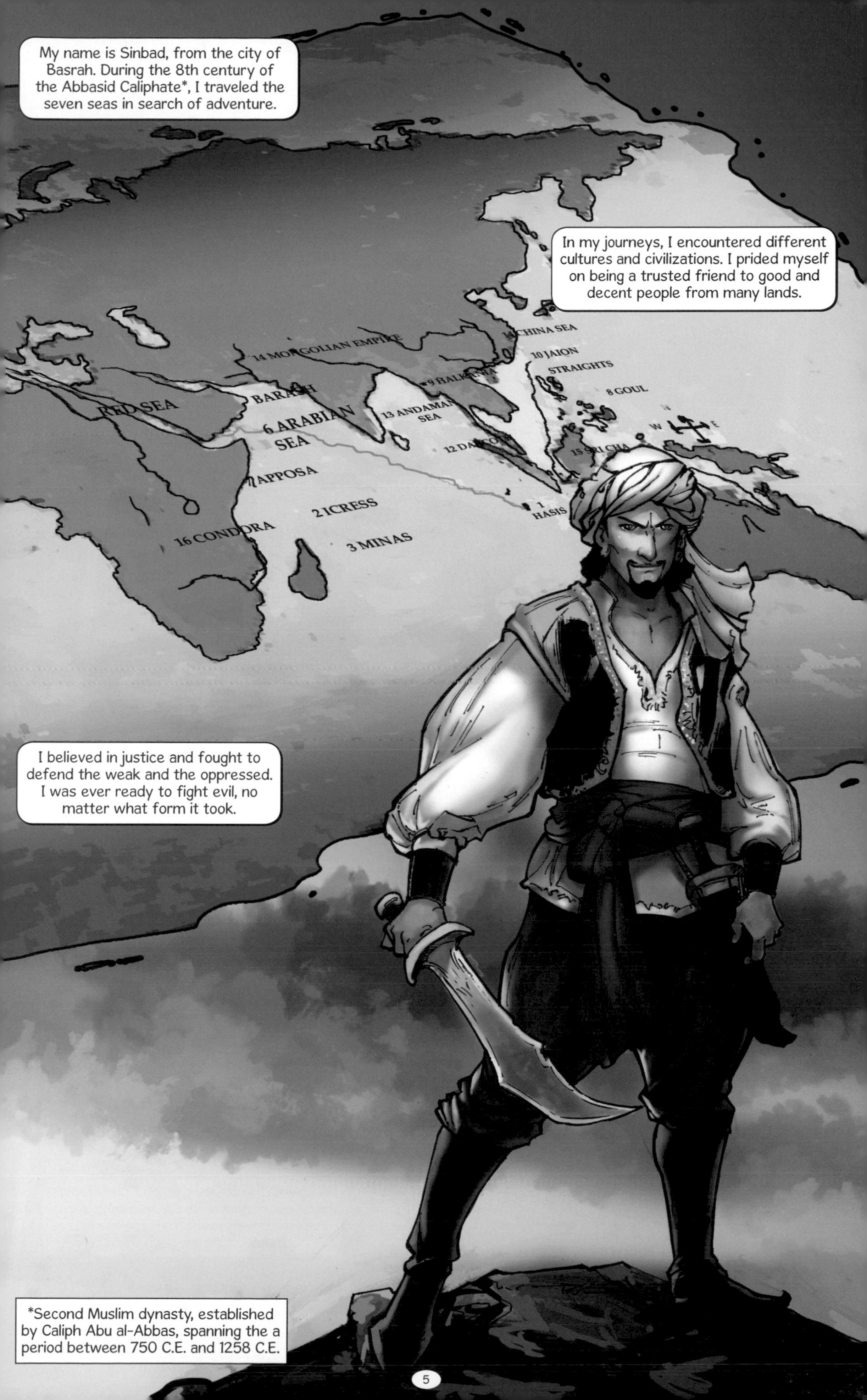
My name is Sinbad, from the city of Basrah. During the 8th century of the Abbasid Caliphate*, I traveled the seven seas in search of adventure.
In my journeys, I encountered different cultures and civilizations. I prided myself on being a trusted friend to good and decent people from many lands.
CHINA SEA
10 JAION STRAIGHTS
8 GOUL
RED SEA
6 ARABIAN SEA
13 ANDAMAN SEA
APPOSA
2 ICRESS
1 HASIS
16 CONDORA
3 MINAS
I believed in justice and fought to defend the weak and the oppressed. I was ever ready to fight evil, no matter what form it took.

*Second Muslim dynasty, established by Caliph Abu al-Abbas, spanning the a period between 750 C.E. and 1258 C.E.

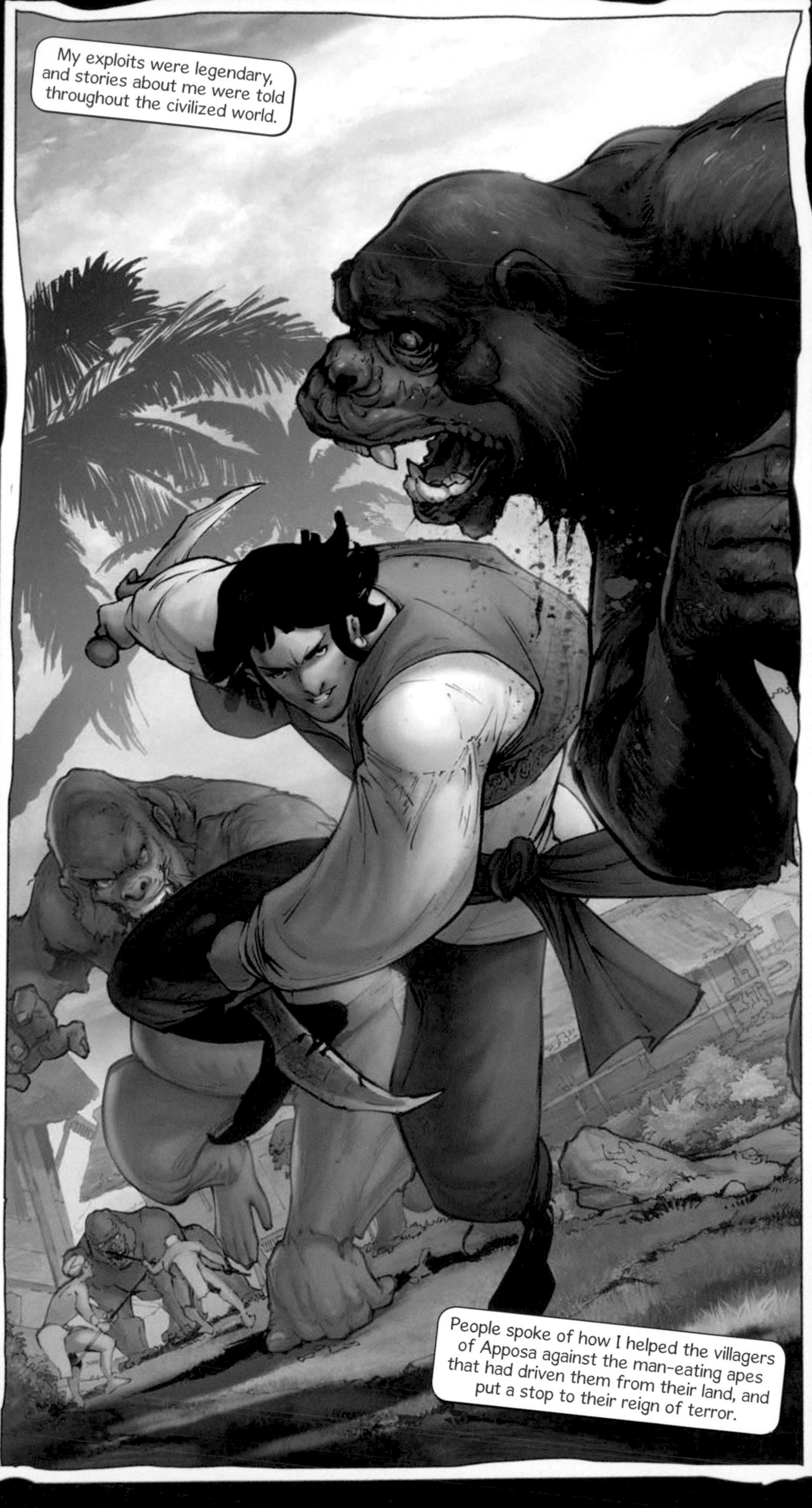
My exploits were legendary, and stories about me were told throughout the civilized world.
People spoke of how I helped the villagers of Apposa against the man-eating apes that had driven them from their land, and put a stop to their reign of terror.

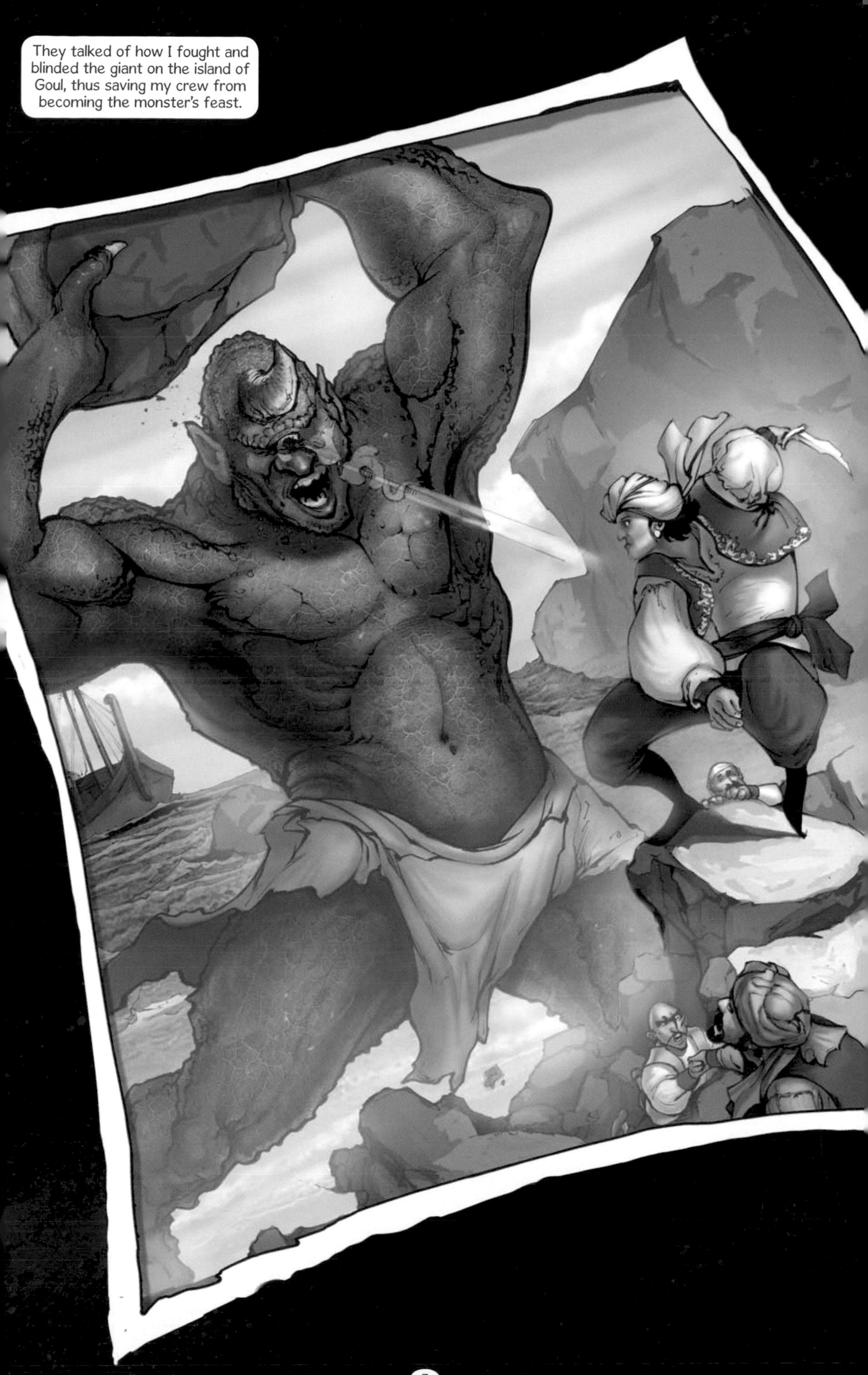
They talked of how I fought and blinded the giant on the island of Goul, thus saving my crew from becoming the monster's feast.

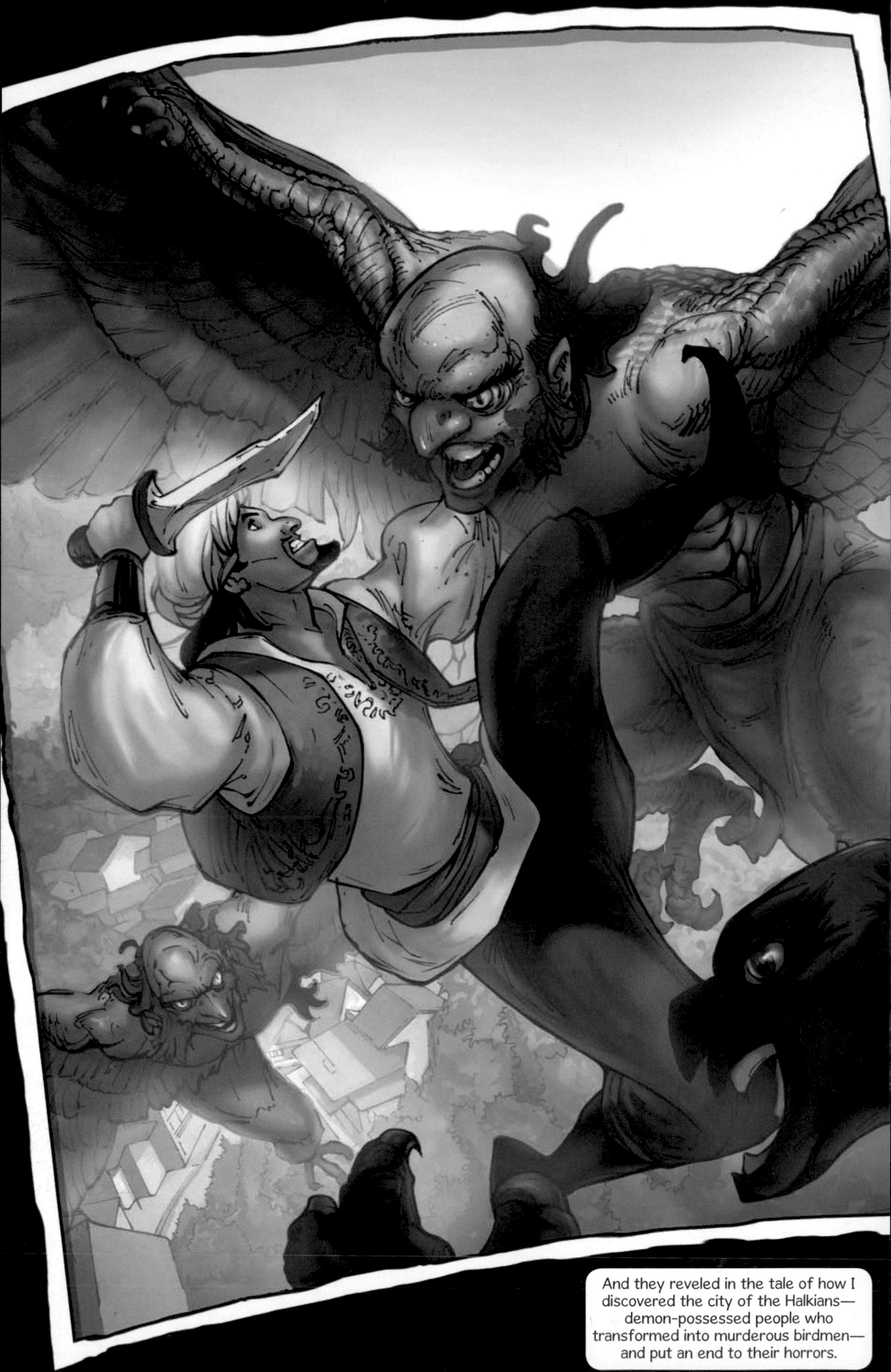
And they reveled in the tale of how I discovered the city of the Halkians—demon-possessed people who transformed into murderous birdmen—and put an end to their horrors.

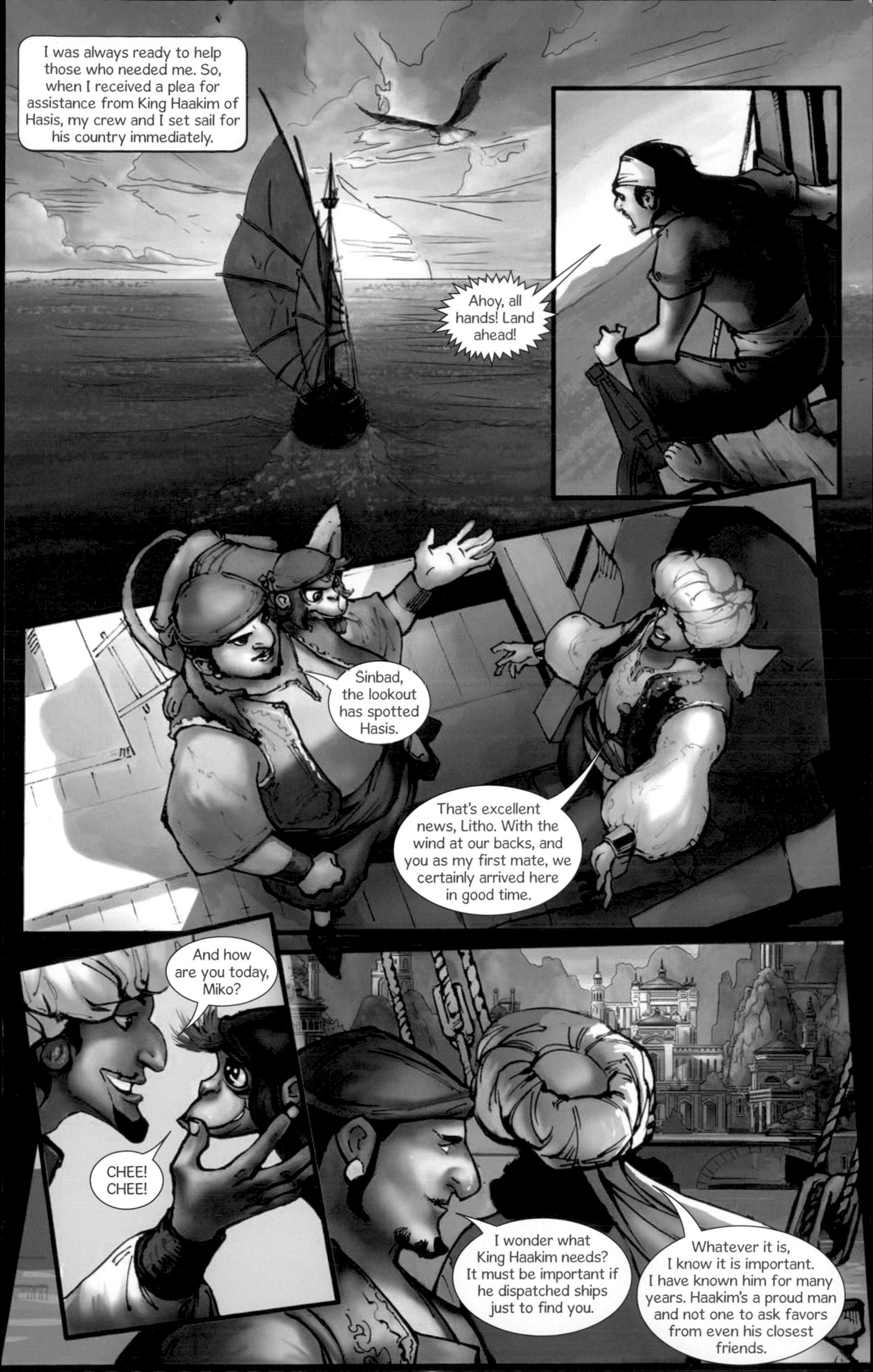
I was always ready to help those who needed me. So, when I received a plea for assistance from King Haakim of Hasis, my crew and I set sail for his country immediately.
Ahoy, all hands! Land ahead!
Sinbad, the lookout has spotted Hasis.
That's excellent news, Litho. With the wind at our backs, and you as my first mate, we certainly arrived here in good time.
And how are you today, Miko?
CHEE! CHEE!
I wonder what King Haakim needs? It must be important if he dispatched ships just to find you.
Whatever it is, I know it is important. I have known him for many years. Haakim's a proud man and not one to ask favors from even his closest friends.

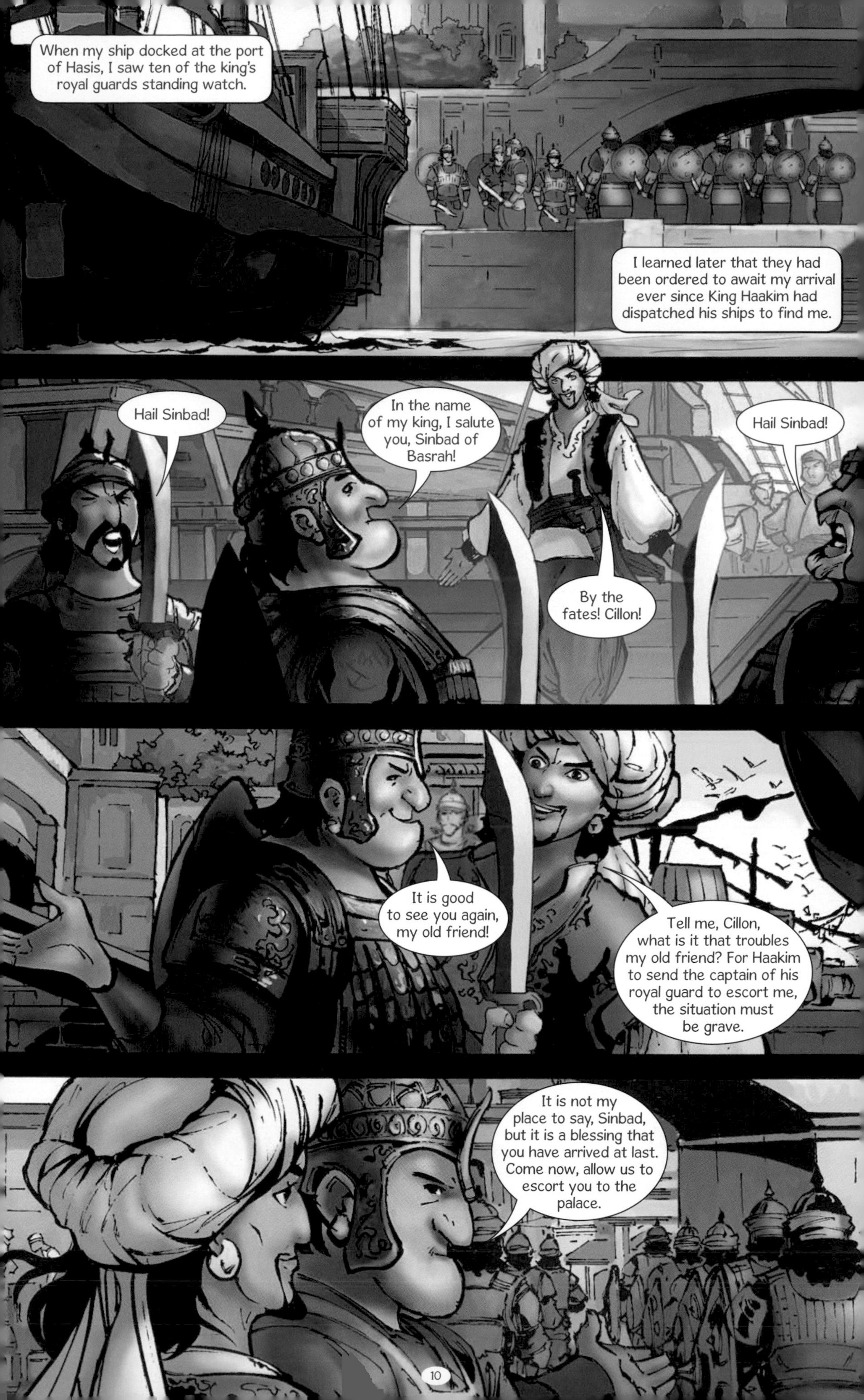
When my ship docked at the port of Hasis, I saw ten of the king's royal guards standing watch.
I learned later that they had been ordered to await my arrival ever since King Haakim had dispatched his ships to find me.
Hail Sinbad!
In the name of my king, I salute you, Sinbad of Basrah!
Hail Sinbad!
By the fates! Cillon!
It is good to see you again, my old friend!
Tell me, Cillon, what is it that troubles my old friend? For Haakim to send the captain of his royal guard to escort me, the situation must be grave.
It is not my place to say, Sinbad, but it is a blessing that you have arrived at last. Come now, allow us to escort you to the palace.

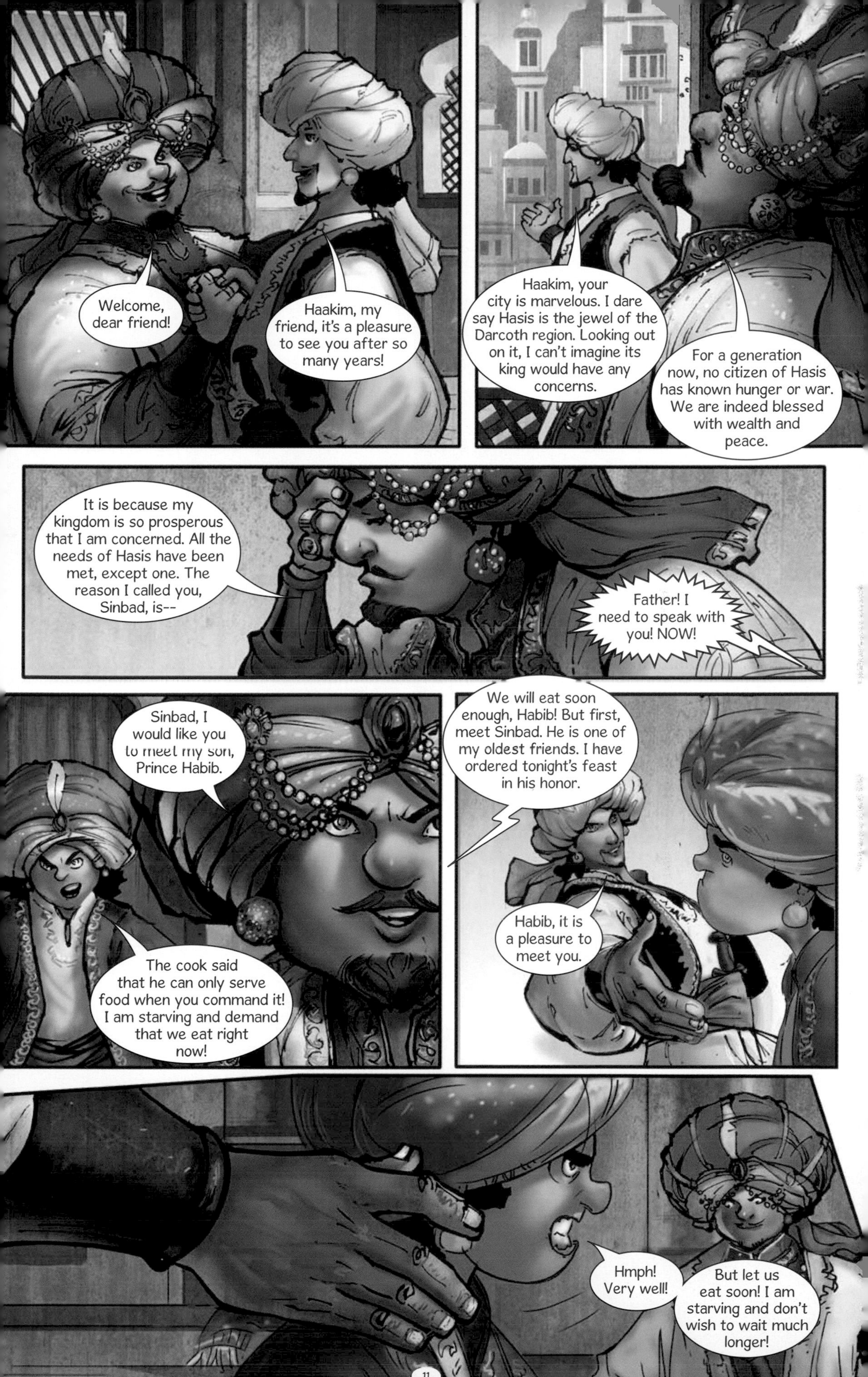

Welcome, dear friend!
Haakim, my friend, it's a pleasure to see you after so many years!
Haakim, your city is marvelous. I dare say Hasis is the jewel of the Darcoth region. Looking out on it, I can't imagine its king would have any concerns.
For a generation now, no citizen of Hasis has known hunger or war. We are indeed blessed with wealth and peace.
It is because my kingdom is so prosperous that I am concerned. All the needs of Hasis have been met, except one. The reason I called you, Sinbad, is--
Father! I need to speak with you! NOW!
Sinbad, I would like you to meet my son, Prince Habib.
The cook said that he can only serve food when you command it! I am starving and demand that we eat right now!
We will eat soon enough, Habib! But first, meet Sinbad. He is one of my oldest friends. I have ordered tonight's feast in his honor.
Habib, it is a pleasure to meet you.
Hmph! Very well!
But let us eat soon! I am starving and don't wish to wait much longer!

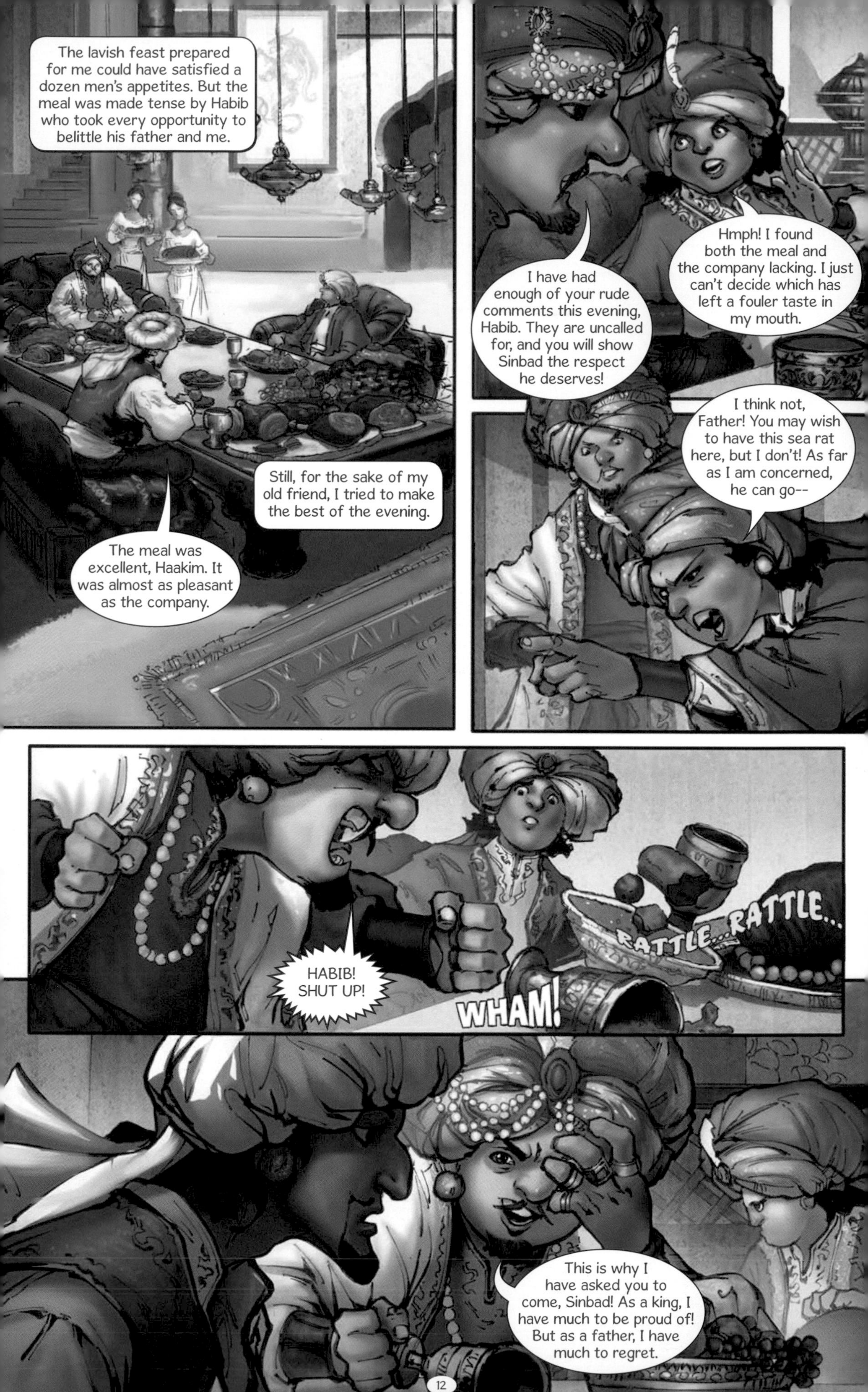

The lavish feast prepared for me could have satisfied a dozen men's appetites. But the meal was made tense by Habib who took every opportunity to belittle his father and me.
Still, for the sake of my old friend, I tried to make the best of the evening.
The meal was excellent, Haakim. It was almost as pleasant as the company.
I have had enough of your rude comments this evening, Habib. They are uncalled for, and you will show Sinbad the respect he deserves!
Hmph! I found both the meal and the company lacking. I just can't decide which has left a fouler taste in my mouth.
I think not, Father! You may wish to have this sea rat here, but I don't! As far as I am concerned, he can go--
HABIB! SHUT UP!
WHAM!
RATTLE... RATTLE...
This is why I have asked you to come, Sinbad! As a king, I have much to be proud of! But as a father, I have much to regret.

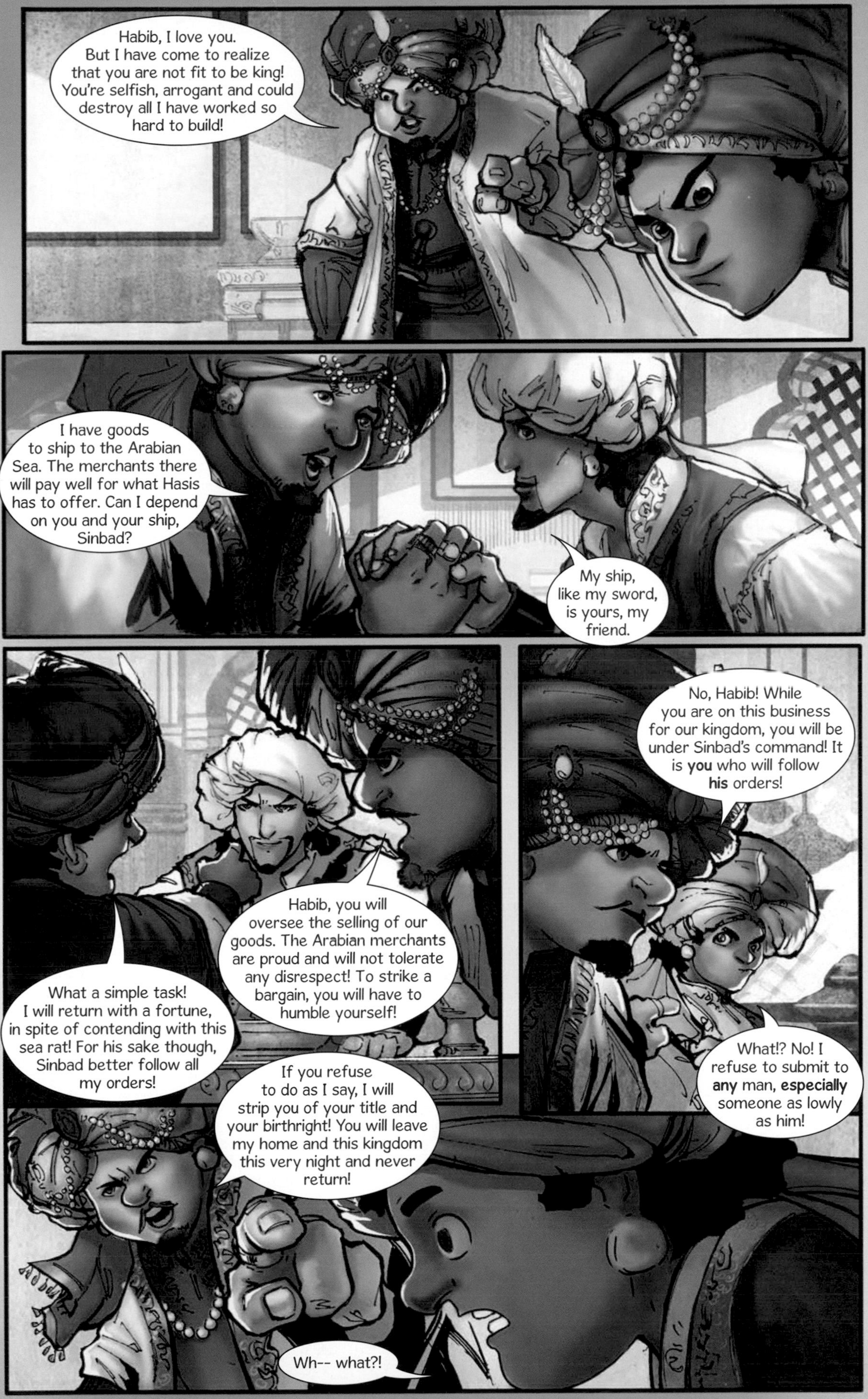
Habib, I love you. But I have come to realize that you are not fit to be king! You're selfish, arrogant and could destroy all I have worked so hard to build!
I have goods to ship to the Arabian Sea. The merchants there will pay well for what Hasis has to offer. Can I depend on you and your ship, Sinbad?
My ship, like my sword, is yours, my friend.
Habib, you will oversee the selling of our goods. The Arabian merchants are proud and will not tolerate any disrespect! To strike a bargain, you will have to humble yourself!
What a simple task! I will return with a fortune, in spite of contending with this sea rat! For his sake though, Sinbad better follow all my orders!
No, Habib! While you are on this business for our kingdom, you will be under Sinbad's command! It is **you** who will follow **his** orders!
What!? No! I refuse to submit to **any** man, **especially** someone as lowly as him!
If you refuse to do as I say, I will strip you of your title and your birthright! You will leave my home and this kingdom this very night and never return!
Wh-- what?!

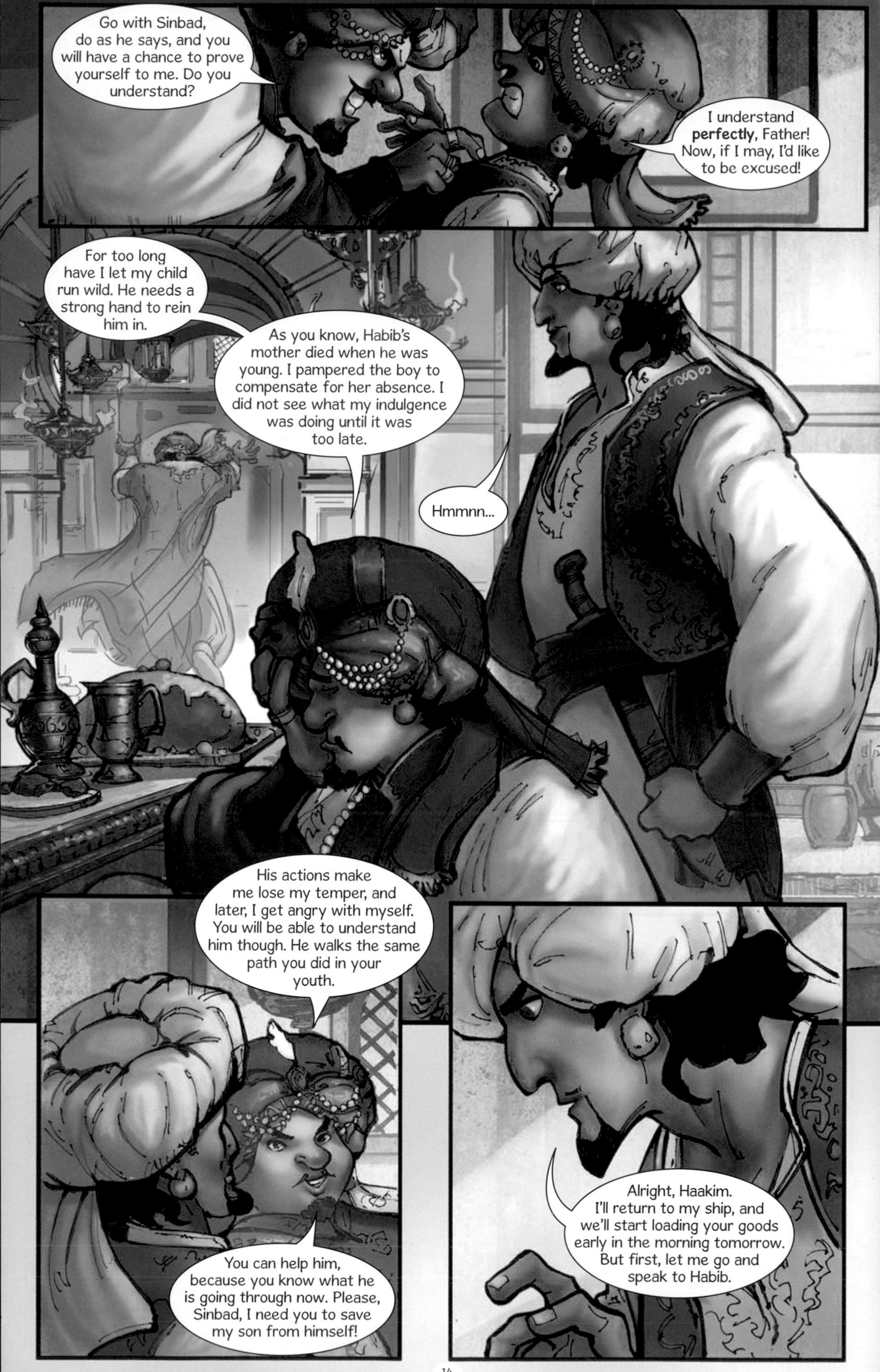

Go with Sinbad, do as he says, and you will have a chance to prove yourself to me. Do you understand?
I understand **perfectly**, Father! Now, if I may, I'd like to be excused!
For too long have I let my child run wild. He needs a strong hand to rein him in.
As you know, Habib's mother died when he was young. I pampered the boy to compensate for her absence. I did not see what my indulgence was doing until it was too late.
Hmmnn...
His actions make me lose my temper, and later, I get angry with myself. You will be able to understand him though. He walks the same path you did in your youth.
You can help him, because you know what he is going through now. Please, Sinbad, I need you to save my son from himself!
Alright, Haakim. I'll return to my ship, and we'll start loading your goods early in the morning tomorrow. But first, let me go and speak to Habib.

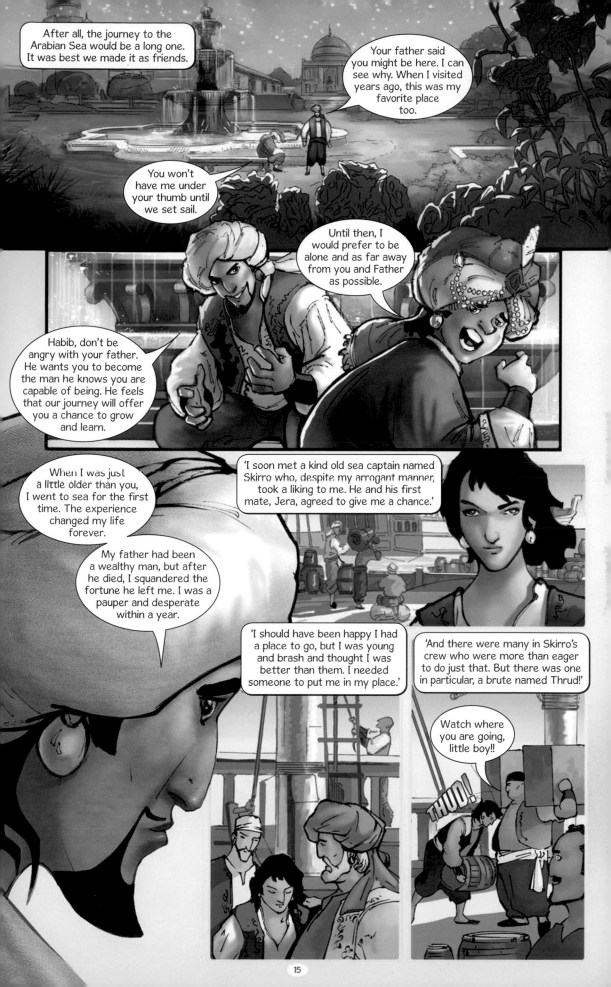

After all, the journey to the Arabian Sea would be a long one. It was best we made it as friends.

Your father said you might be here. I can see why. When I visited years ago, this was my favorite place too.

You won't have me under your thumb until we set sail.

Until then, I would prefer to be alone and as far away from you and Father as possible.

Habib, don't be angry with your father. He wants you to become the man he knows you are capable of being. He feels that our journey will offer you a chance to grow and learn.

When I was just a little older than you, I went to sea for the first time. The experience changed my life forever.

My father had been a wealthy man, but after he died, I squandered the fortune he left me. I was a pauper and desperate within a year.

'I soon met a kind old sea captain named Skirro who, despite my arrogant manner, took a liking to me. He and his first mate, Jera, agreed to give me a chance.'

'I should have been happy I had a place to go, but I was young and brash and thought I was better than them. I needed someone to put me in my place.'

'And there were many in Skirro's crew who were more than eager to do just that. But there was one in particular, a brute named Thrud!'

Watch where you are going, little boy!!

THUD!

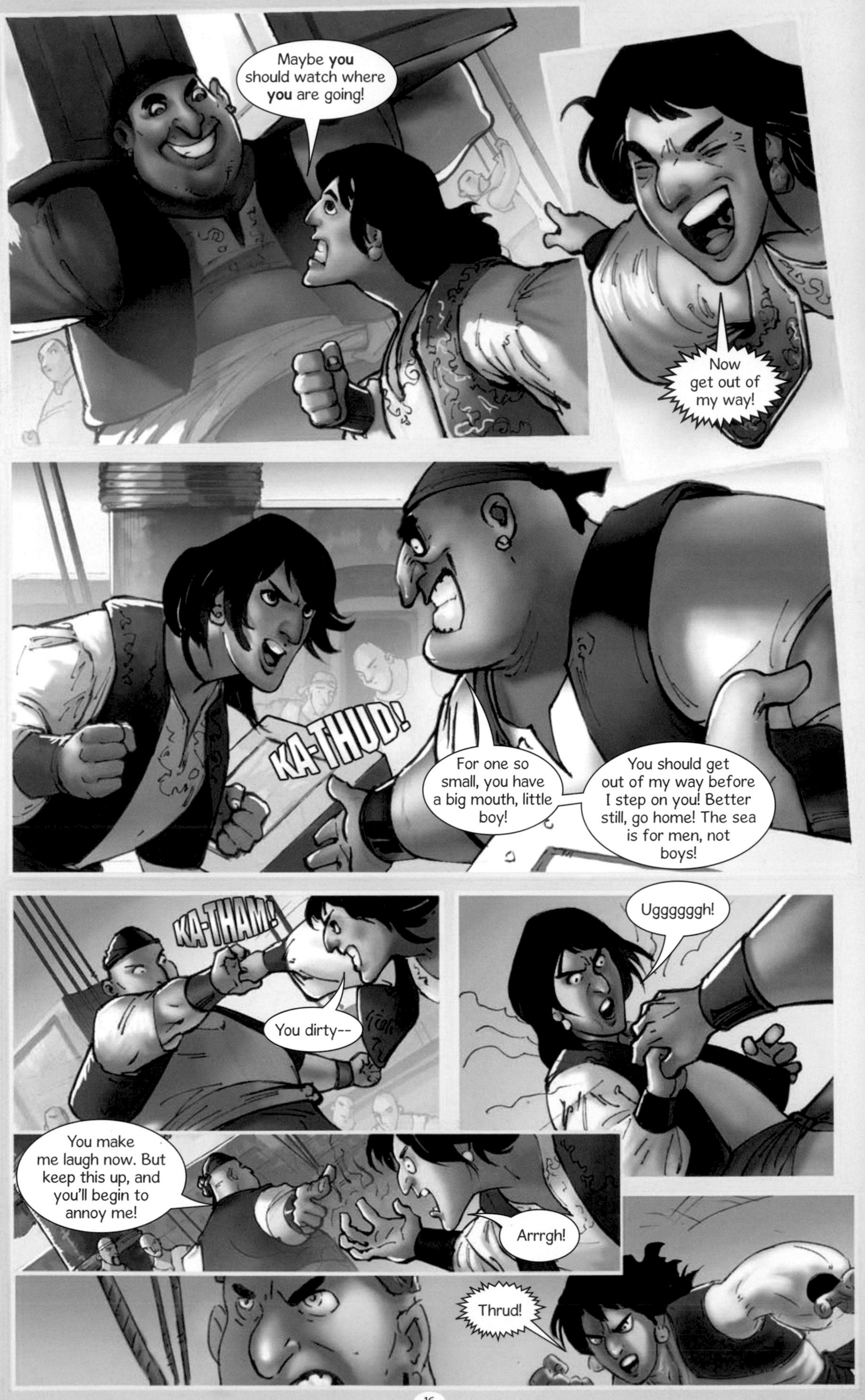
Maybe **you** should watch where **you** are going!
Now get out of my way!
KA-THUD!
For one so small, you have a big mouth, little boy!
You should get out of my way before I step on you! Better still, go home! The sea is for men, not boys!
KA-THAM!
You dirty--
Uggggggh!
You make me laugh now. But keep this up, and you'll begin to annoy me!
Arrrgh!
Thrud!

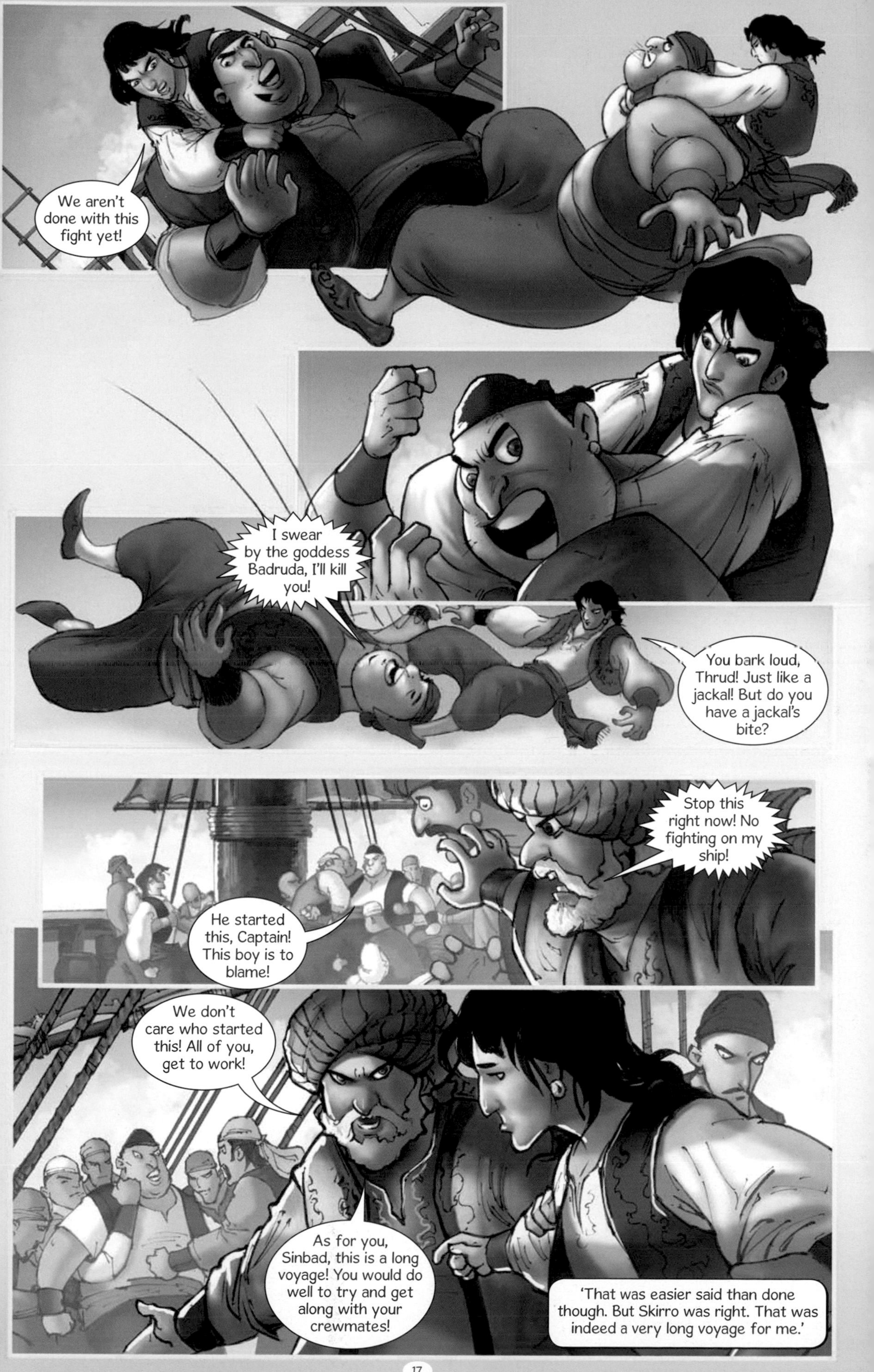

We aren't done with this fight yet!
I swear by the goddess Badruda, I'll kill you!
You bark loud, Thrud! Just like a jackal! But do you have a jackal's bite?
Stop this right now! No fighting on my ship!
He started this, Captain! This boy is to blame!
We don't care who started this! All of you, get to work!
As for you, Sinbad, this is a long voyage! You would do well to try and get along with your crewmates!
'That was easier said than done though. But Skirro was right. That was indeed a very long voyage for me.'

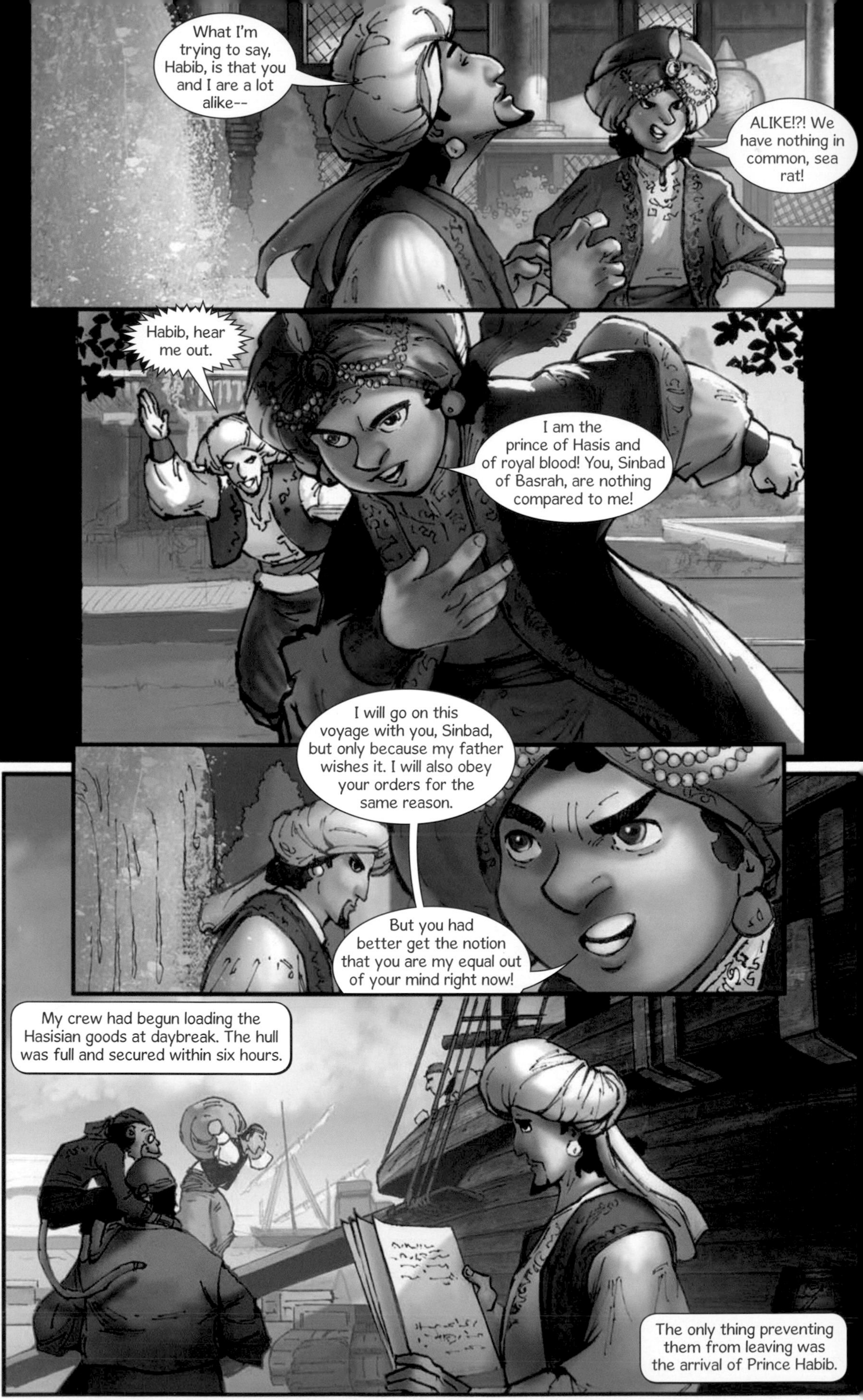
What I'm trying to say, Habib, is that you and I are a lot alike--
ALIKE!?! We have nothing in common, sea rat!
Habib, hear me out.
I am the prince of Hasis and of royal blood! You, Sinbad of Basrah, are nothing compared to me!
I will go on this voyage with you, Sinbad, but only because my father wishes it. I will also obey your orders for the same reason.
But you had better get the notion that you are my equal out of your mind right now!
My crew had begun loading the Hasisian goods at daybreak. The hull was full and secured within six hours.
The only thing preventing them from leaving was the arrival of Prince Habib.

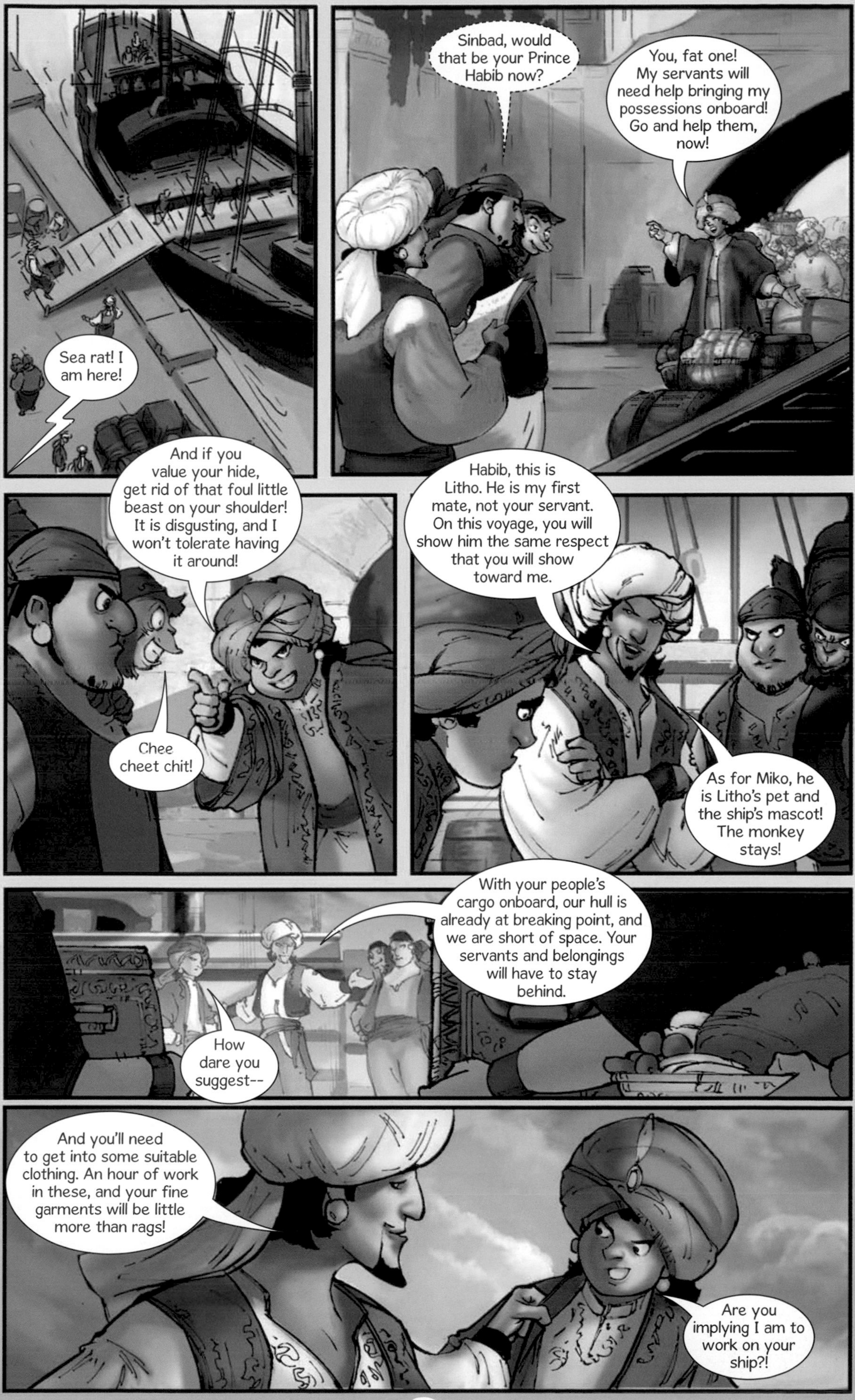
Sea rat! I am here!
Sinbad, would that be your Prince Habib now?
You, fat one! My servants will need help bringing my possessions onboard! Go and help them, now!
And if you value your hide, get rid of that foul little beast on your shoulder! It is disgusting, and I won't tolerate having it around!
Chee cheet chit!
Habib, this is Litho. He is my first mate, not your servant. On this voyage, you will show him the same respect that you will show toward me.
As for Miko, he is Litho's pet and the ship's mascot! The monkey stays!
With your people's cargo onboard, our hull is already at breaking point, and we are short of space. Your servants and belongings will have to stay behind.
How dare you suggest--
And you'll need to get into some suitable clothing. An hour of work in these, and your fine garments will be little more than rags!
Are you implying I am to work on your ship?!

Every man who sails with me must pull his own weight. You're no exception.
I am carrying your father's cargo as a favor to him. You, though, must earn your passage.
I will leave you in Dango's hands! He is the overseer of my crew, and my most trusted man next to Litho!
Dango! Take our young friend here and find him some clothes he won't mind getting dirty.
When you're done, put him to work on the ship's rigging. He is young and strong and will do well handling the ropes.
Ha! The boy looks like a peacock! Come, Your Highness! Time to change your plumage to something less grand!
A short time later, my crew and I were ready to get underway. To the surprise of none, our newest crewman had some difficulties with the task assigned to him.
No, no, peacock! That's all wrong! Don't be afraid to put your back into it!

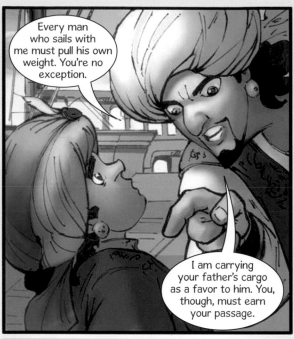

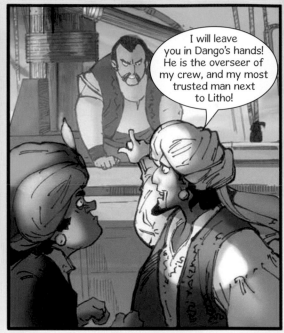

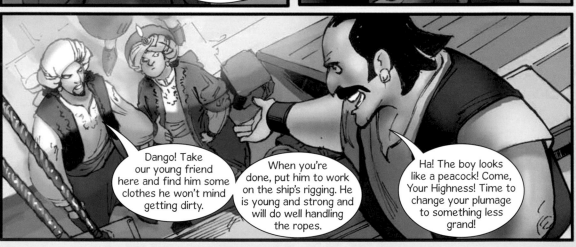

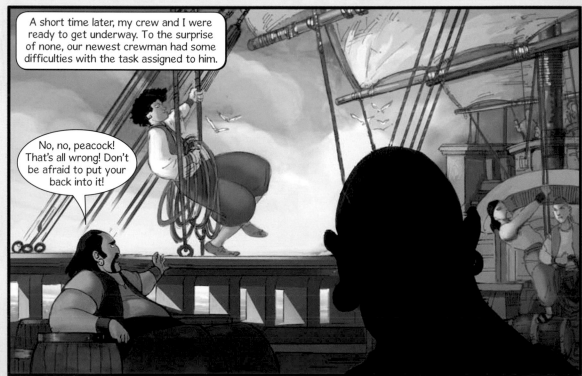

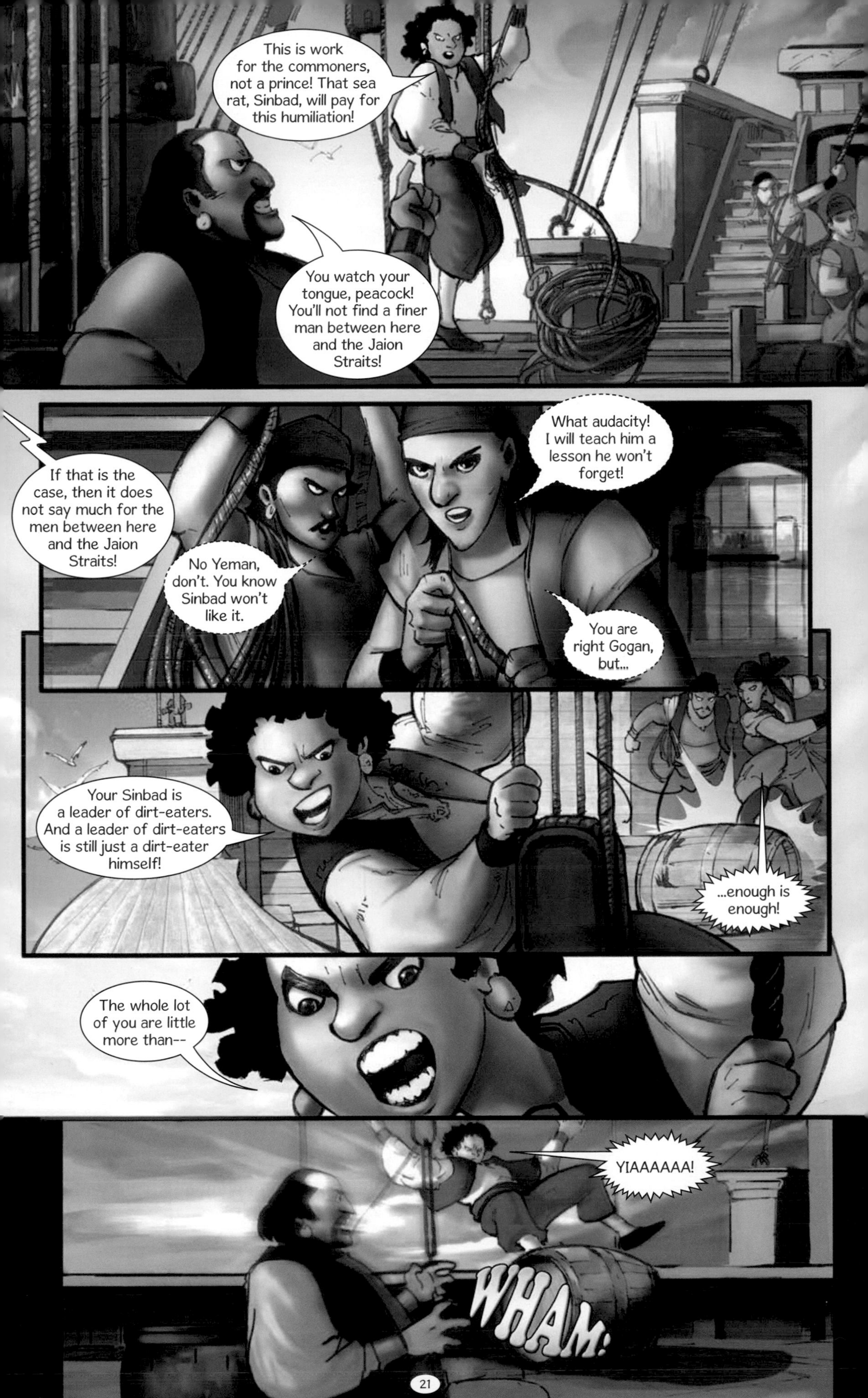

This is work for the commoners, not a prince! That sea rat, Sinbad, will pay for this humiliation!
You watch your tongue, peacock! You'll not find a finer man between here and the Jaion Straits!
If that is the case, then it does not say much for the men between here and the Jaion Straits!
What audacity! I will teach him a lesson he won't forget!
No Yeman, don't. You know Sinbad won't like it.
You are right Gogan, but...
Your Sinbad is a leader of dirt-eaters. And a leader of dirt-eaters is still just a dirt-eater himself!
...enough is enough!
The whole lot of you are little more than--
YIAAAAAA!
WHAM!

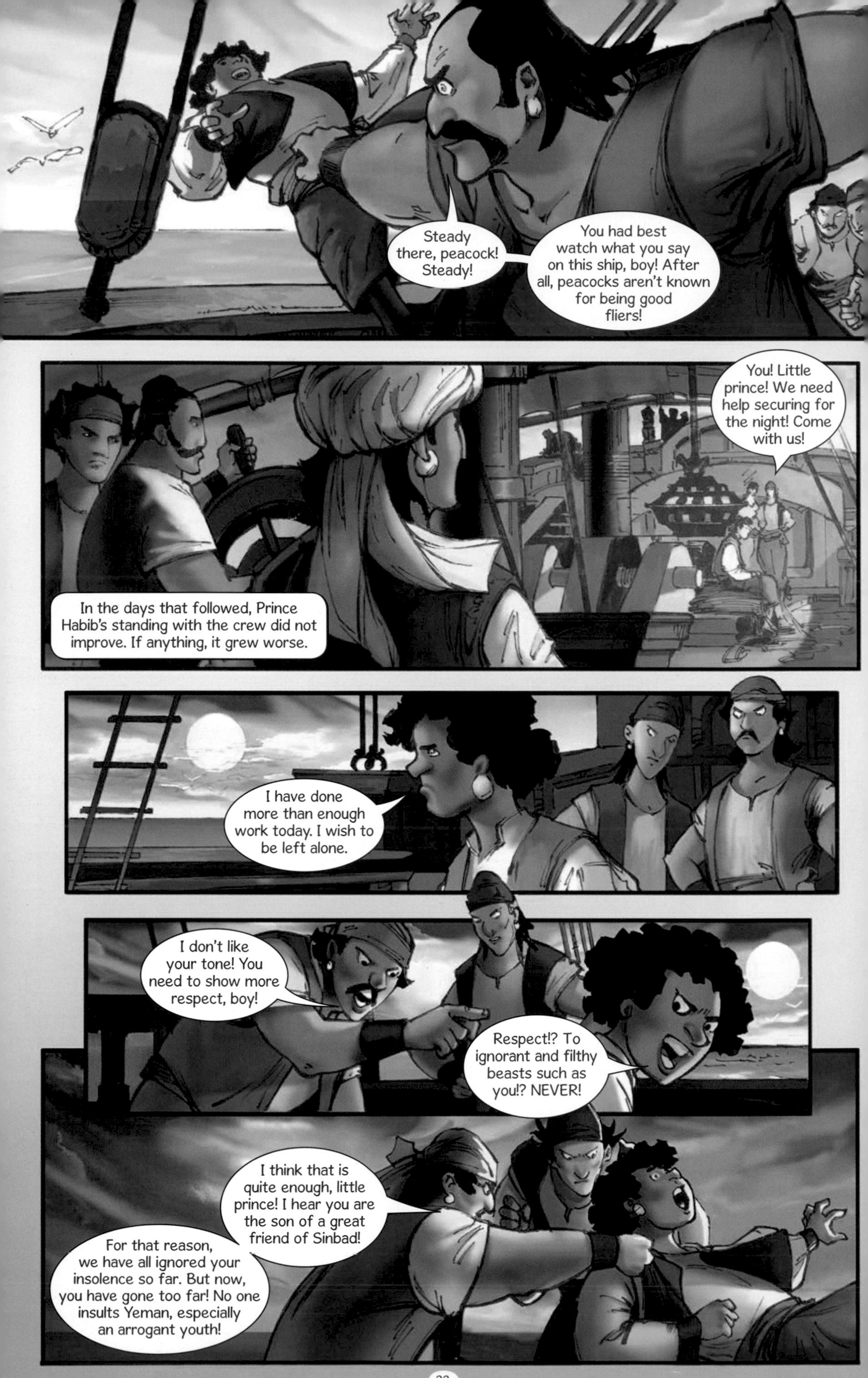
Steady there, peacock! Steady!
You had best watch what you say on this ship, boy! After all, peacocks aren't known for being good fliers!
You! Little prince! We need help securing for the night! Come with us!
In the days that followed, Prince Habib's standing with the crew did not improve. If anything, it grew worse.
I have done more than enough work today. I wish to be left alone.
I don't like your tone! You need to show more respect, boy!
Respect!? To ignorant and filthy beasts such as you!? NEVER!
I think that is quite enough, little prince! I hear you are the son of a great friend of Sinbad!
For that reason, we have all ignored your insolence so far. But now, you have gone too far! No one insults Yeman, especially an arrogant youth!

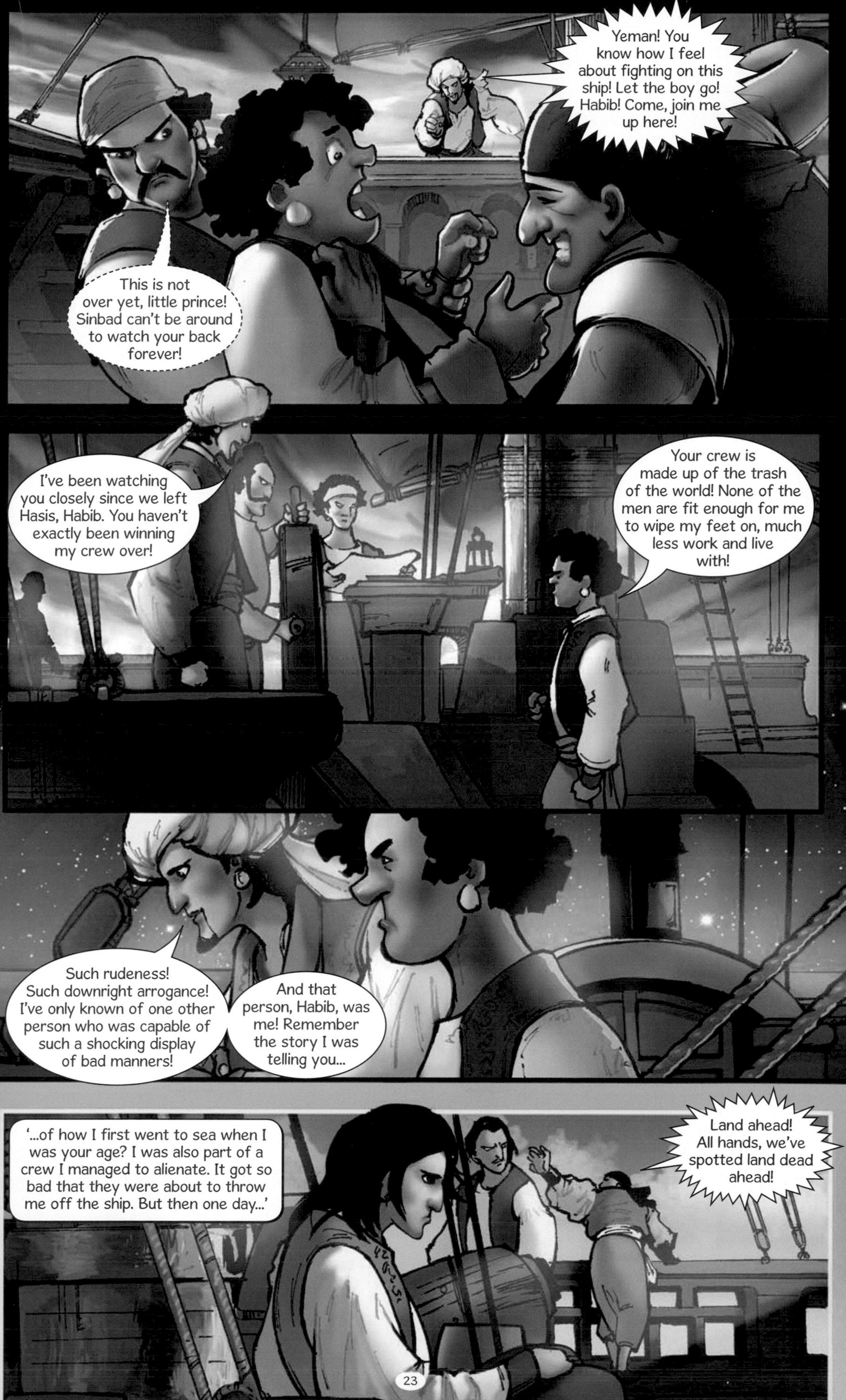
Yeman! You know how I feel about fighting on this ship! Let the boy go! Habib! Come, join me up here!
This is not over yet, little prince! Sinbad can't be around to watch your back forever!
I've been watching you closely since we left Hasis, Habib. You haven't exactly been winning my crew over!
Your crew is made up of the trash of the world! None of the men are fit enough for me to wipe my feet on, much less work and live with!
Such rudeness! Such downright arrogance! I've only known of one other person who was capable of such a shocking display of bad manners!
And that person, Habib, was me! Remember the story I was telling you...
'...of how I first went to sea when I was your age? I was also part of a crew I managed to alienate. It got so bad that they were about to throw me off the ship. But then one day...'
Land ahead! All hands, we've spotted land dead ahead!

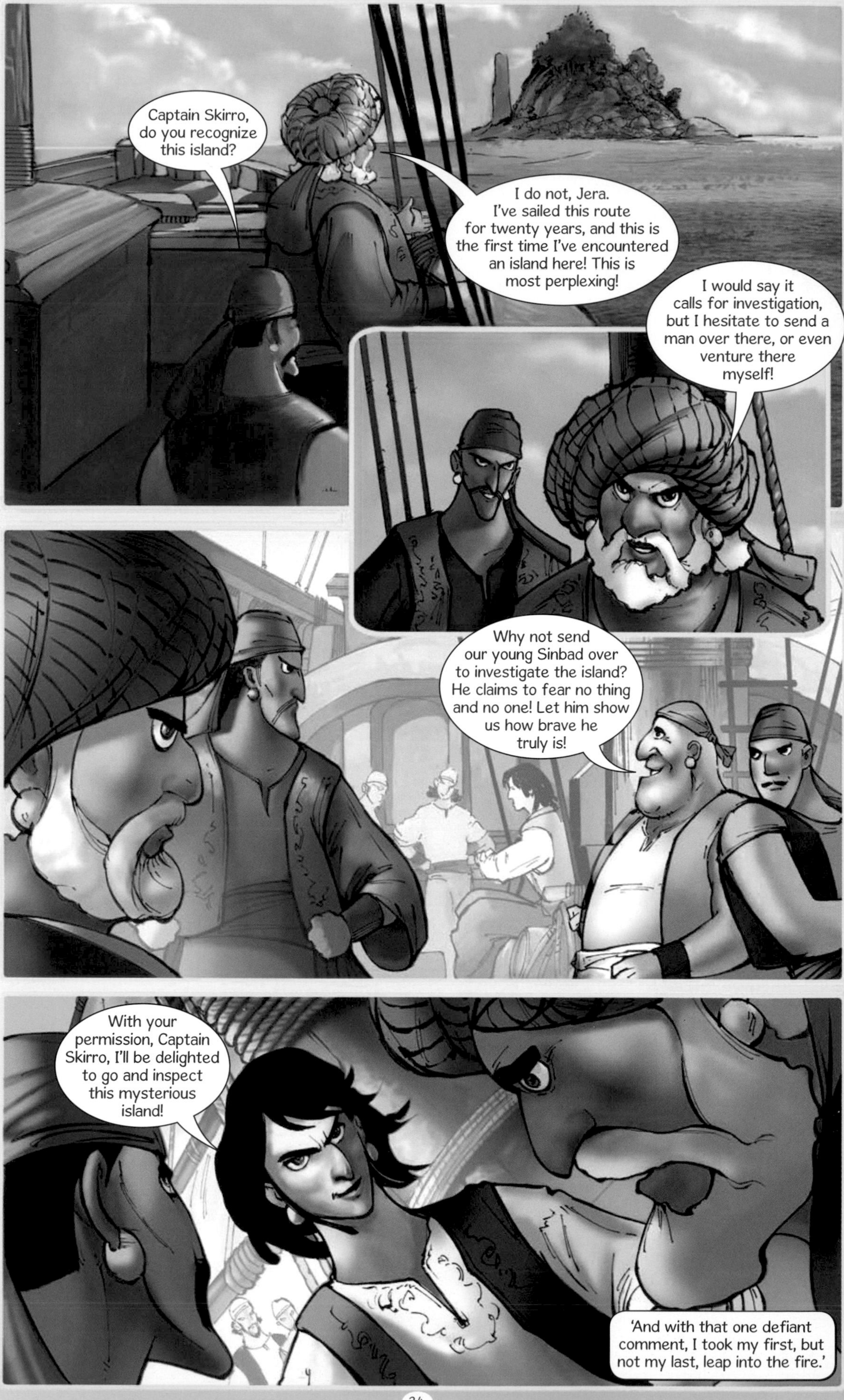
Captain Skirro, do you recognize this island?
I do not, Jera. I've sailed this route for twenty years, and this is the first time I've encountered an island here! This is most perplexing!
I would say it calls for investigation, but I hesitate to send a man over there, or even venture there myself!
Why not send our young Sinbad over to investigate the island? He claims to fear no thing and no one! Let him show us how brave he truly is!
With your permission, Captain Skirro, I'll be delighted to go and inspect this mysterious island!
'And with that one defiant comment, I took my first, but not my last, leap into the fire.'

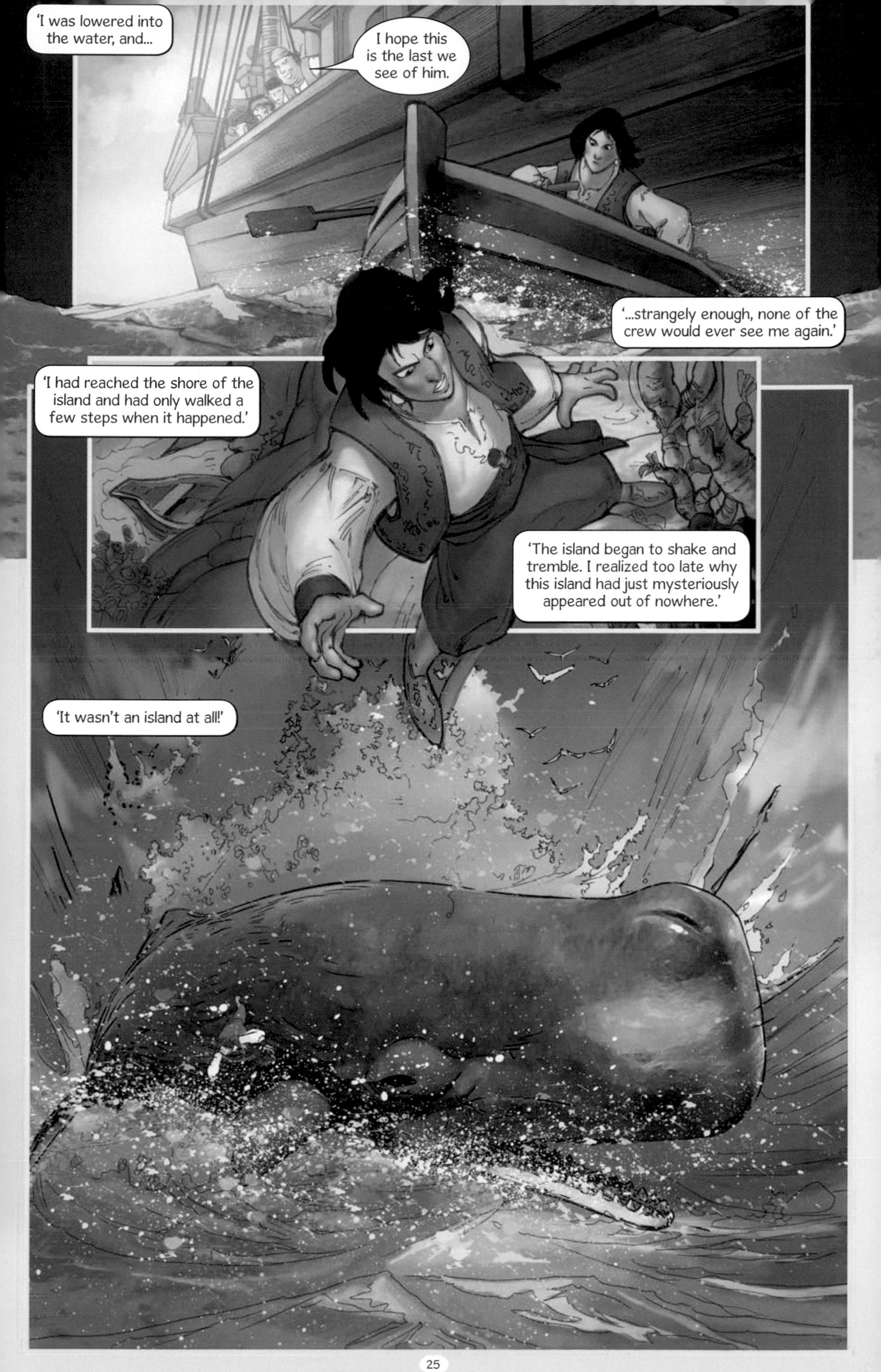
'I was lowered into the water, and...
I hope this is the last we see of him.
'...strangely enough, none of the crew would ever see me again.'
'I had reached the shore of the island and had only walked a few steps when it happened.'
'The island began to shake and tremble. I realized too late why this island had just mysteriously appeared out of nowhere.'
'It wasn't an island at all!'

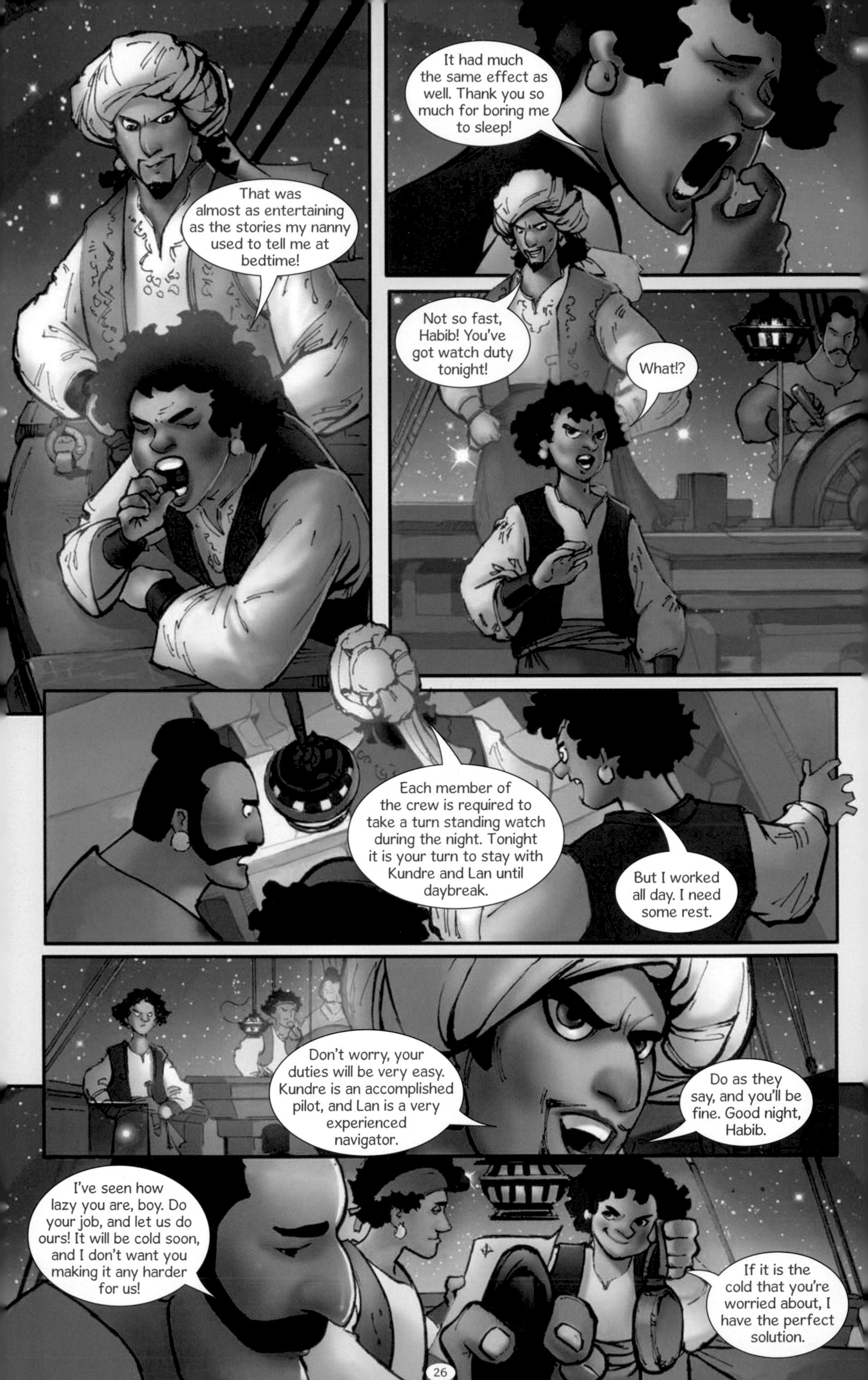
That was almost as entertaining as the stories my nanny used to tell me at bedtime!
It had much the same effect as well. Thank you so much for boring me to sleep!
Not so fast, Habib! You've got watch duty tonight!
What!?
Each member of the crew is required to take a turn standing watch during the night. Tonight it is your turn to stay with Kundre and Lan until daybreak.
But I worked all day. I need some rest.
Don't worry, your duties will be very easy. Kundre is an accomplished pilot, and Lan is a very experienced navigator.
Do as they say, and you'll be fine. Good night, Habib.
I've seen how lazy you are, boy. Do your job, and let us do ours! It will be cold soon, and I don't want you making it any harder for us!
If it is the cold that you're worried about, I have the perfect solution.

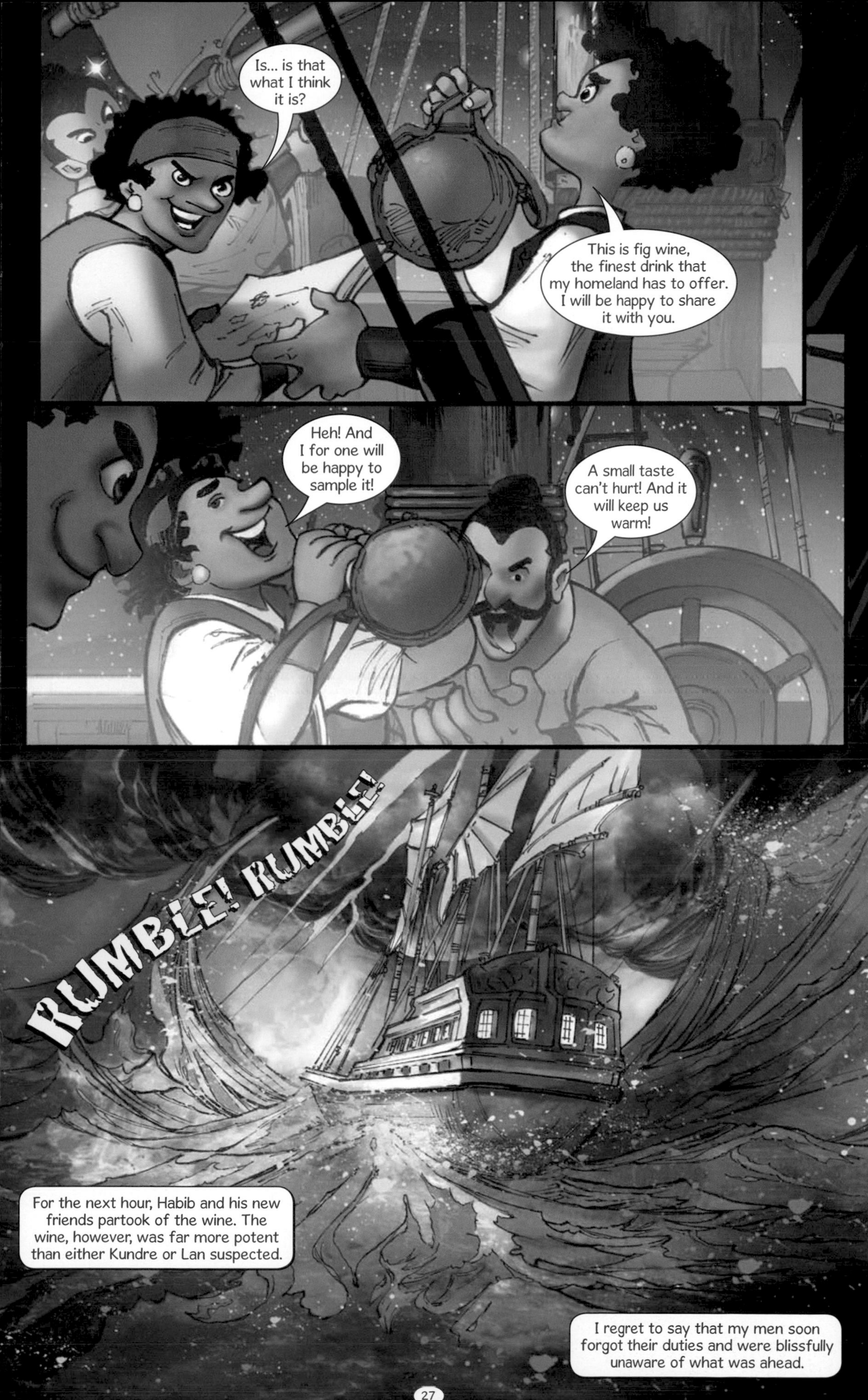
Is... is that what I think it is?
This is fig wine, the finest drink that my homeland has to offer. I will be happy to share it with you.
Heh! And I for one will be happy to sample it!
A small taste can't hurt! And it will keep us warm!
RUMBLE! RUMBLE!
For the next hour, Habib and his new friends partook of the wine. The wine, however, was far more potent than either Kundre or Lan suspected.
I regret to say that my men soon forgot their duties and were blissfully unaware of what was ahead.

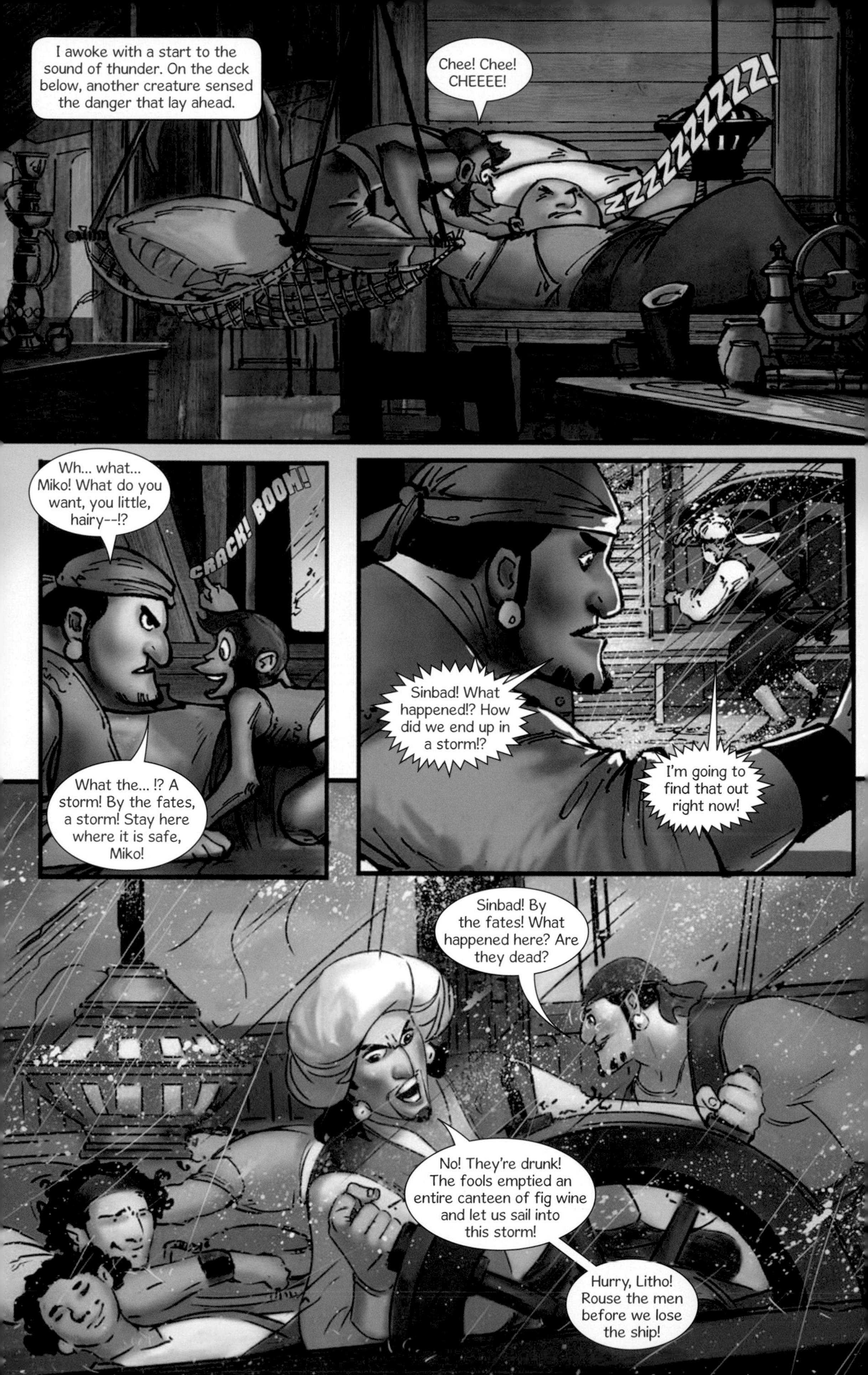
I awoke with a start to the sound of thunder. On the deck below, another creature sensed the danger that lay ahead.
Chee! Chee! CHEEEE!
ZZZZZZZZZZZ!
Wh... what... Miko! What do you want, you little, hairy--!?
CRACK! BOOM!
What the... !? A storm! By the fates, a storm! Stay here where it is safe, Miko!
Sinbad! What happened!? How did we end up in a storm!?
I'm going to find that out right now!
Sinbad! By the fates! What happened here? Are they dead?
No! They're drunk! The fools emptied an entire canteen of fig wine and let us sail into this storm!
Hurry, Litho! Rouse the men before we lose the ship!

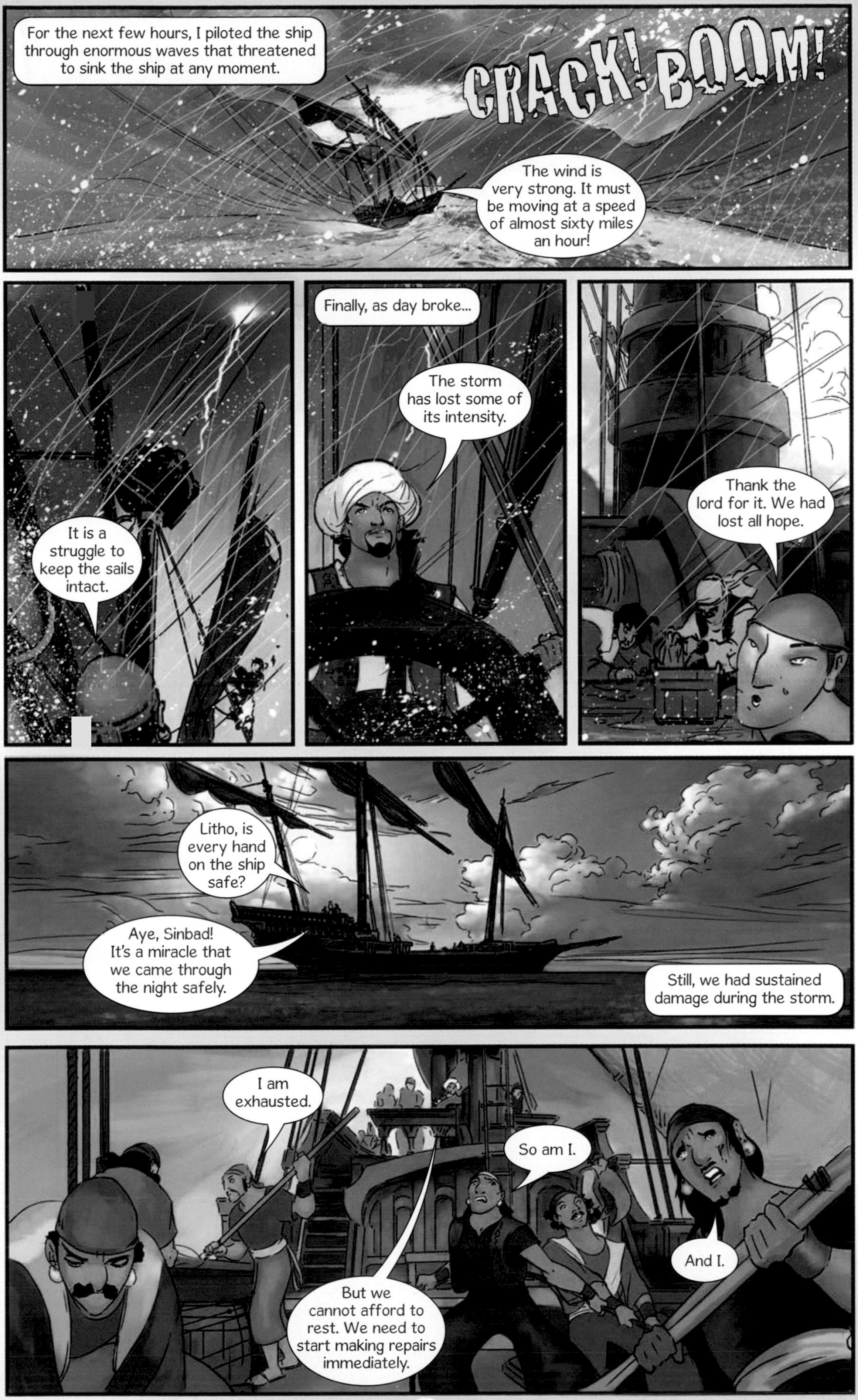

For the next few hours, I piloted the ship through enormous waves that threatened to sink the ship at any moment.
CRACK! BOOM!
The wind is very strong. It must be moving at a speed of almost sixty miles an hour!
It is a struggle to keep the sails intact.
Finally, as day broke...
The storm has lost some of its intensity.
Thank the lord for it. We had lost all hope.
Litho, is every hand on the ship safe?
Aye, Sinbad! It's a miracle that we came through the night safely.
Still, we had sustained damage during the storm.
I am exhausted.
So am I.
And I.
But we cannot afford to rest. We need to start making repairs immediately.

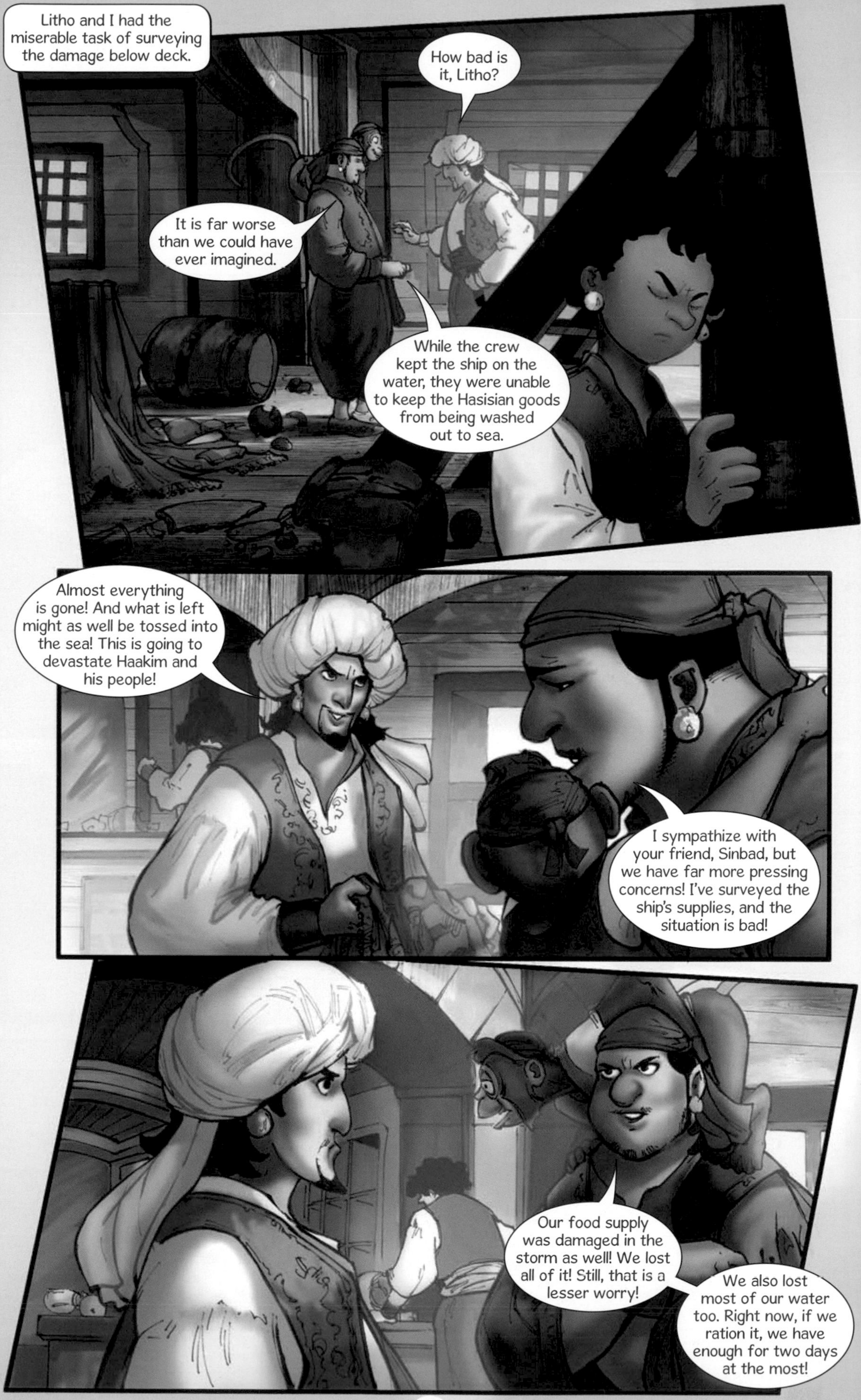

Litho and I had the miserable task of surveying the damage below deck.
How bad is it, Litho?
It is far worse than we could have ever imagined.
While the crew kept the ship on the water, they were unable to keep the Hasisian goods from being washed out to sea.
Almost everything is gone! And what is left might as well be tossed into the sea! This is going to devastate Haakim and his people!
I sympathize with your friend, Sinbad, but we have far more pressing concerns! I've surveyed the ship's supplies, and the situation is bad!
Our food supply was damaged in the storm as well! We lost all of it! Still, that is a lesser worry!
We also lost most of our water too. Right now, if we ration it, we have enough for two days at the most!

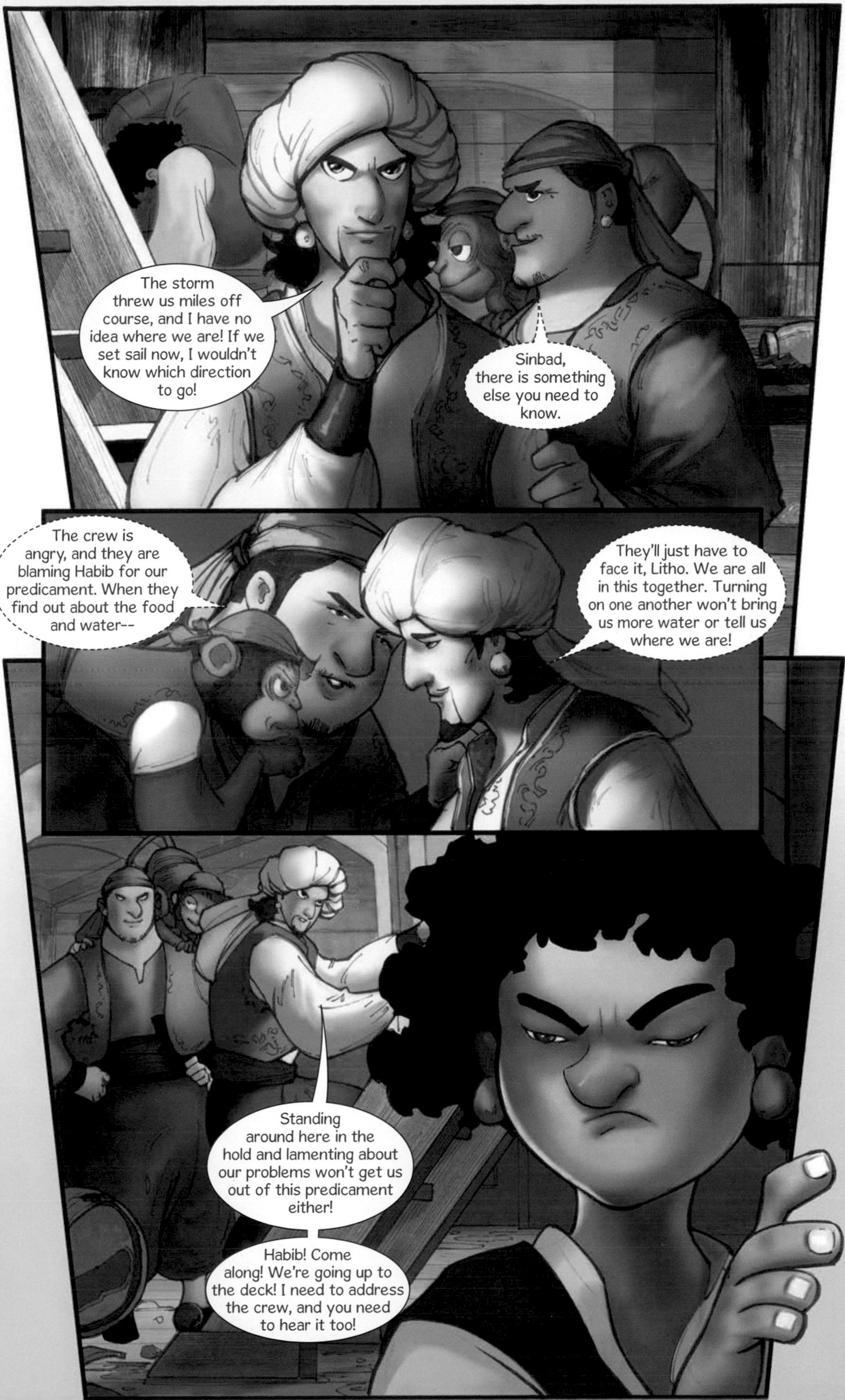

The storm threw us miles off course, and I have no idea where we are! If we set sail now, I wouldn't know which direction to go!
Sinbad, there is something else you need to know.
The crew is angry, and they are blaming Habib for our predicament. When they find out about the food and water--
They'll just have to face it, Litho. We are all in this together. Turning on one another won't bring us more water or tell us where we are!
Standing around here in the hold and lamenting about our problems won't get us out of this predicament either!
Habib! Come along! We're going up to the deck! I need to address the crew, and you need to hear it too!

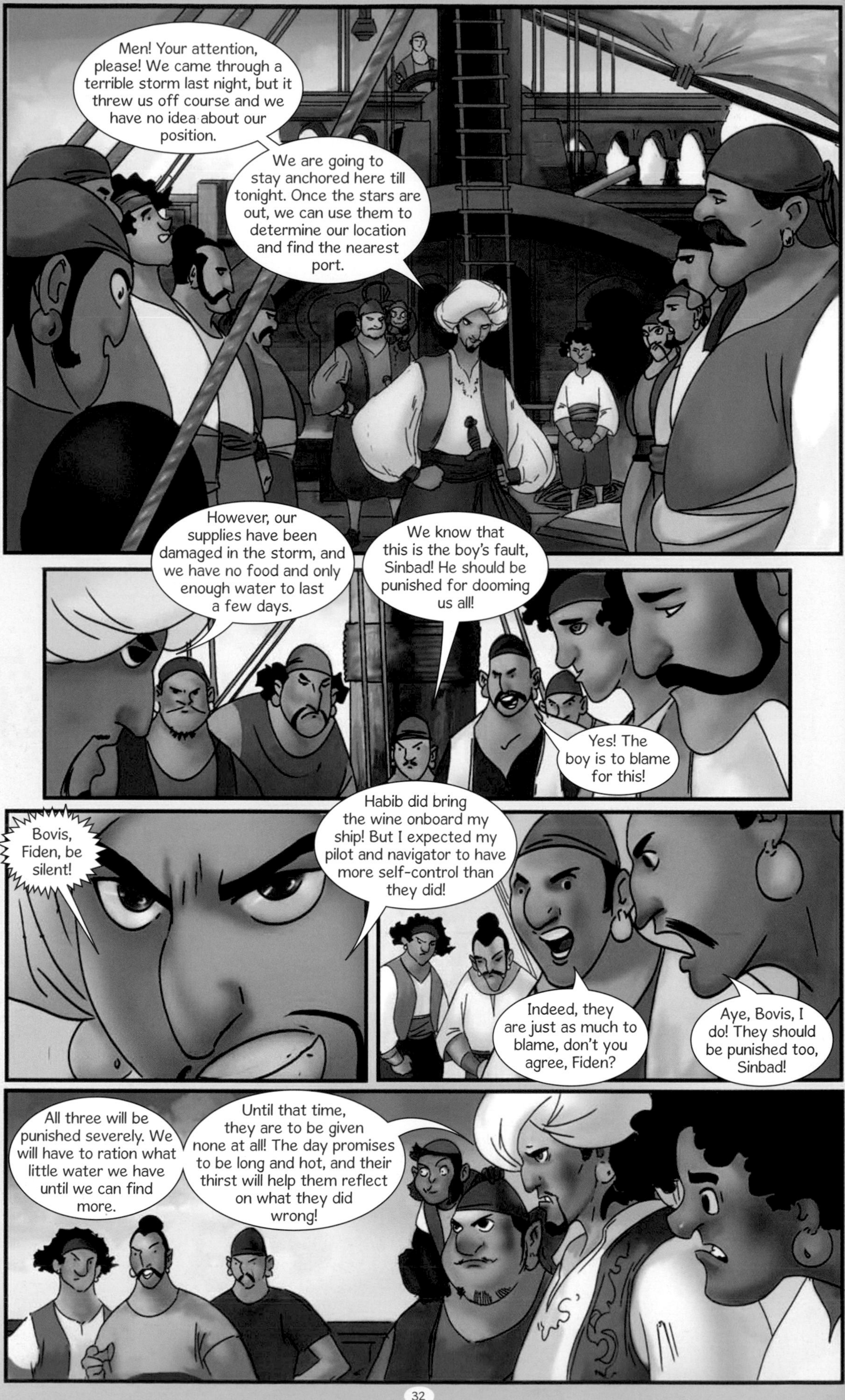
Men! Your attention, please! We came through a terrible storm last night, but it threw us off course and we have no idea about our position.
We are going to stay anchored here till tonight. Once the stars are out, we can use them to determine our location and find the nearest port.
However, our supplies have been damaged in the storm, and we have no food and only enough water to last a few days.
We know that this is the boy's fault, Sinbad! He should be punished for dooming us all!
Yes! The boy is to blame for this!
Bovis, Fiden, be silent!
Habib did bring the wine onboard my ship! But I expected my pilot and navigator to have more self-control than they did!
Indeed, they are just as much to blame, don't you agree, Fiden?
Aye, Bovis, I do! They should be punished too, Sinbad!
All three will be punished severely. We will have to ration what little water we have until we can find more.
Until that time, they are to be given none at all! The day promises to be long and hot, and their thirst will help them reflect on what they did wrong!

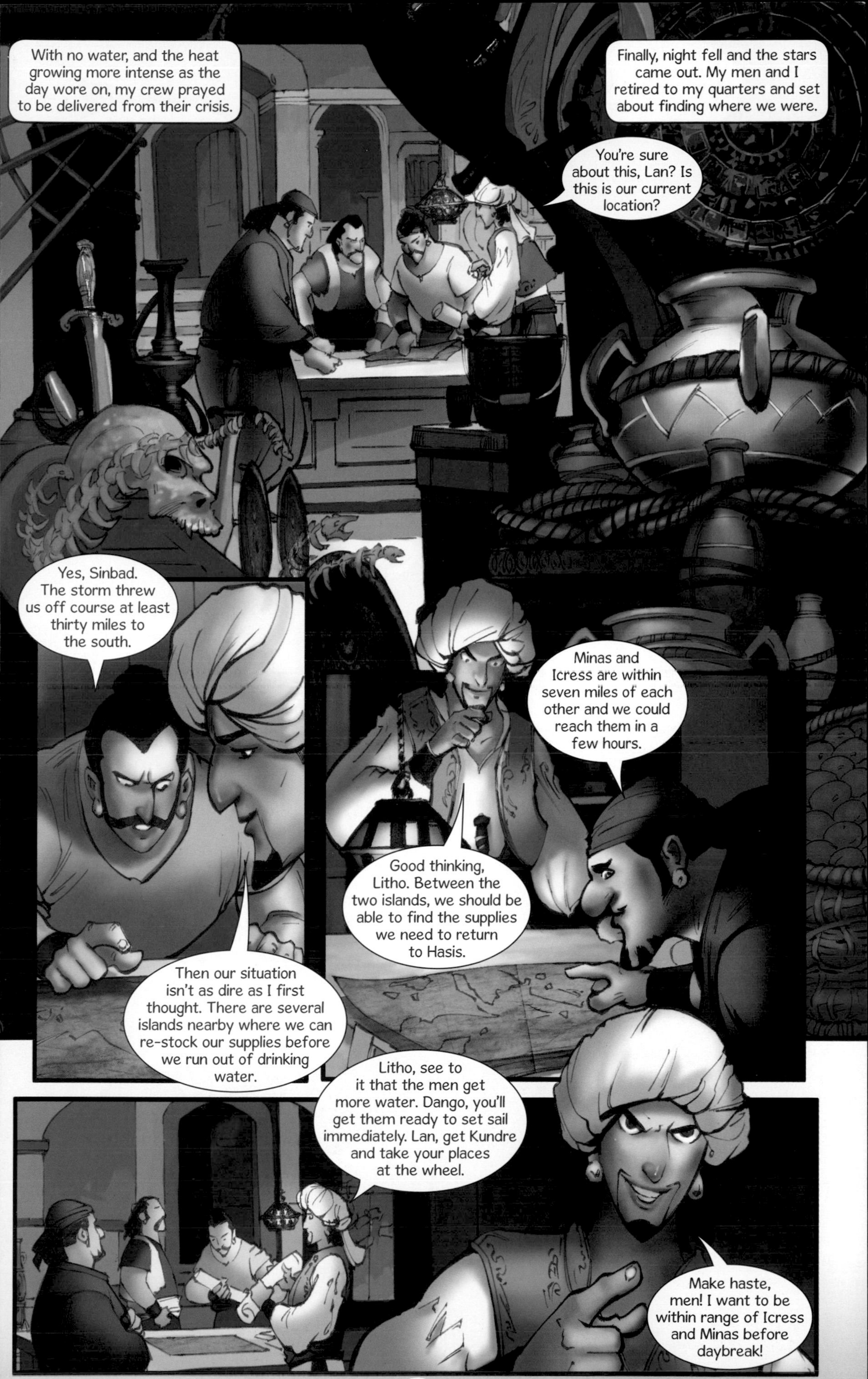

With no water, and the heat growing more intense as the day wore on, my crew prayed to be delivered from their crisis.
Finally, night fell and the stars came out. My men and I retired to my quarters and set about finding where we were.
You're sure about this, Lan? Is this is our current location?
Yes, Sinbad. The storm threw us off course at least thirty miles to the south.
Then our situation isn't as dire as I first thought. There are several islands nearby where we can re-stock our supplies before we run out of drinking water.
Minas and Icress are within seven miles of each other and we could reach them in a few hours.
Good thinking, Litho. Between the two islands, we should be able to find the supplies we need to return to Hasis.
Litho, see to it that the men get more water. Dango, you'll get them ready to set sail immediately. Lan, get Kundre and take your places at the wheel.
Make haste, men! I want to be within range of Icress and Minas before daybreak!

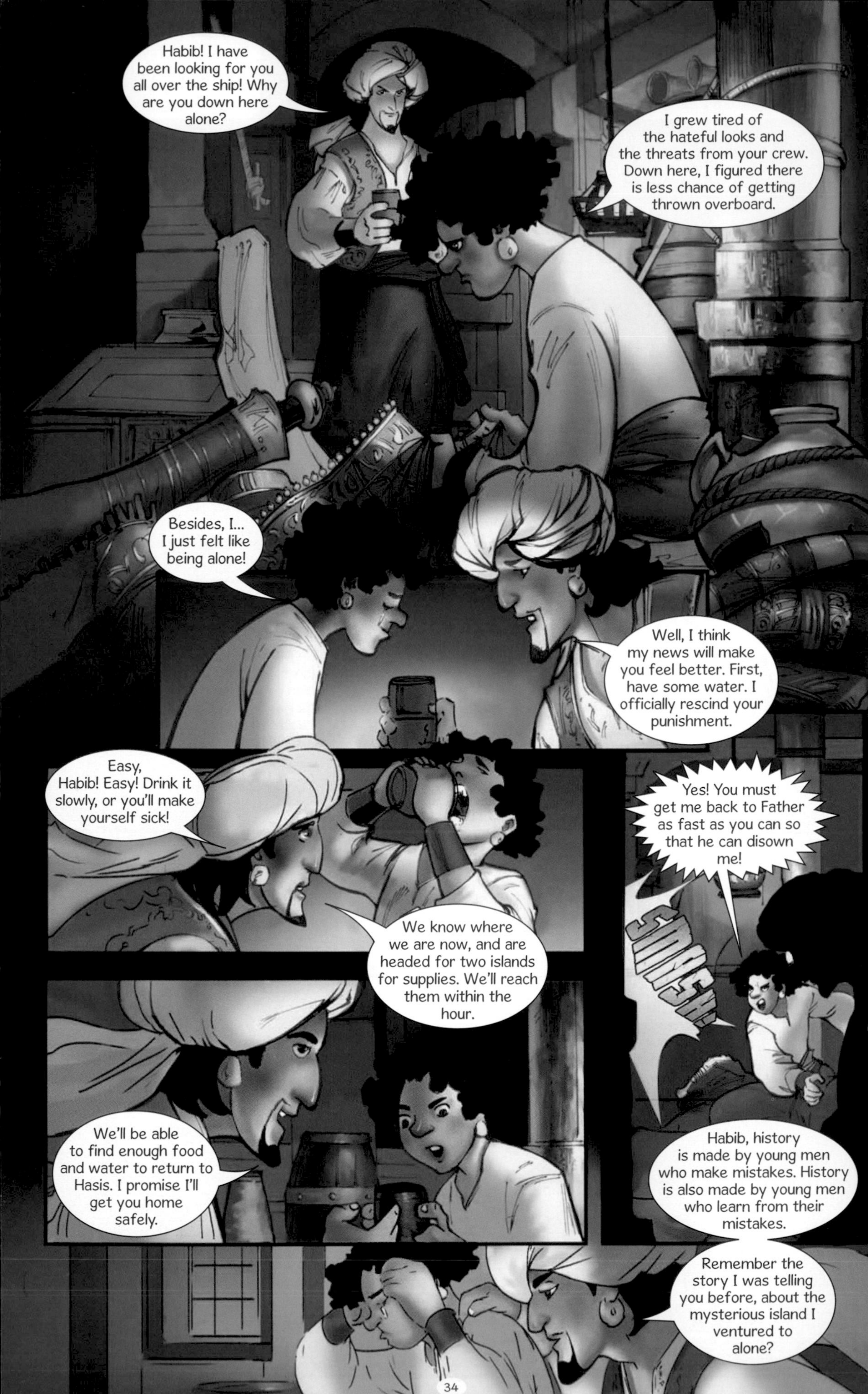
Habib! I have been looking for you all over the ship! Why are you down here alone?
I grew tired of the hateful looks and the threats from your crew. Down here, I figured there is less chance of getting thrown overboard.
Besides, I... I just felt like being alone!
Well, I think my news will make you feel better. First, have some water. I officially rescind your punishment.
Easy, Habib! Easy! Drink it slowly, or you'll make yourself sick!
We know where we are now, and are headed for two islands for supplies. We'll reach them within the hour.
We'll be able to find enough food and water to return to Hasis. I promise I'll get you home safely.
Yes! You must get me back to Father as fast as you can so that he can disown me!
Habib, history is made by young men who make mistakes. History is also made by young men who learn from their mistakes.
Remember the story I was telling you before, about the mysterious island I ventured to alone?

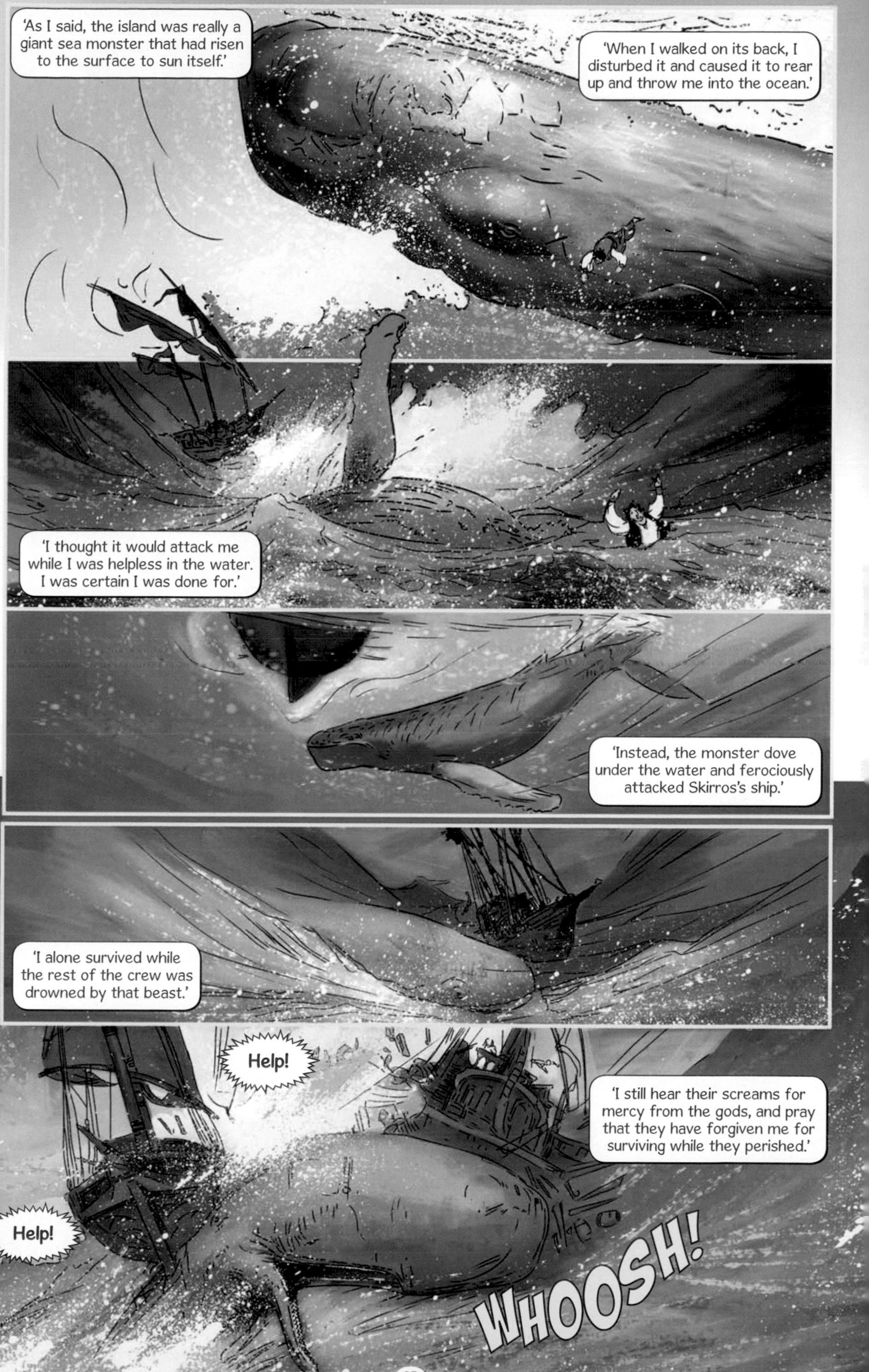

'As I said, the island was really a giant sea monster that had risen to the surface to sun itself.'
'When I walked on its back, I disturbed it and caused it to rear up and throw me into the ocean.'
'I thought it would attack me while I was helpless in the water. I was certain I was done for.'
'Instead, the monster dove under the water and ferociously attacked Skirros's ship.'
'I alone survived while the rest of the crew was drowned by that beast.'
Help!
'I still hear their screams for mercy from the gods, and pray that they have forgiven me for surviving while they perished.'
Help!
WHOOSH!

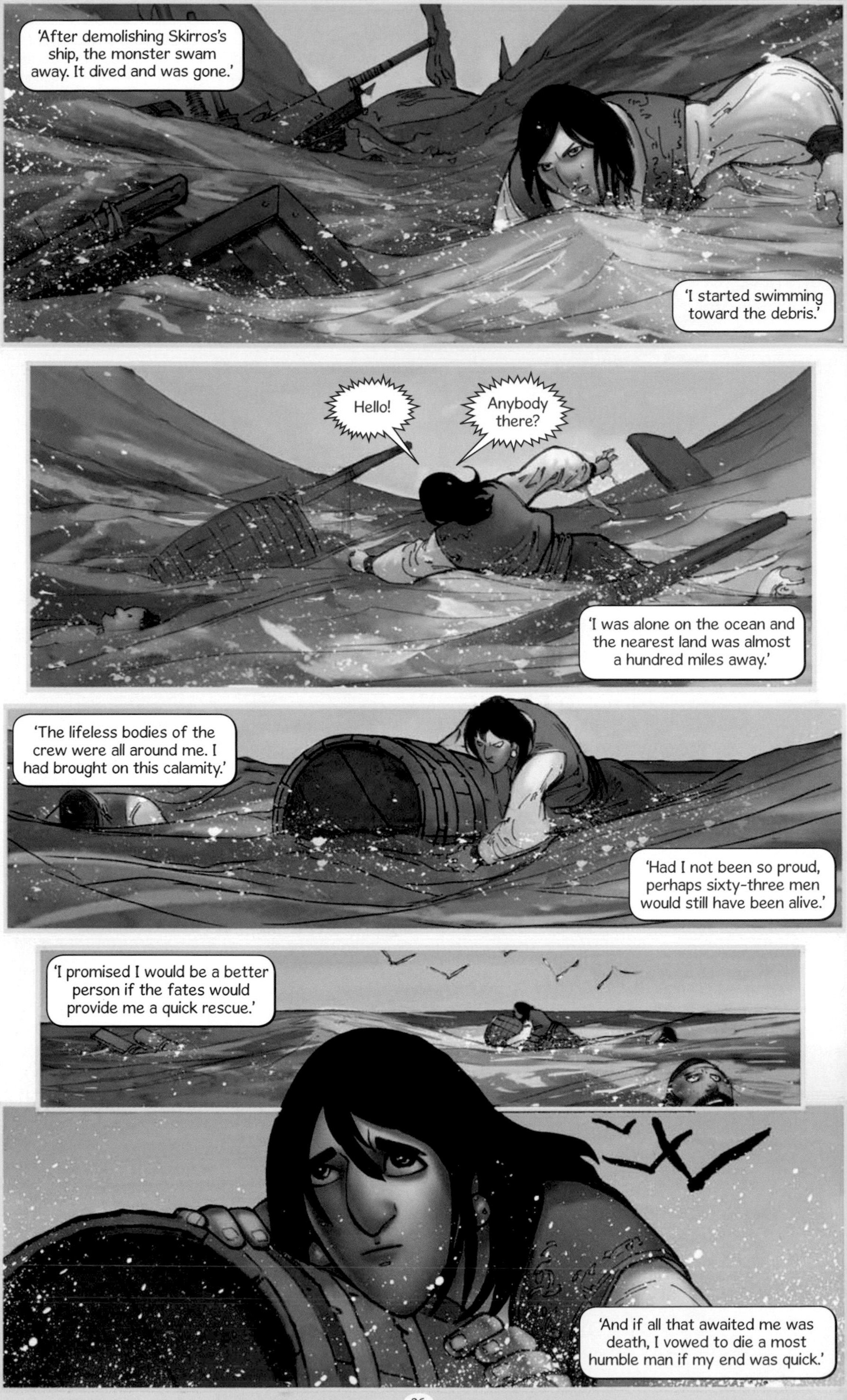
'After demolishing Skirros's ship, the monster swam away. It dived and was gone.'
'I started swimming toward the debris.'
Hello!
Anybody there?
'I was alone on the ocean and the nearest land was almost a hundred miles away.'
'The lifeless bodies of the crew were all around me. I had brought on this calamity.'
'Had I not been so proud, perhaps sixty-three men would still have been alive.'
'I promised I would be a better person if the fates would provide me a quick rescue.'
'And if all that awaited me was death, I vowed to die a most humble man if my end was quick.'

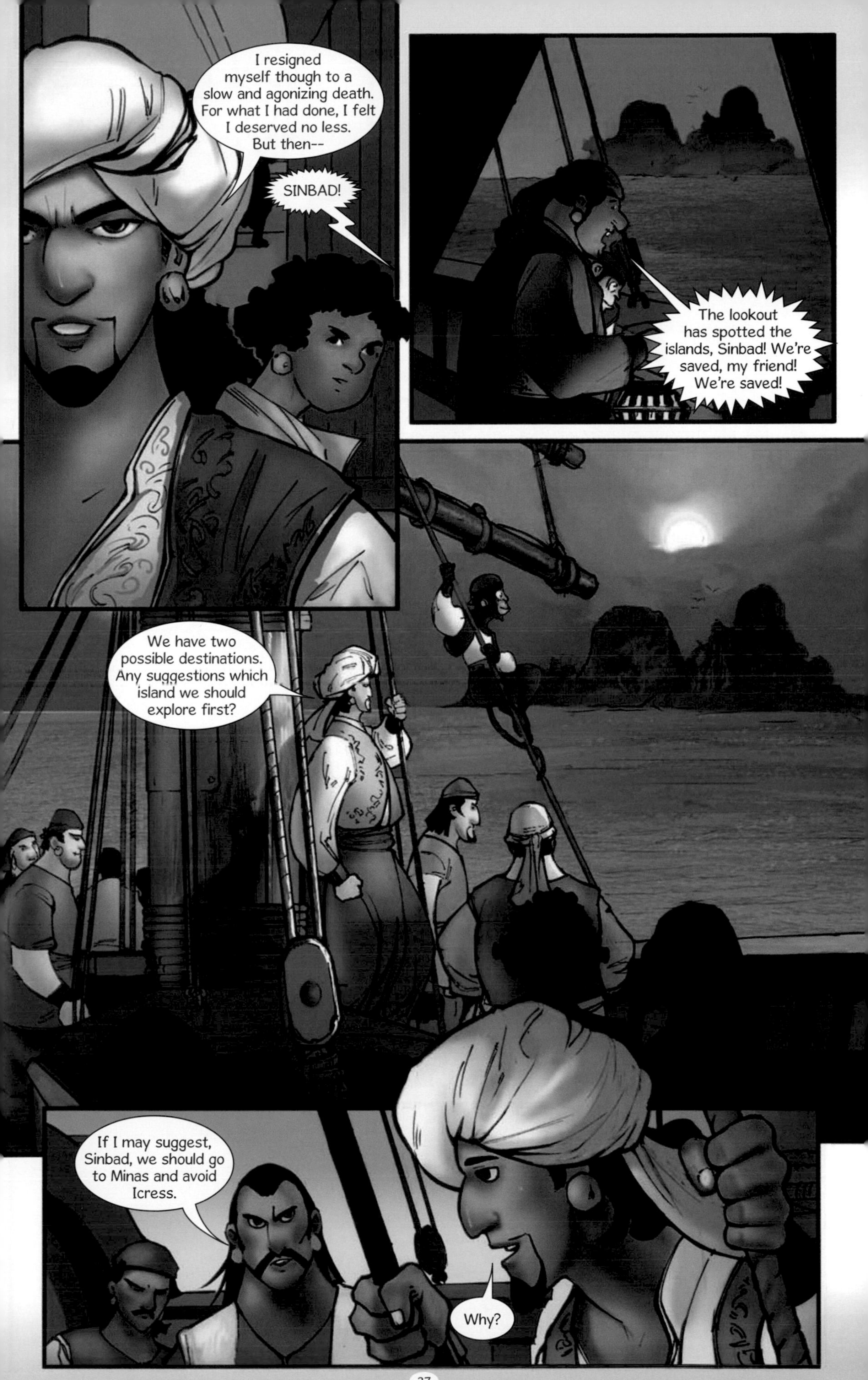
I resigned myself though to a slow and agonizing death. For what I had done, I felt I deserved no less. But then--
SINBAD!
The lookout has spotted the islands, Sinbad! We're saved, my friend! We're saved!
We have two possible destinations. Any suggestions which island we should explore first?
If I may suggest, Sinbad, we should go to Minas and avoid Icress.
Why?

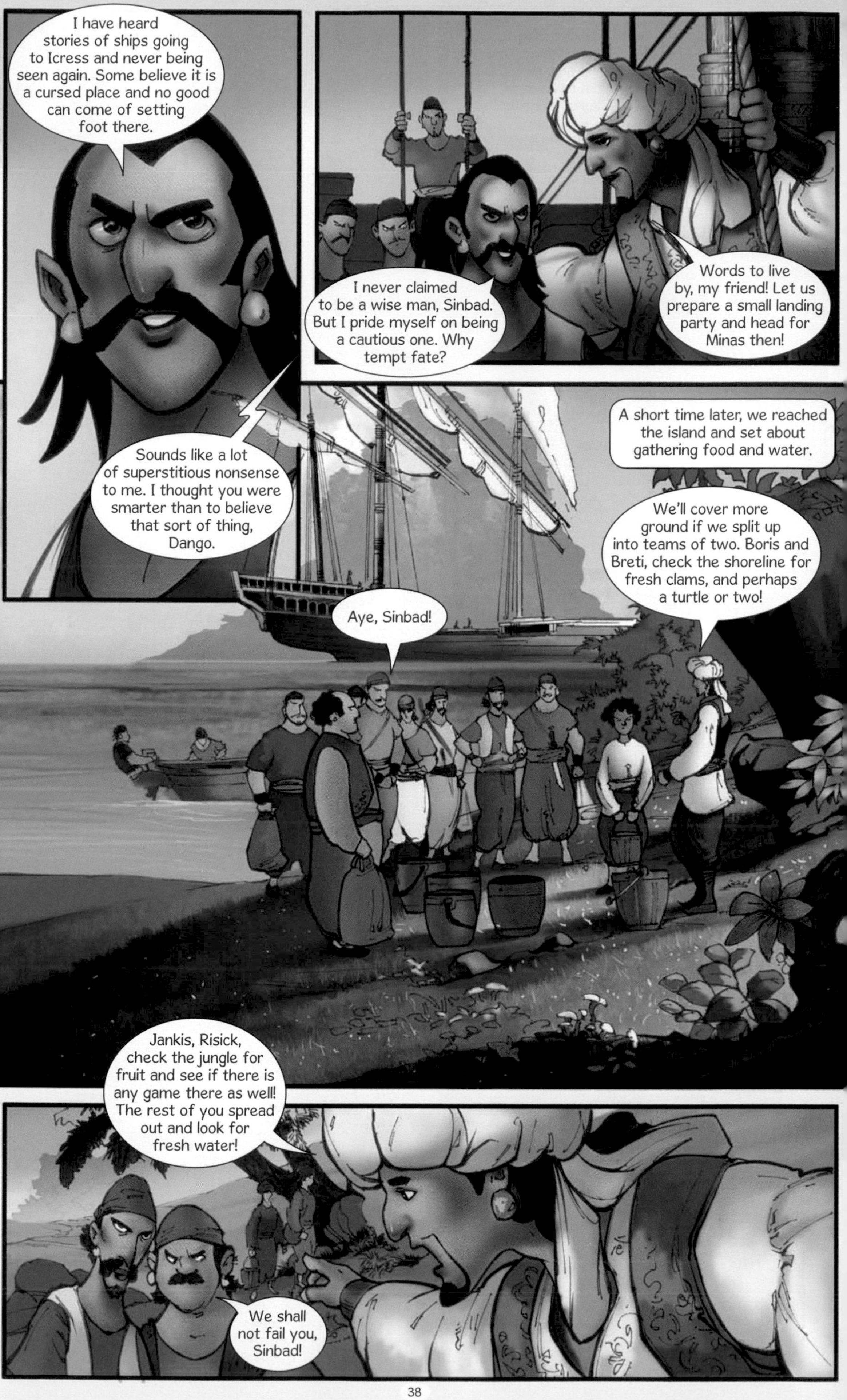
I have heard stories of ships going to Icress and never being seen again. Some believe it is a cursed place and no good can come of setting foot there.
Sounds like a lot of superstitious nonsense to me. I thought you were smarter than to believe that sort of thing, Dango.
I never claimed to be a wise man, Sinbad. But I pride myself on being a cautious one. Why tempt fate?
Words to live by, my friend! Let us prepare a small landing party and head for Minas then!
A short time later, we reached the island and set about gathering food and water.
We'll cover more ground if we split up into teams of two. Boris and Breti, check the shoreline for fresh clams, and perhaps a turtle or two!
Aye, Sinbad!
Jankis, Risick, check the jungle for fruit and see if there is any game there as well! The rest of you spread out and look for fresh water!
We shall not fail you, Sinbad!

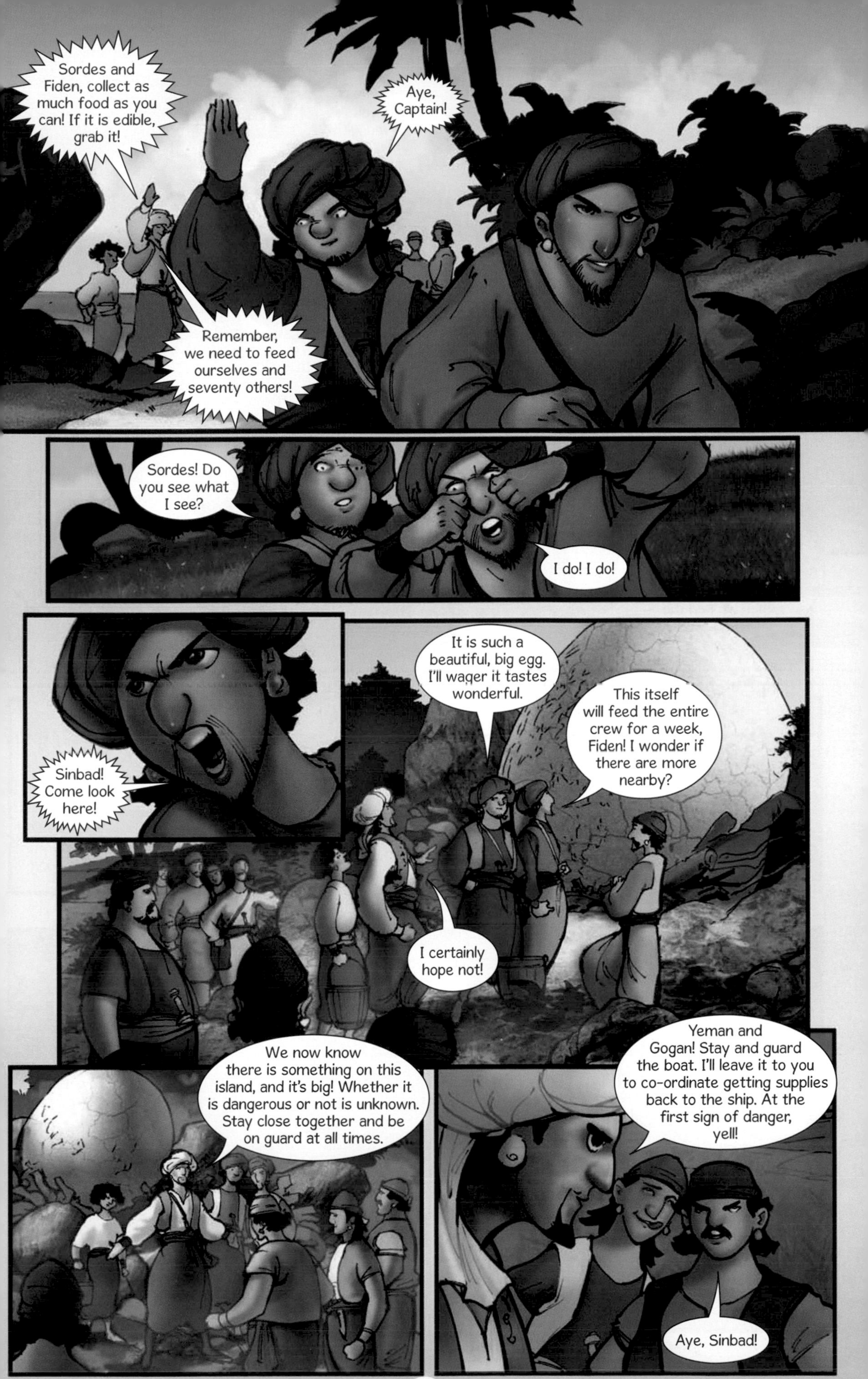
Sordes and Fiden, collect as much food as you can! If it is edible, grab it!
Aye, Captain!
Remember, we need to feed ourselves and seventy others!
Sordes! Do you see what I see?
I do! I do!
Sinbad! Come look here!
It is such a beautiful, big egg. I'll wager it tastes wonderful.
This itself will feed the entire crew for a week, Fiden! I wonder if there are more nearby?
I certainly hope not!
We now know there is something on this island, and it's big! Whether it is dangerous or not is unknown. Stay close together and be on guard at all times.
Yeman and Gogan! Stay and guard the boat. I'll leave it to you to co-ordinate getting supplies back to the ship. At the first sign of danger, yell!
Aye, Sinbad!

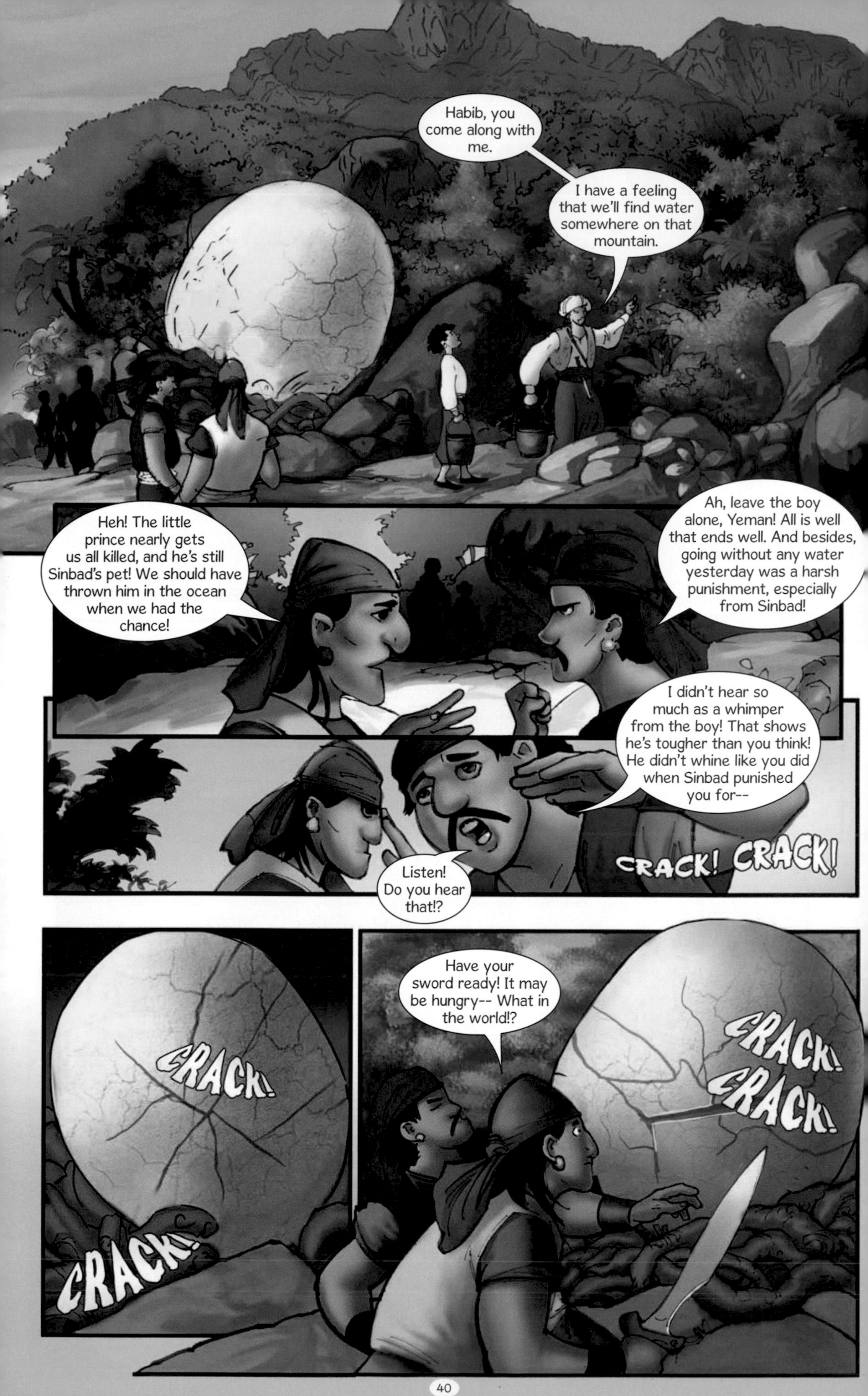

Habib, you come along with me.
I have a feeling that we'll find water somewhere on that mountain.
Heh! The little prince nearly gets us all killed, and he's still Sinbad's pet! We should have thrown him in the ocean when we had the chance!
Ah, leave the boy alone, Yeman! All is well that ends well. And besides, going without any water yesterday was a harsh punishment, especially from Sinbad!
I didn't hear so much as a whimper from the boy! That shows he's tougher than you think! He didn't whine like you did when Sinbad punished you for--
CRACK! CRACK!
Listen! Do you hear that!?
CRACK!
CRACK!
Have your sword ready! It may be hungry-- What in the world!?
CRACK! CRACK!

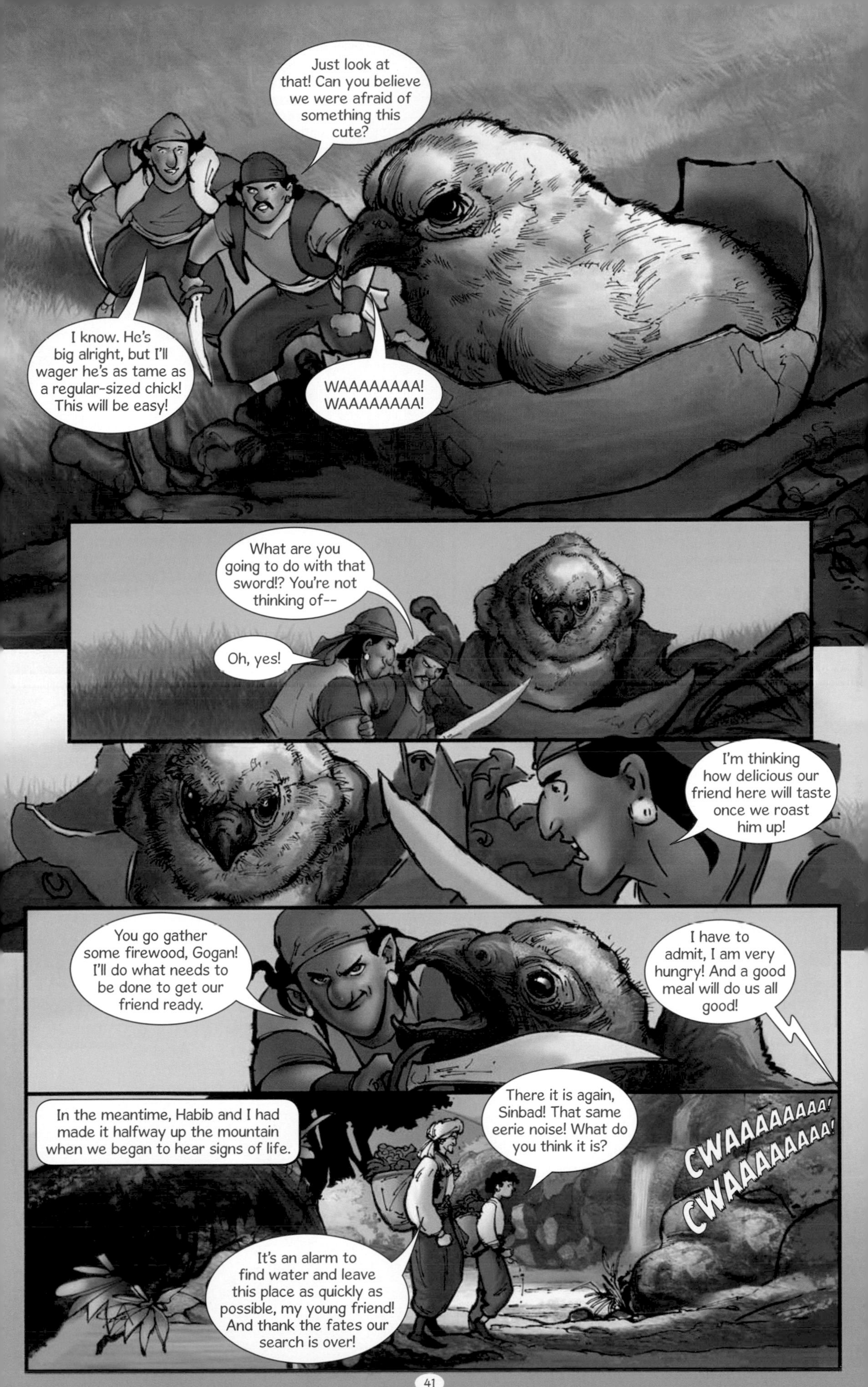
Just look at that! Can you believe we were afraid of something this cute?
I know. He's big alright, but I'll wager he's as tame as a regular-sized chick! This will be easy!
WAAAAAAAA! WAAAAAAAA!
What are you going to do with that sword!? You're not thinking of--
Oh, yes!
I'm thinking how delicious our friend here will taste once we roast him up!
You go gather some firewood, Gogan! I'll do what needs to be done to get our friend ready.
I have to admit, I am very hungry! And a good meal will do us all good!
In the meantime, Habib and I had made it halfway up the mountain when we began to hear signs of life.
There it is again, Sinbad! That same eerie noise! What do you think it is?
CWAAAAAAAA! CWAAAAAAAA!
It's an alarm to find water and leave this place as quickly as possible, my young friend! And thank the fates our search is over!

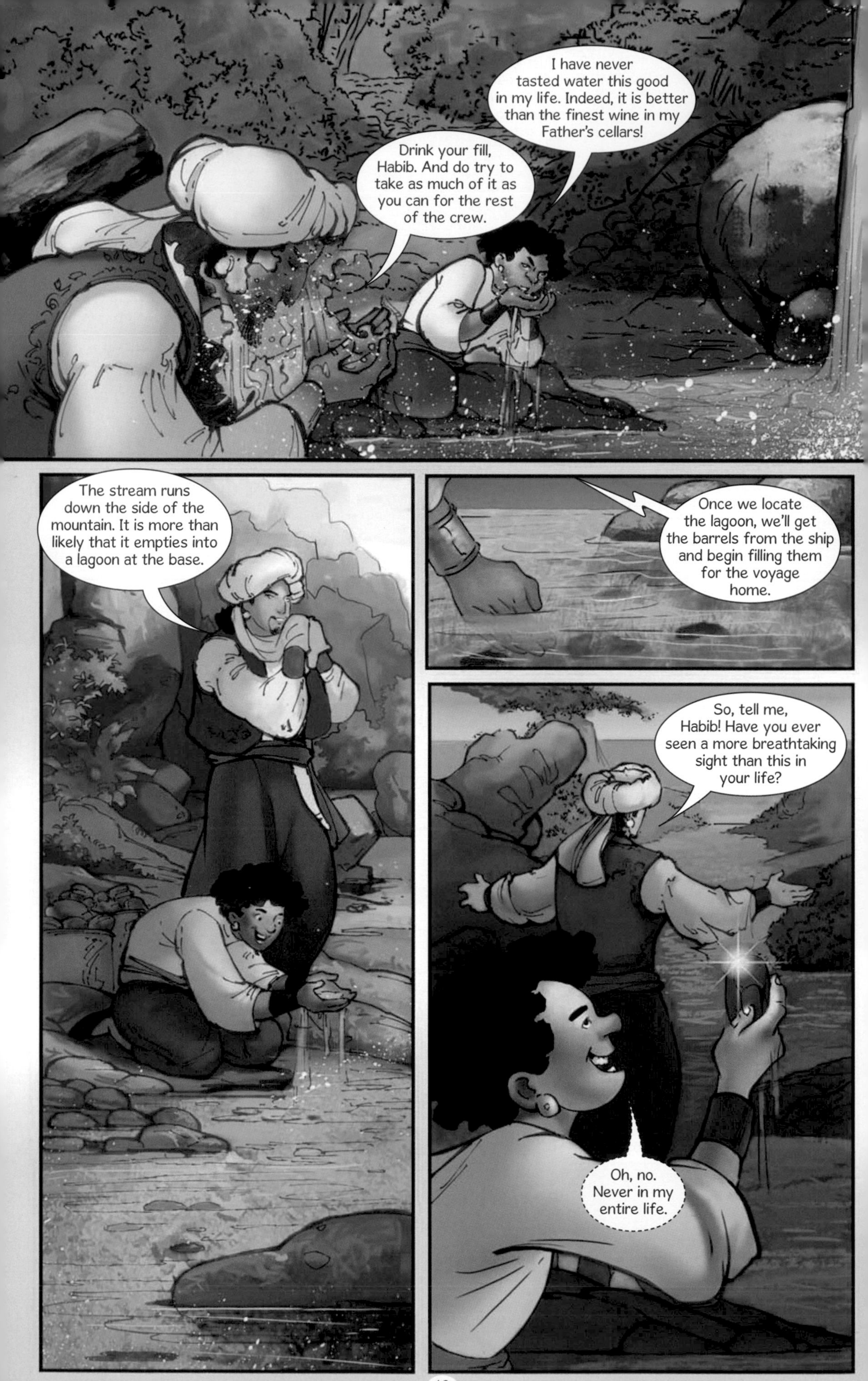
Drink your fill, Habib. And do try to take as much of it as you can for the rest of the crew.
I have never tasted water this good in my life. Indeed, it is better than the finest wine in my Father's cellars!
The stream runs down the side of the mountain. It is more than likely that it empties into a lagoon at the base.
Once we locate the lagoon, we'll get the barrels from the ship and begin filling them for the voyage home.
So, tell me, Habib! Have you ever seen a more breathtaking sight than this in your life?
Oh, no. Never in my entire life.

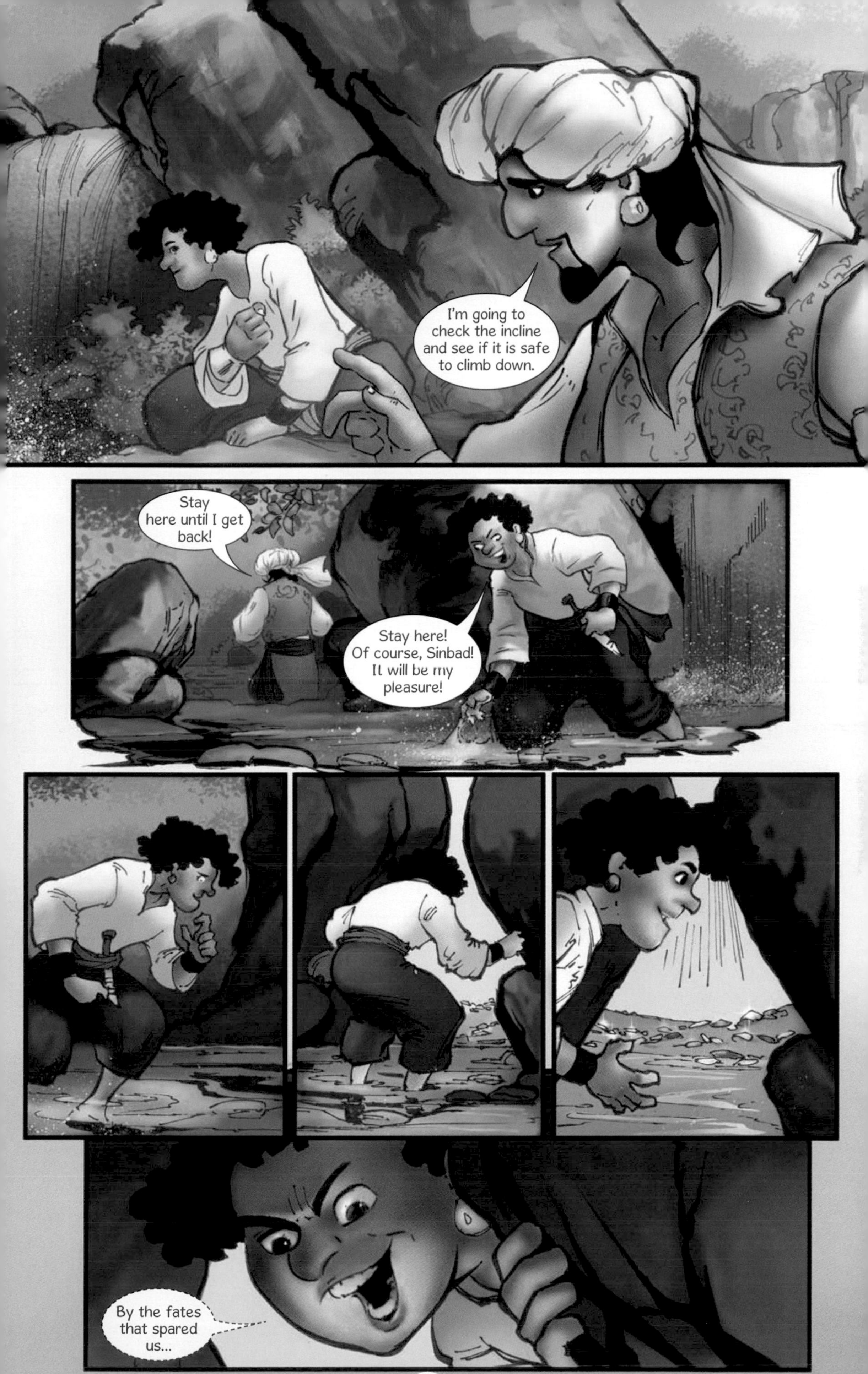
I'm going to check the incline and see if it is safe to climb down.
Stay here until I get back!
Stay here! Of course, Sinbad! It will be my pleasure!
By the fates that spared us...

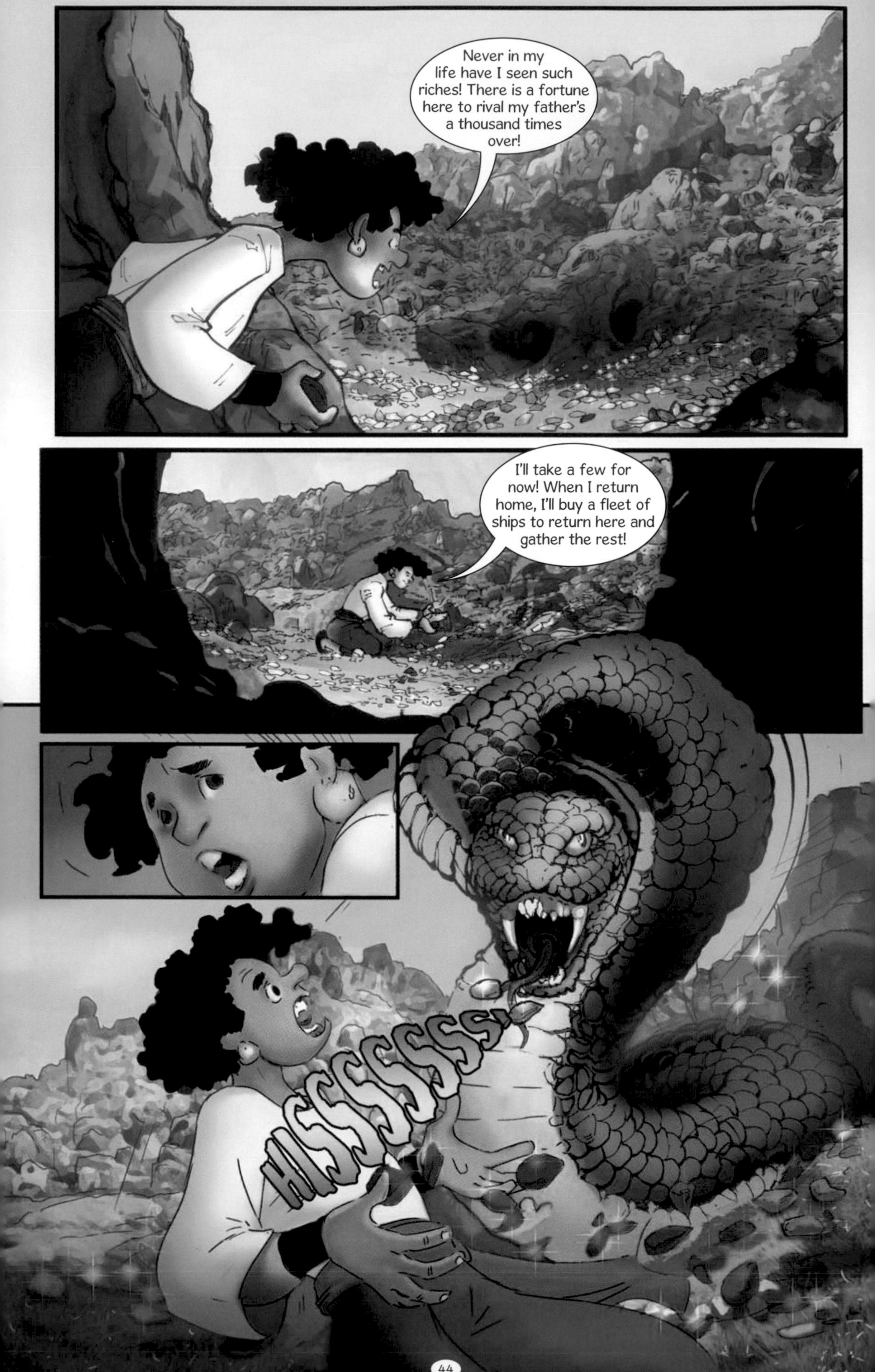
Never in my life have I seen such riches! There is a fortune here to rival my father's a thousand times over!
I'll take a few for now! When I return home, I'll buy a fleet of ships to return here and gather the rest!
HISSSSSSS!

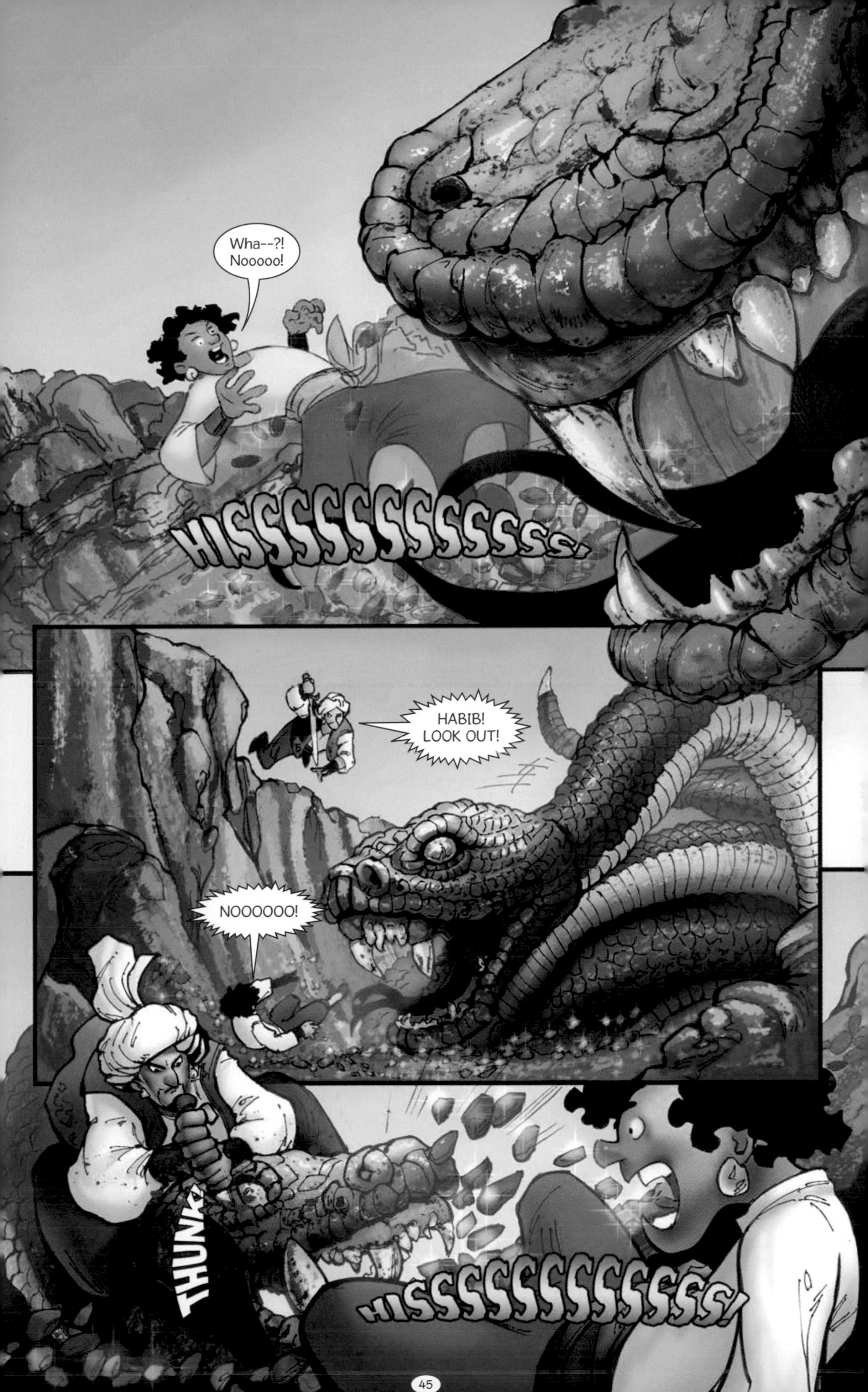
Wha--?! Nooooo!
HISSSSSSSSSSSSSS!
HABIB! LOOK OUT!
NOOOOOO!
THUNK!
HISSSSSSSSSSSSSS!

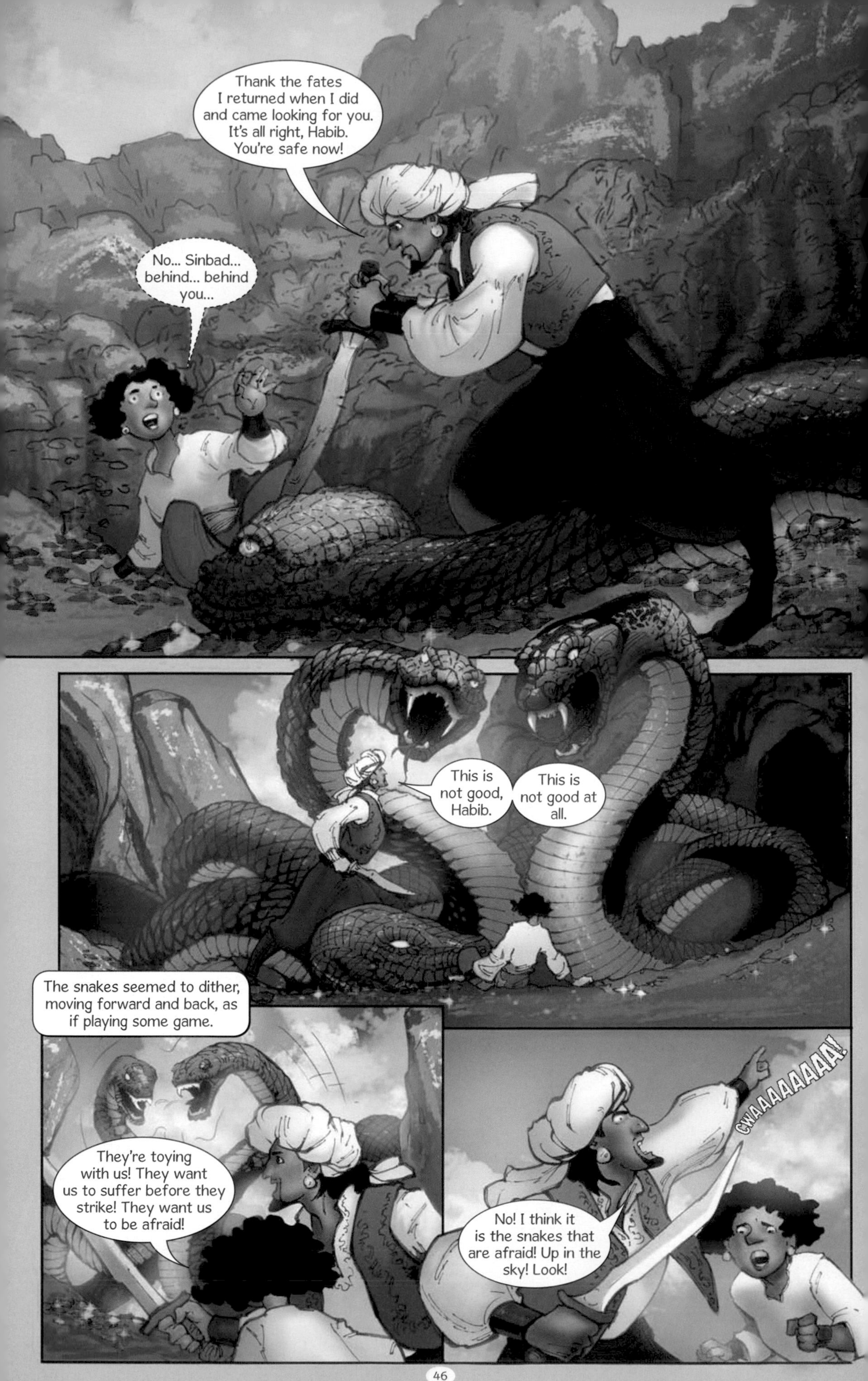
Thank the fates I returned when I did and came looking for you. It's all right, Habib. You're safe now!
No... Sinbad... behind... behind you...
This is not good, Habib.
This is not good at all.
The snakes seemed to dither, moving forward and back, as if playing some game.
They're toying with us! They want us to suffer before they strike! They want us to be afraid!
CWAAAAAAAA!
No! I think it is the snakes that are afraid! Up in the sky! Look!

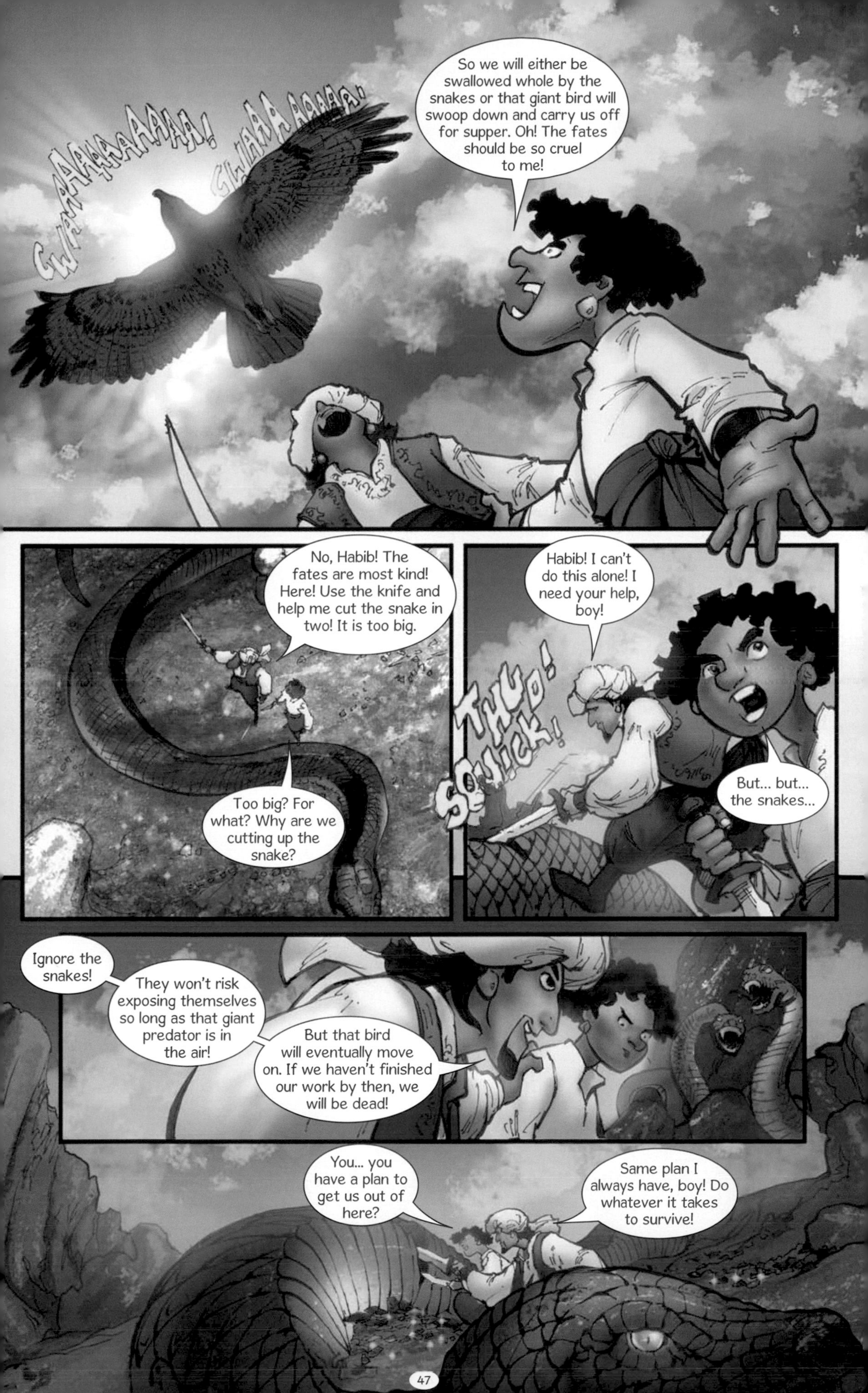
CWRAAAAAAAAA!
CWAAAAAAAA!
So we will either be swallowed whole by the snakes or that giant bird will swoop down and carry us off for supper. Oh! The fates should be so cruel to me!
No, Habib! The fates are most kind! Here! Use the knife and help me cut the snake in two! It is too big.
Too big? For what? Why are we cutting up the snake?
Habib! I can't do this alone! I need your help, boy!
THUD!
SQUICK!
But... but... the snakes...
Ignore the snakes!
They won't risk exposing themselves so long as that giant predator is in the air!
But that bird will eventually move on. If we haven't finished our work by then, we will be dead!
You... you have a plan to get us out of here?
Same plan I always have, boy! Do whatever it takes to survive!

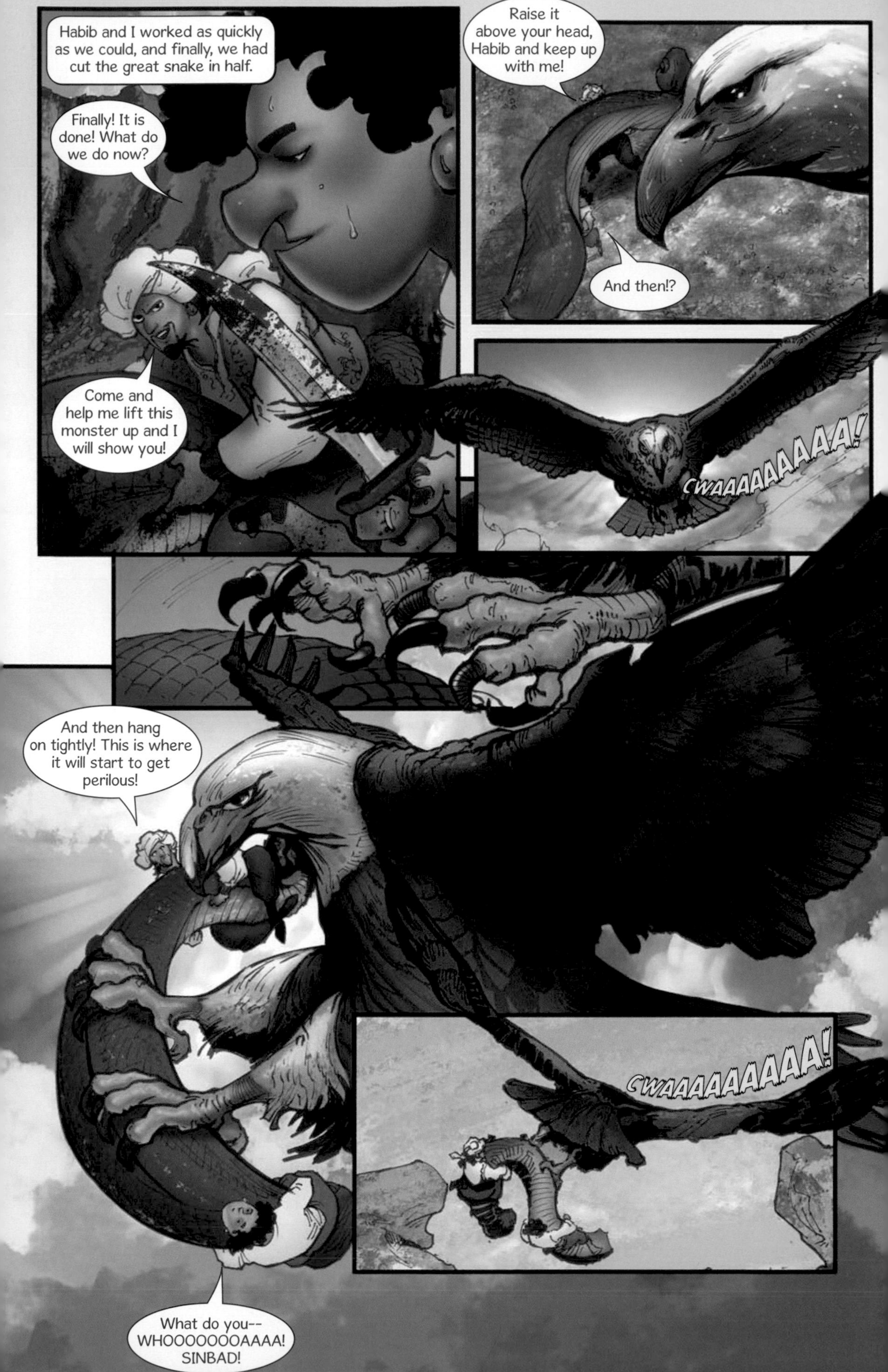
Habib and I worked as quickly as we could, and finally, we had cut the great snake in half.
Finally! It is done! What do we do now?
Come and help me lift this monster up and I will show you!
Raise it above your head, Habib and keep up with me!
And then!?
CWAAAAAAAAAA!
And then hang on tightly! This is where it will start to get perilous!
CWAAAAAAAAAA!
What do you-- WHOOOOOOOAAAA! SINBAD!

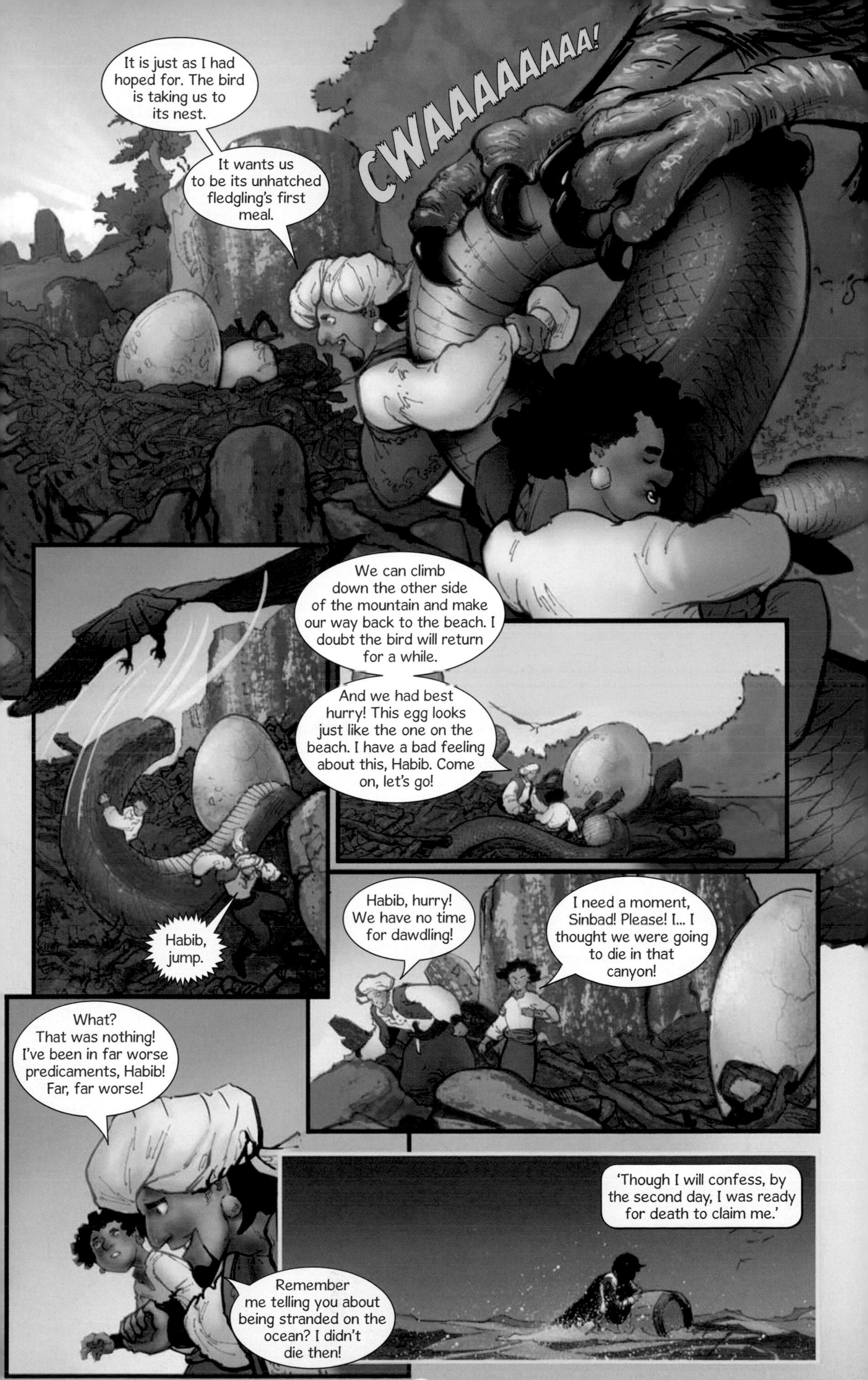

It is just as I had hoped for. The bird is taking us to its nest.
It wants us to be its unhatched fledgling's first meal.
CWAAAAAAAA!
We can climb down the other side of the mountain and make our way back to the beach. I doubt the bird will return for a while.
And we had best hurry! This egg looks just like the one on the beach. I have a bad feeling about this, Habib. Come on, let's go!
Habib, jump.
Habib, hurry! We have no time for dawdling!
I need a moment, Sinbad! Please! I... I thought we were going to die in that canyon!
What? That was nothing! I've been in far worse predicaments, Habib! Far, far worse!
Remember me telling you about being stranded on the ocean? I didn't die then!
'Though I will confess, by the second day, I was ready for death to claim me.'

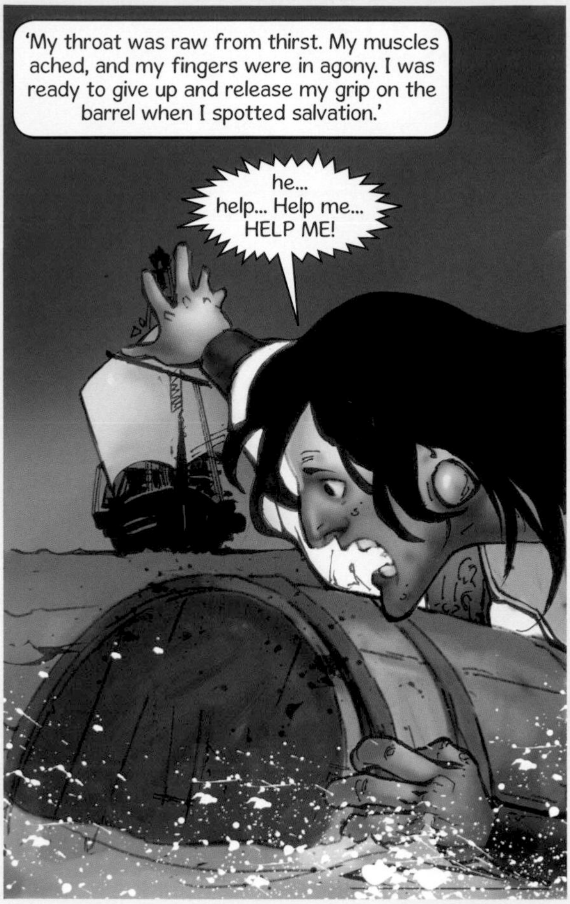
'My throat was raw from thirst. My muscles ached, and my fingers were in agony. I was ready to give up and release my grip on the barrel when I spotted salvation.'
he... help... Help me... HELP ME!

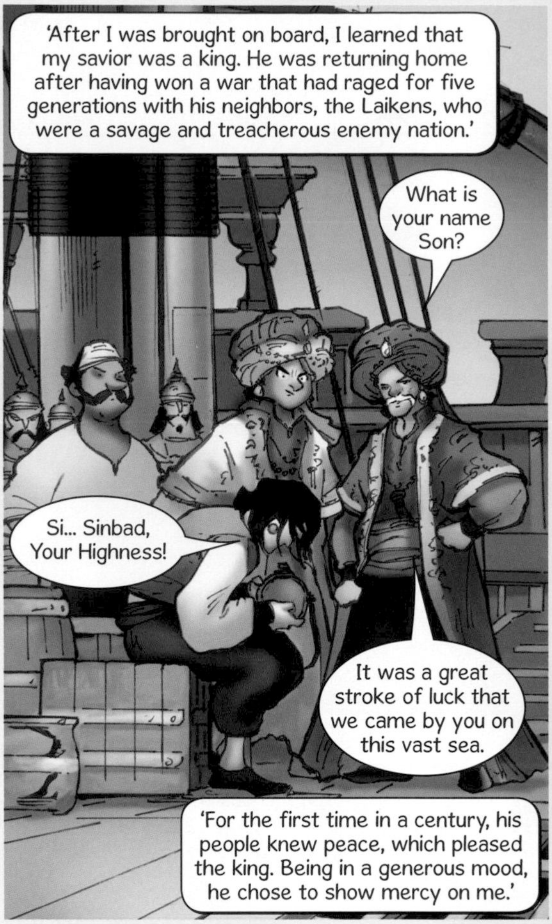
'After I was brought on board, I learned that my savior was a king. He was returning home after having won a war that had raged for five generations with his neighbors, the Laikens, who were a savage and treacherous enemy nation.'
What is your name Son?
Si... Sinbad, Your Highness!
It was a great stroke of luck that we came by you on this vast sea.
'For the first time in a century, his people knew peace, which pleased the king. Being in a generous mood, he chose to show mercy on me.'

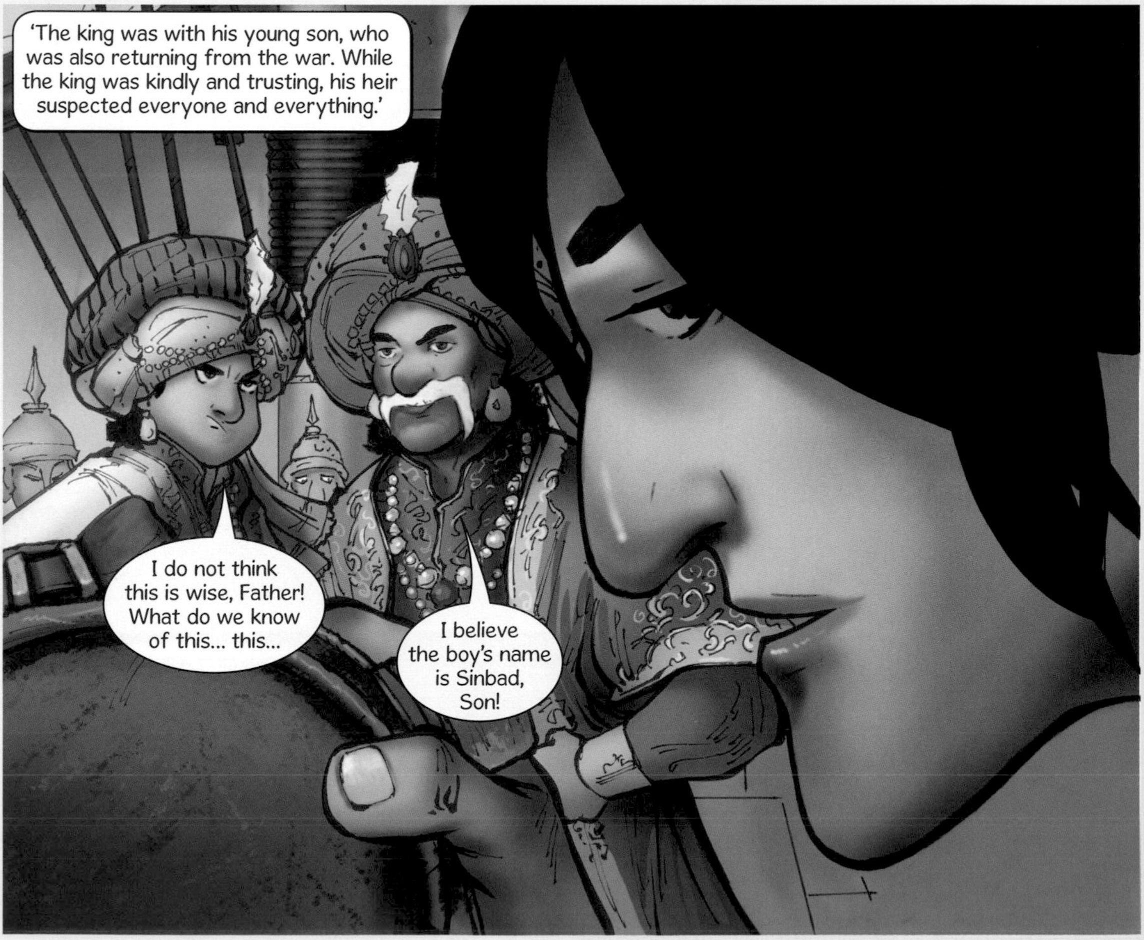
'The king was with his young son, who was also returning from the war. While the king was kindly and trusting, his heir suspected everyone and everything.'
I do not think this is wise, Father! What do we know of this... this...
I believe the boy's name is Sinbad, Son!

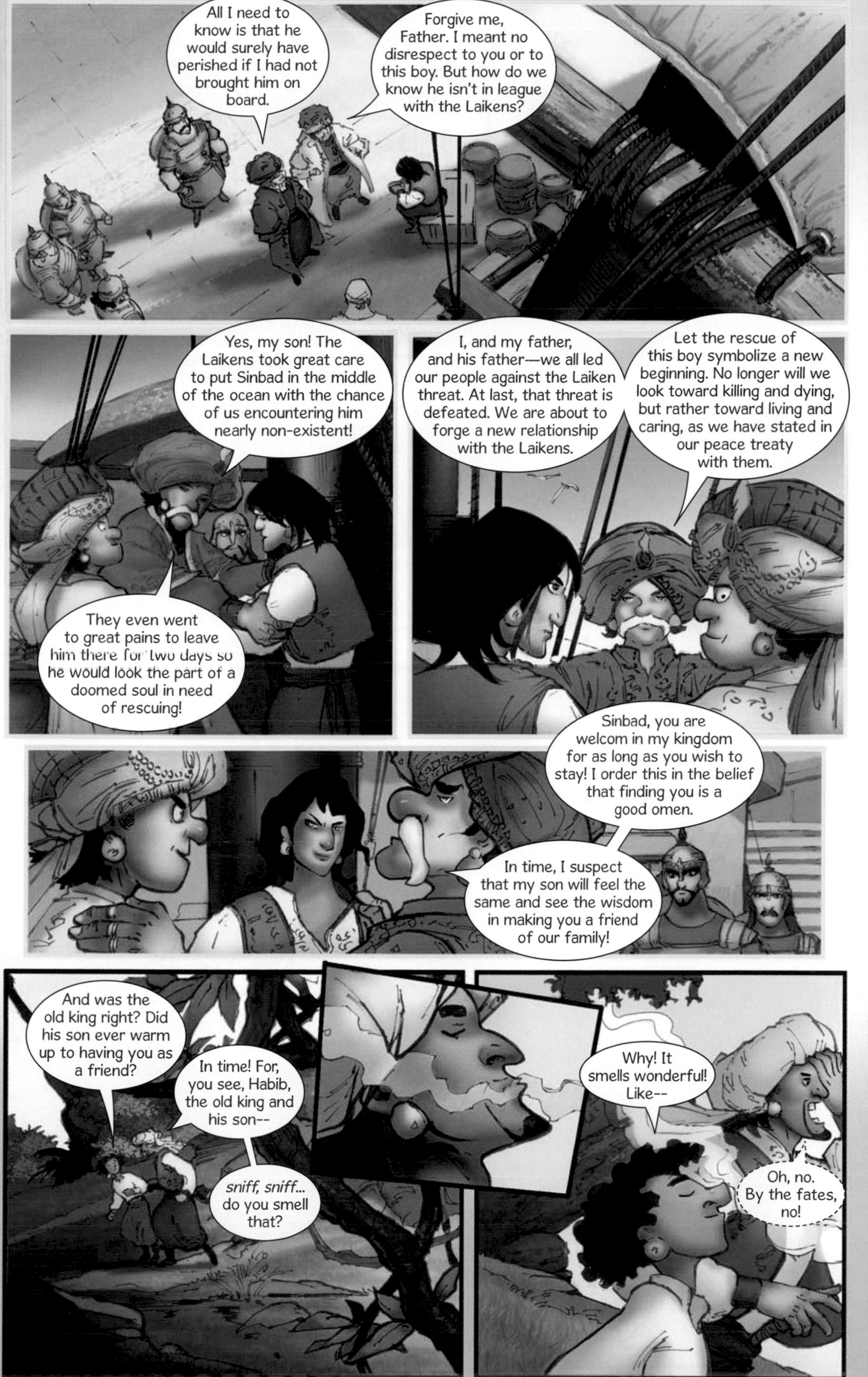
All I need to know is that he would surely have perished if I had not brought him on board.
Forgive me, Father. I meant no disrespect to you or to this boy. But how do we know he isn't in league with the Laikens?
Yes, my son! The Laikens took great care to put Sinbad in the middle of the ocean with the chance of us encountering him nearly non-existent!
They even went to great pains to leave him there for two days so he would look the part of a doomed soul in need of rescuing!
I, and my father, and his father—we all led our people against the Laiken threat. At last, that threat is defeated. We are about to forge a new relationship with the Laikens.
Let the rescue of this boy symbolize a new beginning. No longer will we look toward killing and dying, but rather toward living and caring, as we have stated in our peace treaty with them.
Sinbad, you are welcom in my kingdom for as long as you wish to stay! I order this in the belief that finding you is a good omen.
In time, I suspect that my son will feel the same and see the wisdom in making you a friend of our family!
And was the old king right? Did his son ever warm up to having you as a friend?
In time! For, you see, Habib, the old king and his son--
sniff, sniff... do you smell that?
Why! It smells wonderful! Like--
Oh, no. By the fates, no!

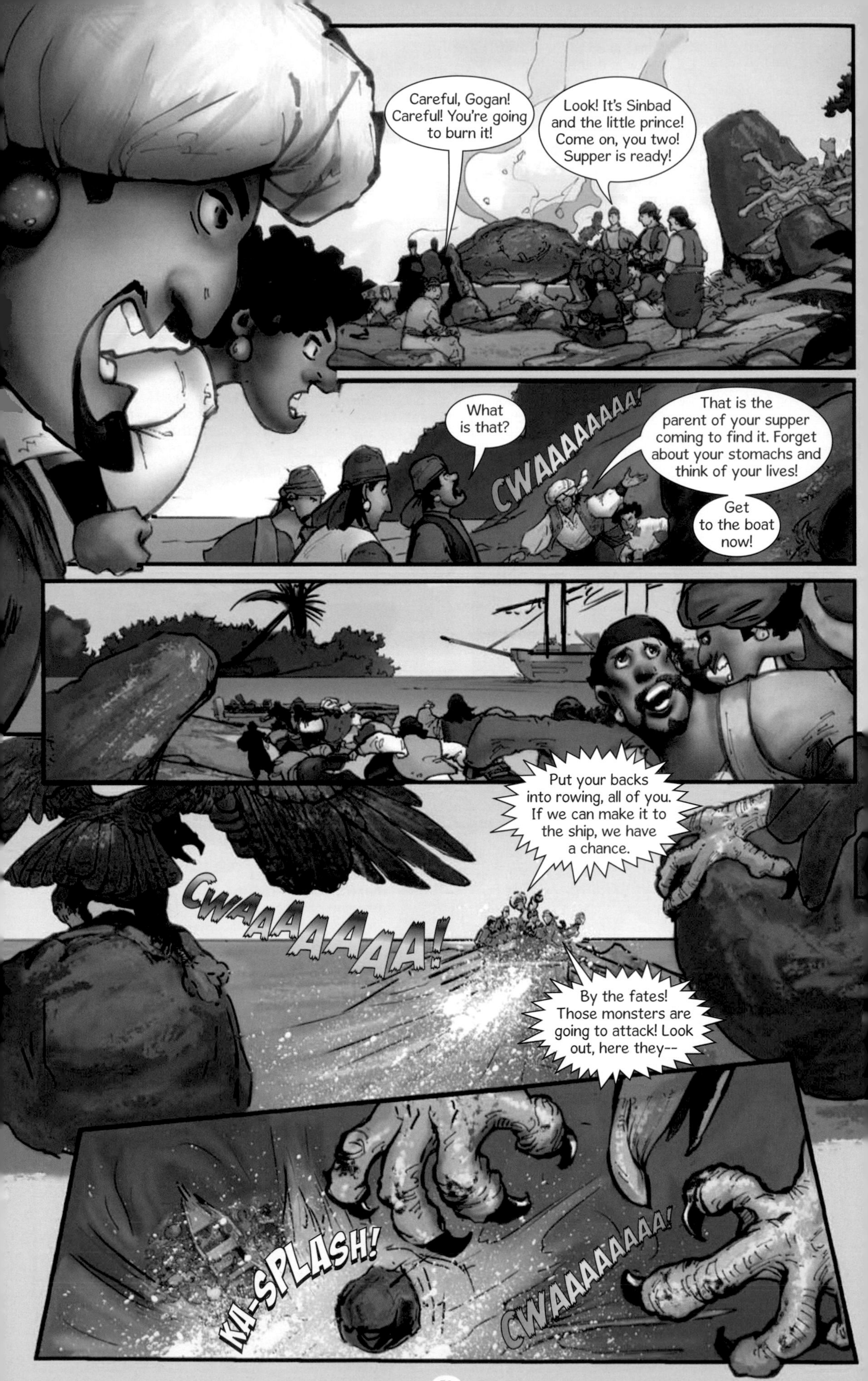
Careful, Gogan! Careful! You're going to burn it!
Look! It's Sinbad and the little prince! Come on, you two! Supper is ready!
What is that?
CWAAAAAAAA!
That is the parent of your supper coming to find it. Forget about your stomachs and think of your lives!
Get to the boat now!
Put your backs into rowing, all of you. If we can make it to the ship, we have a chance.
CWAAAAAAAA!
By the fates! Those monsters are going to attack! Look out, here they--
KA-SPLASH!
CWAAAAAAAA!

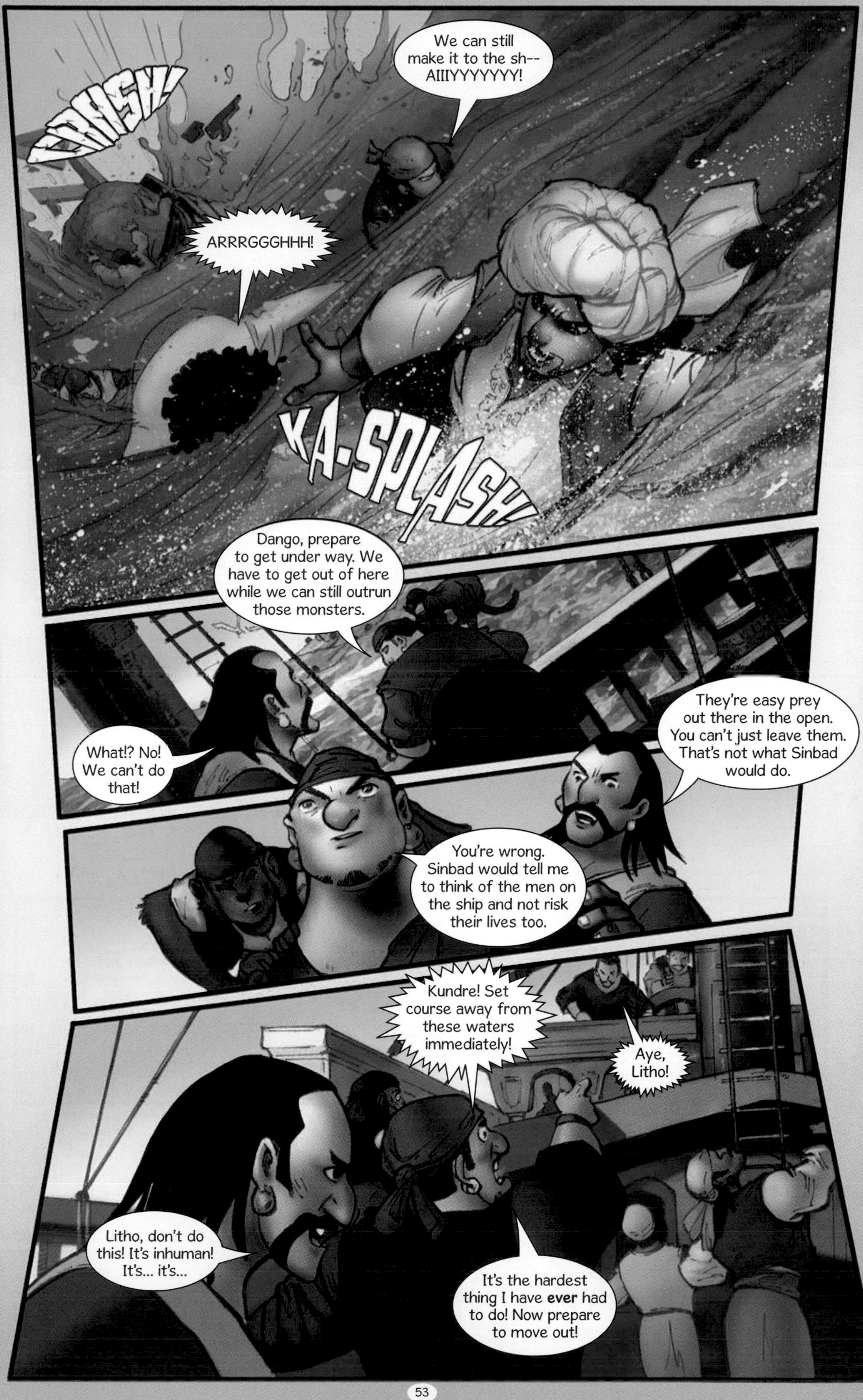
We can still make it to the sh-- AIIIYYYYYYY!
ARRRGGGHHH!
KA-SPLASH!
Dango, prepare to get under way. We have to get out of here while we can still outrun those monsters.
What!? No! We can't do that!
They're easy prey out there in the open. You can't just leave them. That's not what Sinbad would do.
You're wrong. Sinbad would tell me to think of the men on the ship and not risk their lives too.
Kundre! Set course away from these waters immediately!
Aye, Litho!
Litho, don't do this! It's inhuman! It's... it's...
It's the hardest thing I have **ever** had to do! Now prepare to move out!

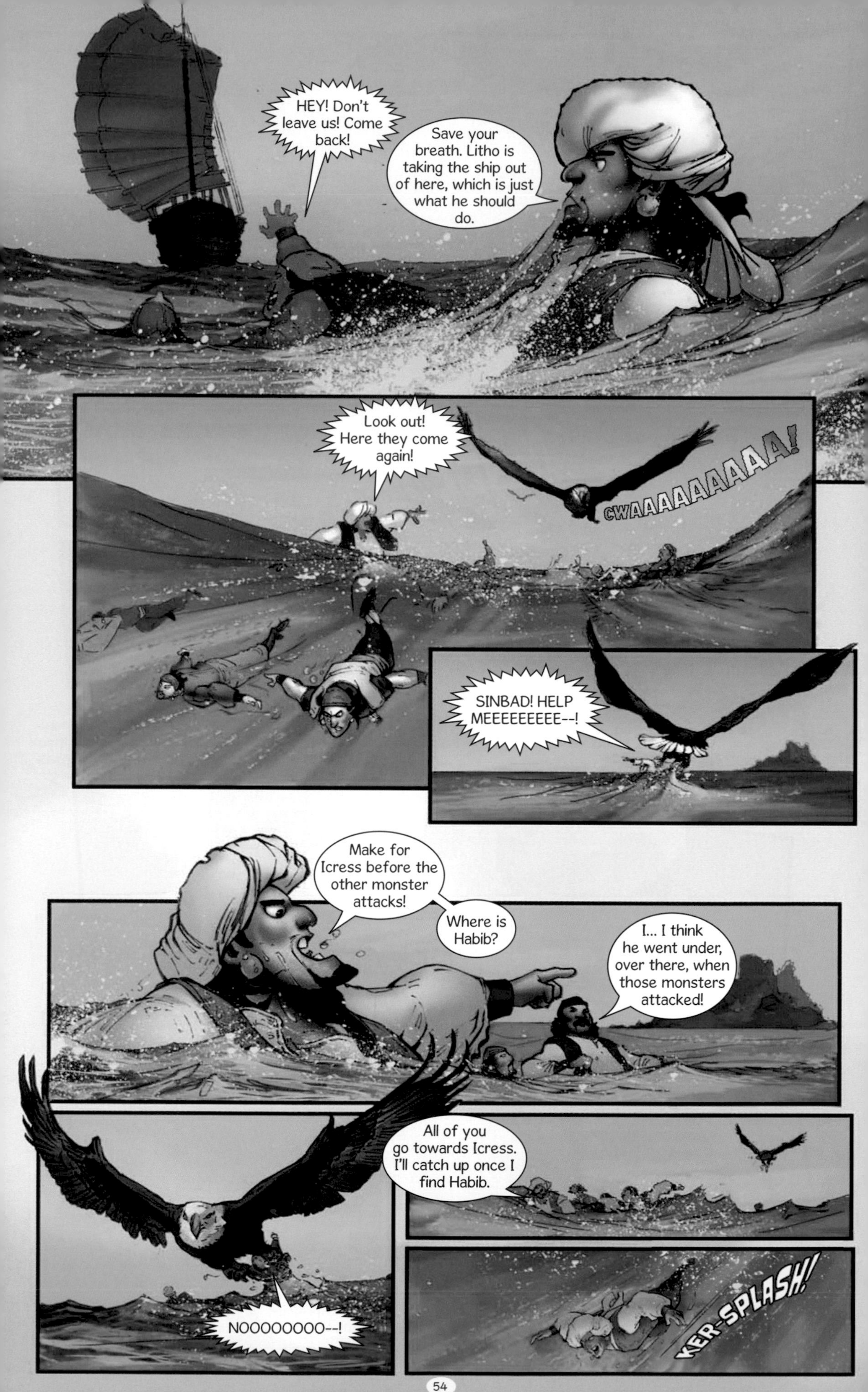

HEY! Don't leave us! Come back!
Save your breath. Litho is taking the ship out of here, which is just what he should do.
Look out! Here they come again!
CWAAAAAAAAAA!
SINBAD! HELP MEEEEEEEEE--!
Make for Icress before the other monster attacks!
Where is Habib?
I... I think he went under, over there, when those monsters attacked!
All of you go towards Icress. I'll catch up once I find Habib.
NOOOOOOOO--!
KER-SPLASH!

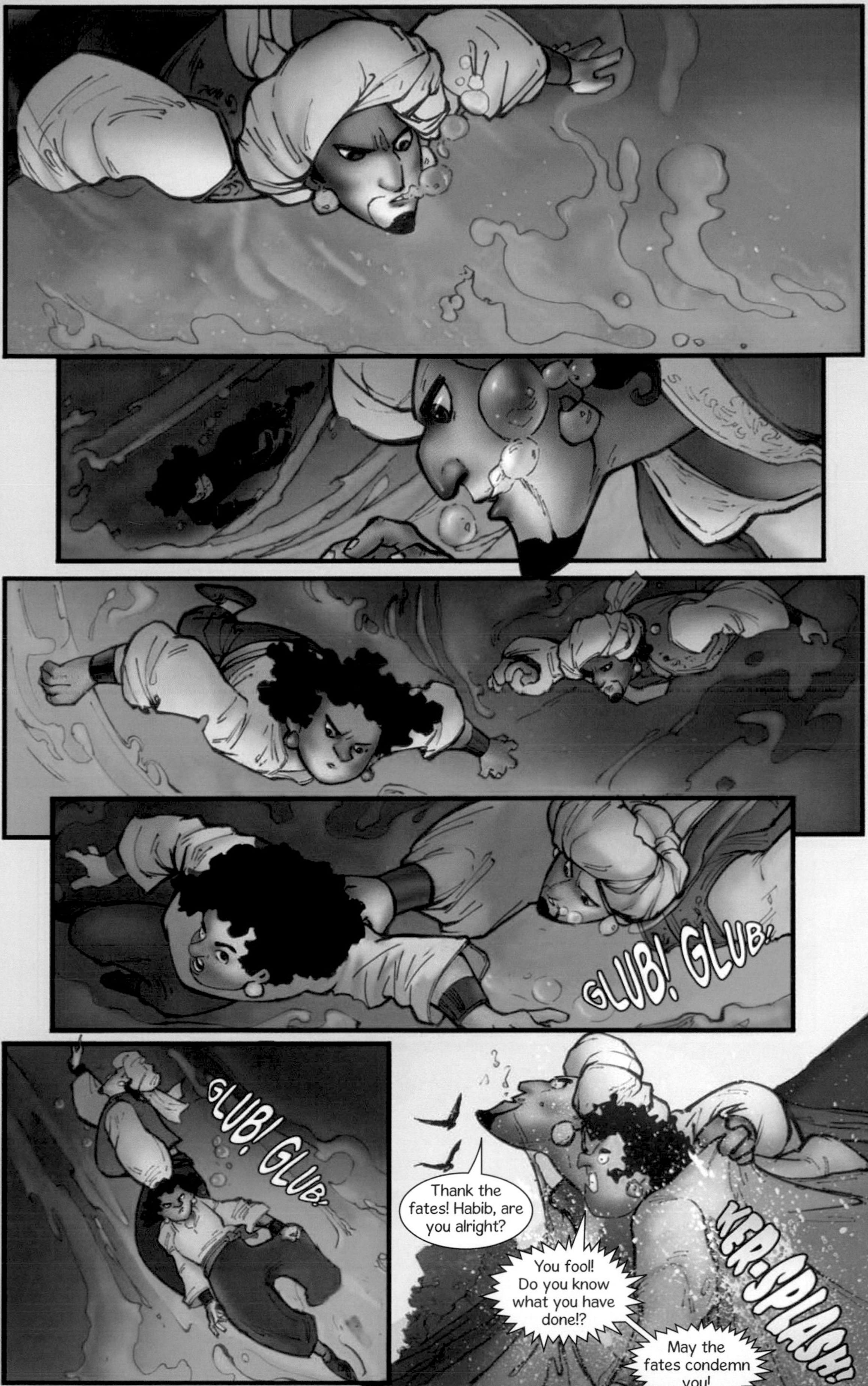
GLUB! GLUB!
GLUB! GLUB!
Thank the fates! Habib, are you alright?
You fool! Do you know what you have done!?
May the fates condemn you!
KER-SPLASH!

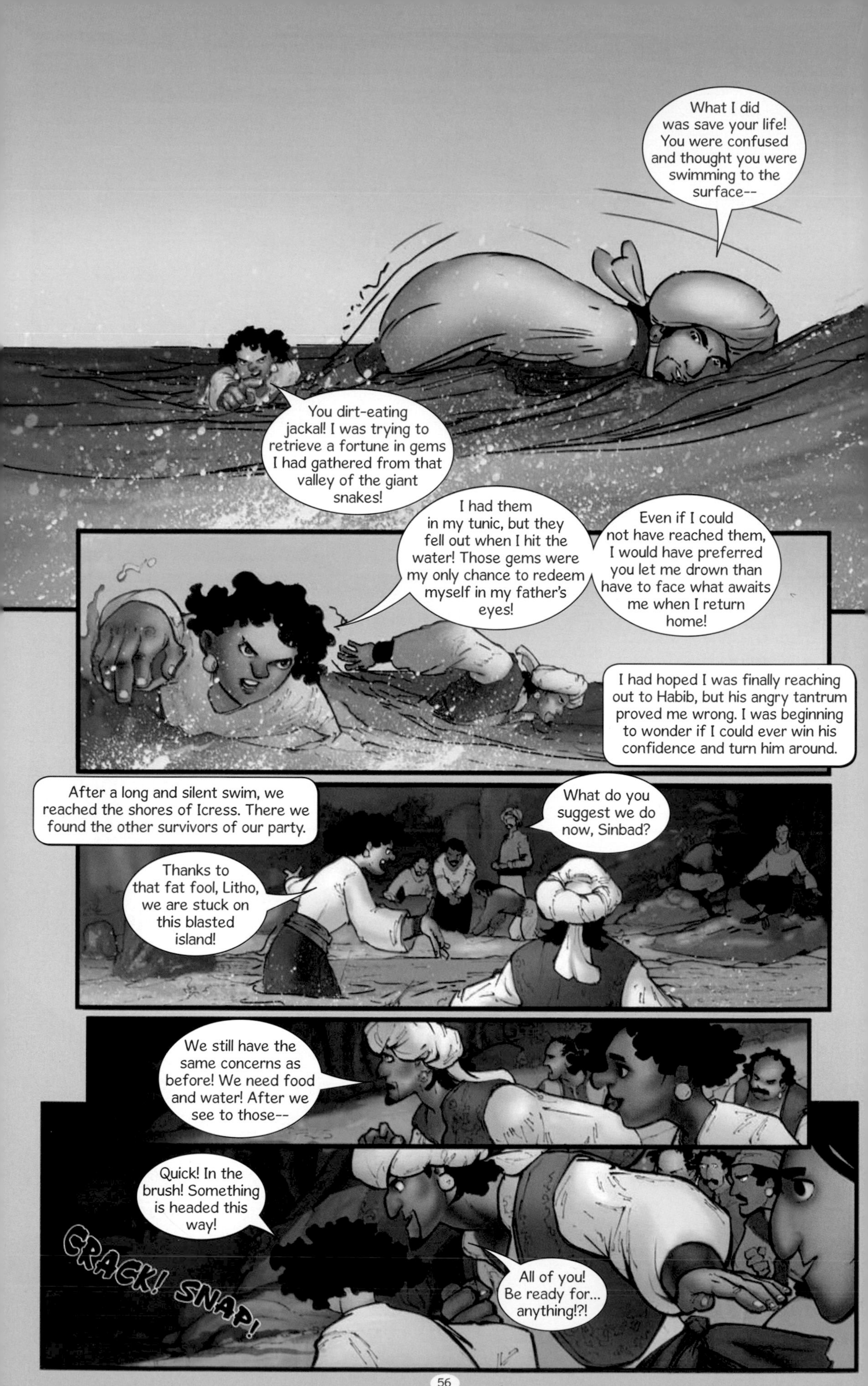
What I did was save your life! You were confused and thought you were swimming to the surface--
You dirt-eating jackal! I was trying to retrieve a fortune in gems I had gathered from that valley of the giant snakes!
I had them in my tunic, but they fell out when I hit the water! Those gems were my only chance to redeem myself in my father's eyes!
Even if I could not have reached them, I would have preferred you let me drown than have to face what awaits me when I return home!
I had hoped I was finally reaching out to Habib, but his angry tantrum proved me wrong. I was beginning to wonder if I could ever win his confidence and turn him around.
After a long and silent swim, we reached the shores of Icress. There we found the other survivors of our party.
What do you suggest we do now, Sinbad?
Thanks to that fat fool, Litho, we are stuck on this blasted island!
We still have the same concerns as before! We need food and water! After we see to those--
Quick! In the brush! Something is headed this way!
CRACK! SNAP!
All of you! Be ready for... anything!?!

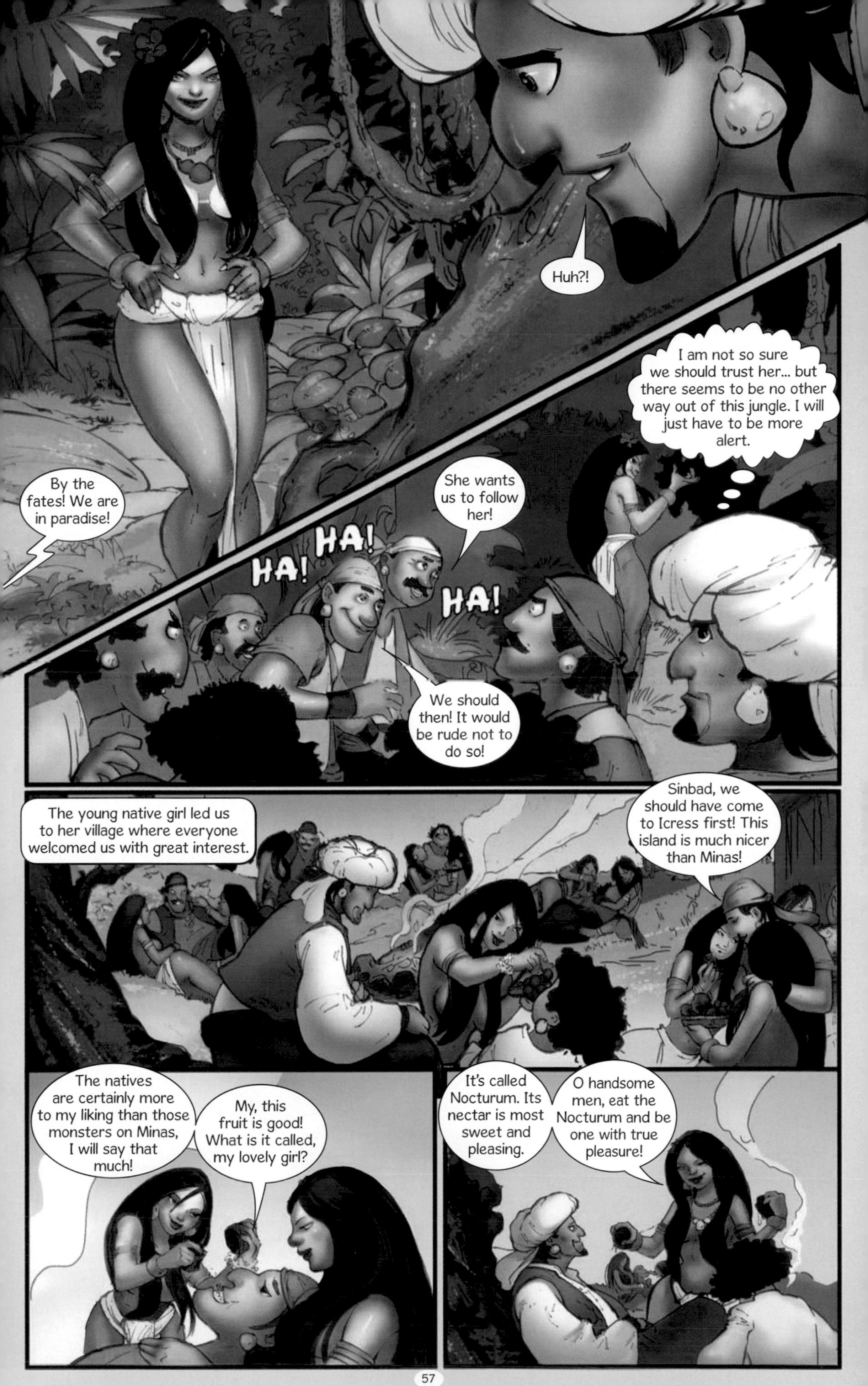
Huh?!
By the fates! We are in paradise!
HA! HA!
She wants us to follow her!
HA!
I am not so sure we should trust her... but there seems to be no other way out of this jungle. I will just have to be more alert.
We should then! It would be rude not to do so!
The young native girl led us to her village where everyone welcomed us with great interest.
Sinbad, we should have come to Icress first! This island is much nicer than Minas!
The natives are certainly more to my liking than those monsters on Minas, I will say that much!
My, this fruit is good! What is it called, my lovely girl?
It's called Nocturum. Its nectar is most sweet and pleasing.
O handsome men, eat the Nocturum and be one with true pleasure!

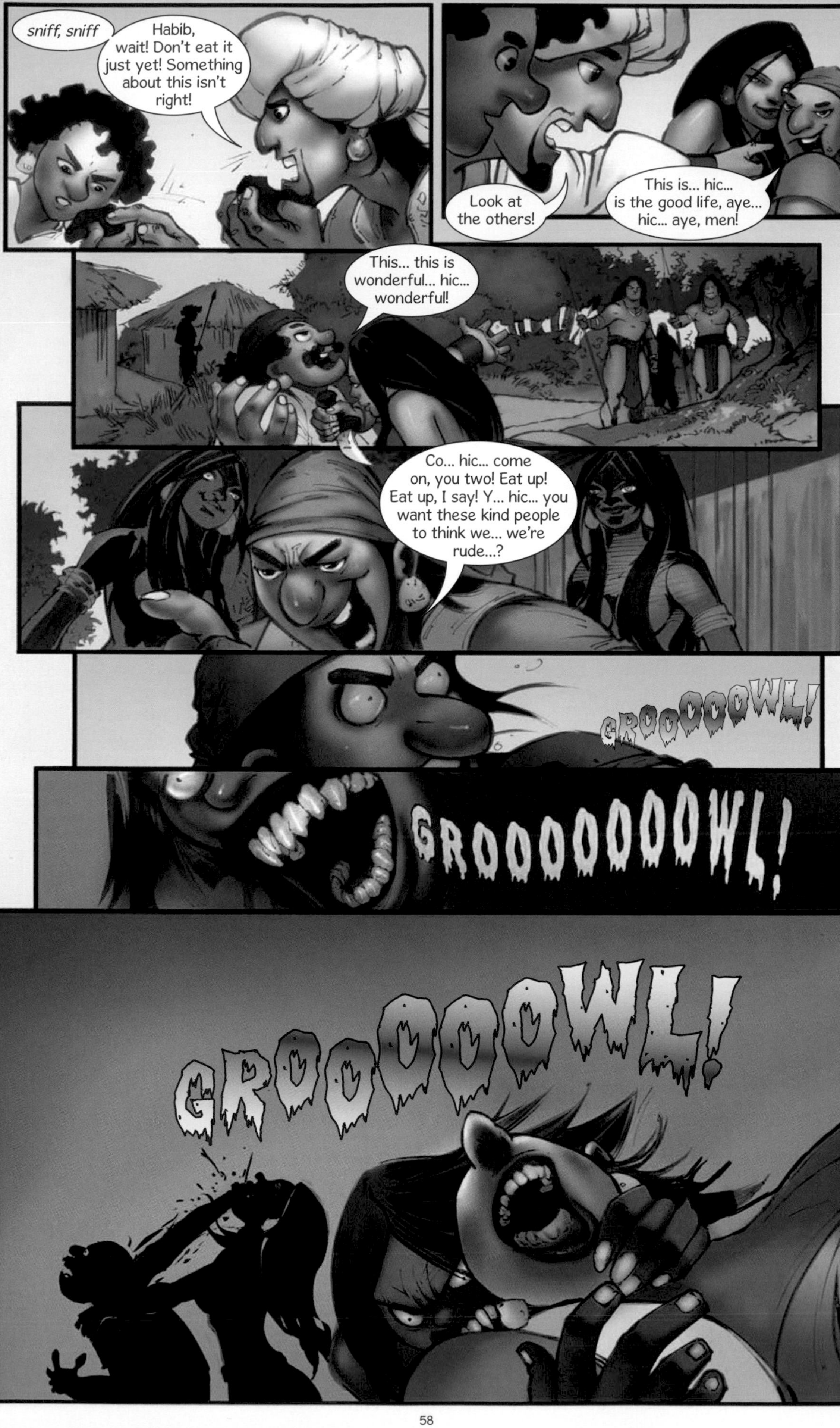
sniff, sniff
Habib, wait! Don't eat it just yet! Something about this isn't right!
Look at the others!
This is... hic... is the good life, aye... hic... aye, men!
This... this is wonderful... hic... wonderful!
Co... hic... come on, you two! Eat up! Eat up, I say! Y... hic... you want these kind people to think we... we're rude...?
GROOOOOOWL!
GROOOOOOOWL!
GROOOOOOWL!

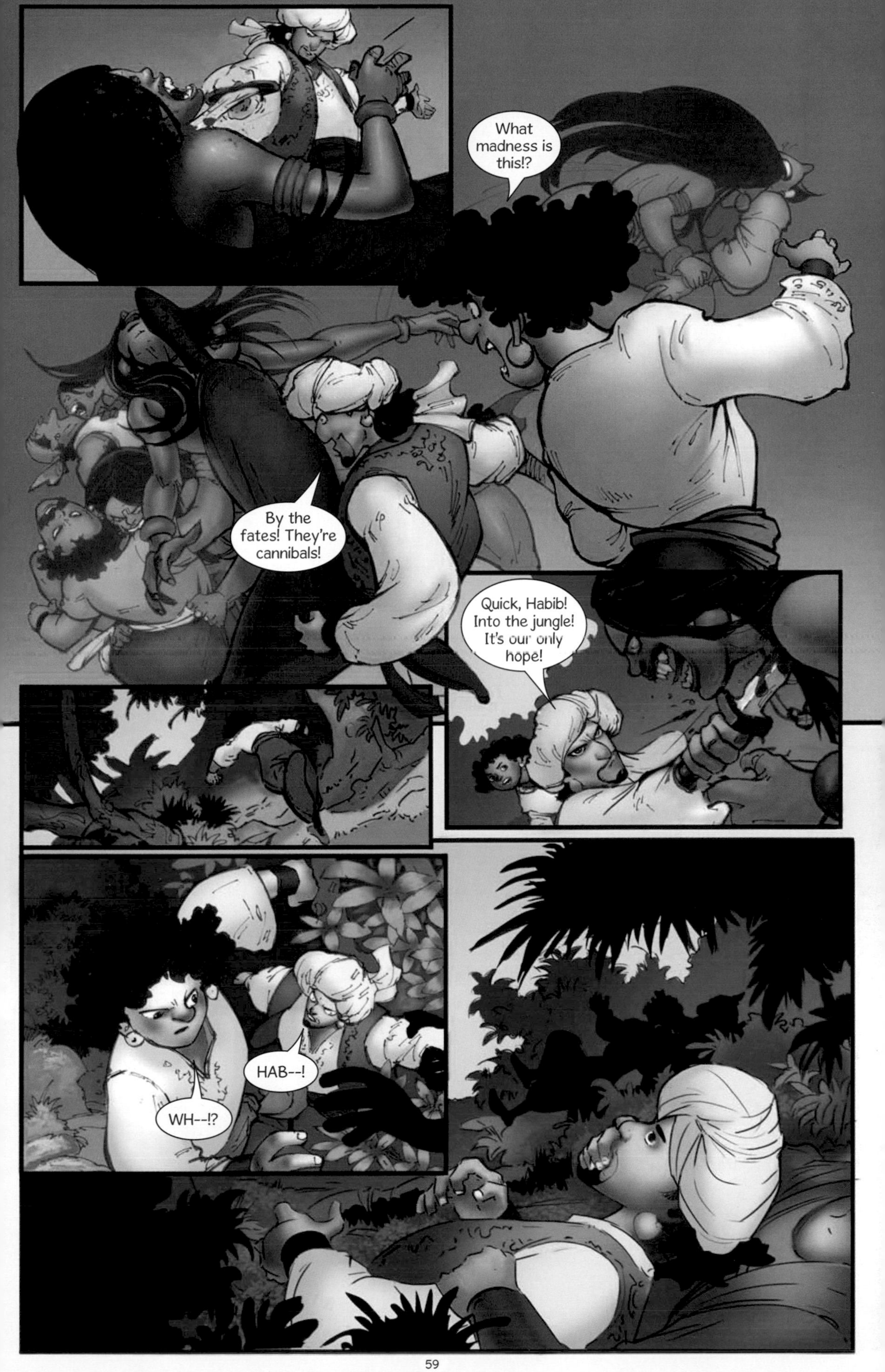
What madness is this!?
By the fates! They're cannibals!
Quick, Habib! Into the jungle! It's our only hope!
HAB--!
WH--!?

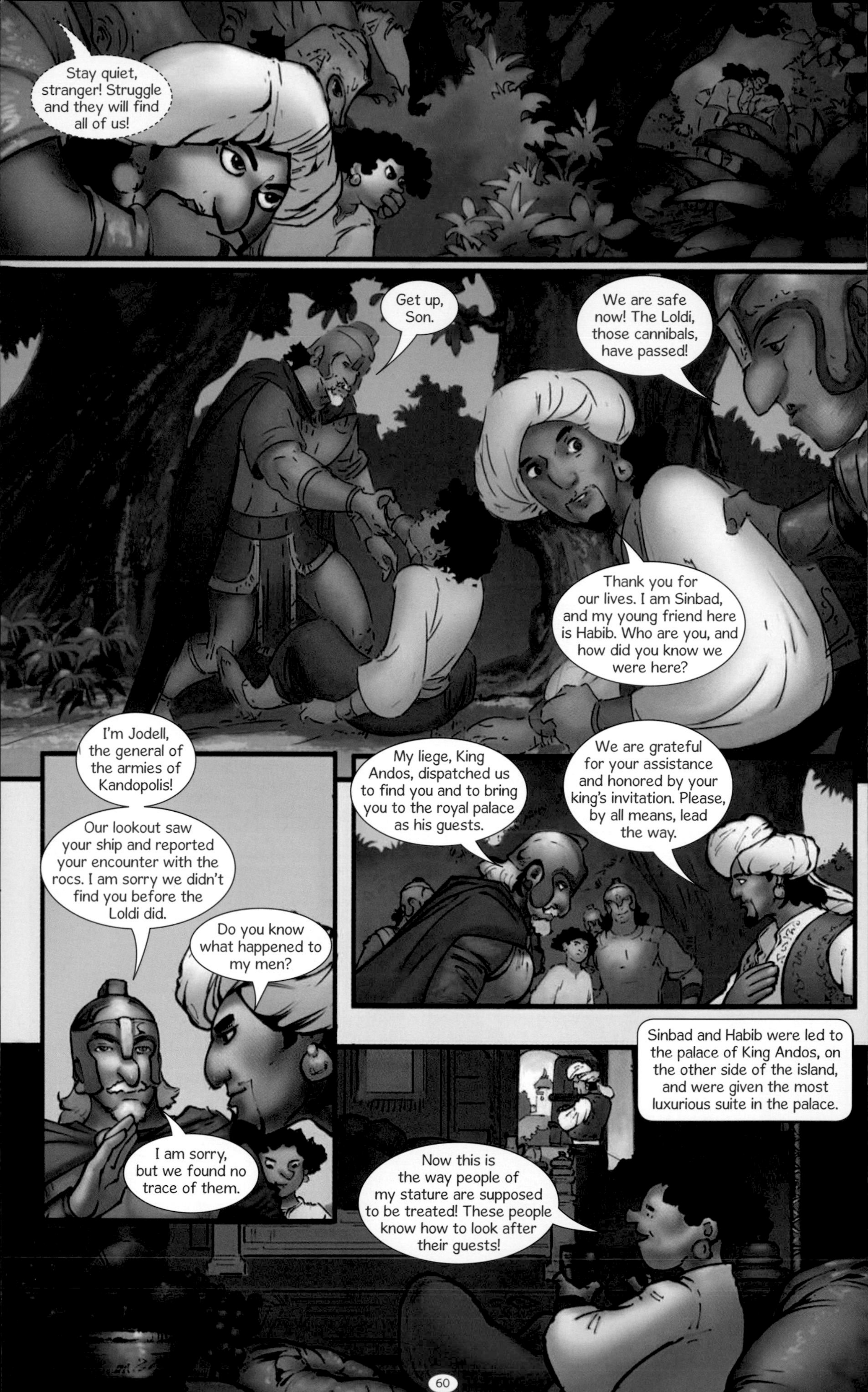

Stay quiet, stranger! Struggle and they will find all of us!
Get up, Son.
We are safe now! The Loldi, those cannibals, have passed!
Thank you for our lives. I am Sinbad, and my young friend here is Habib. Who are you, and how did you know we were here?
I'm Jodell, the general of the armies of Kandopolis!
Our lookout saw your ship and reported your encounter with the rocs. I am sorry we didn't find you before the Loldi did.
Do you know what happened to my men?
I am sorry, but we found no trace of them.
My liege, King Andos, dispatched us to find you and to bring you to the royal palace as his guests.
We are grateful for your assistance and honored by your king's invitation. Please, by all means, lead the way.
Sinbad and Habib were led to the palace of King Andos, on the other side of the island, and were given the most luxurious suite in the palace.
Now this is the way people of my stature are supposed to be treated! These people know how to look after their guests!

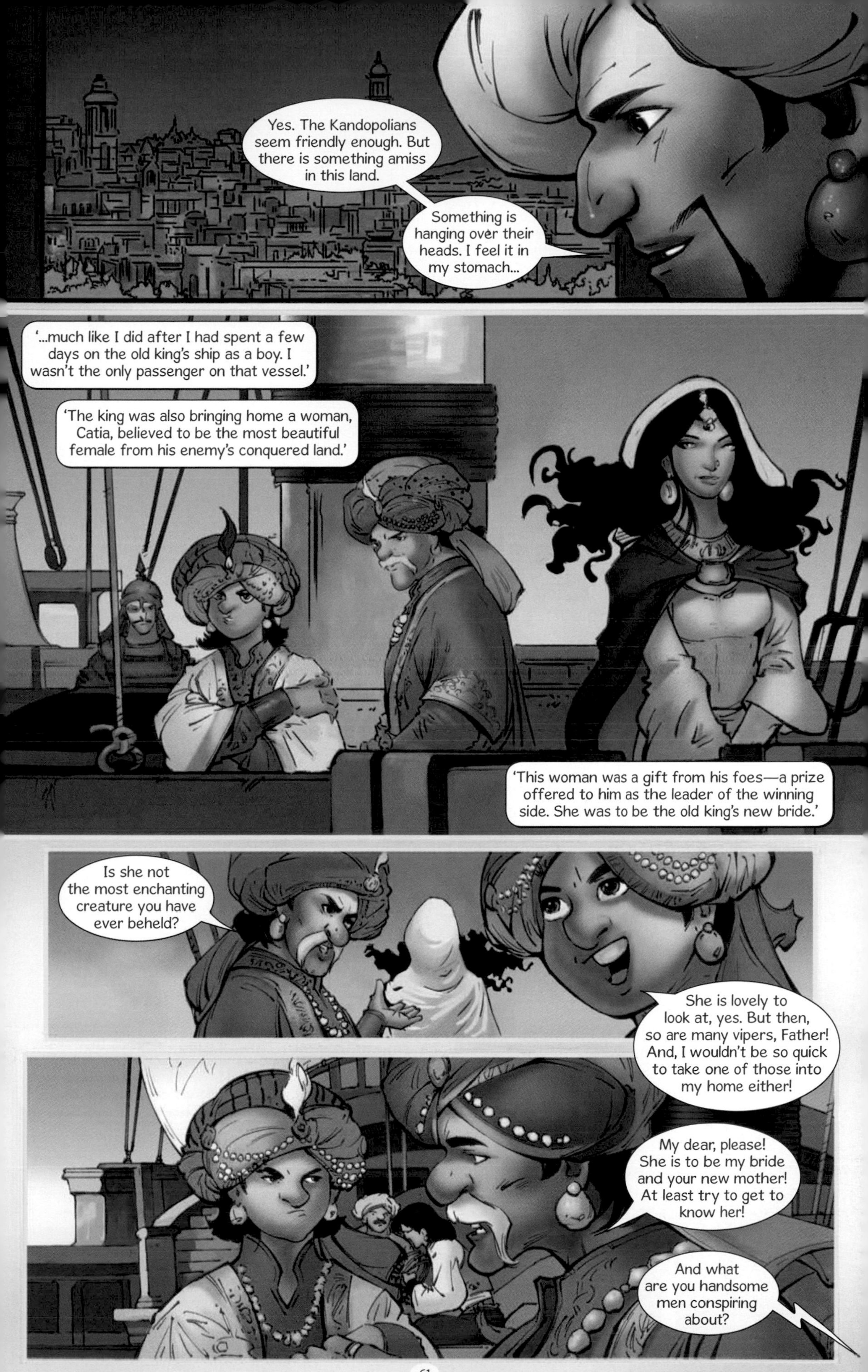
Yes. The Kandopolians seem friendly enough. But there is something amiss in this land.
Something is hanging over their heads. I feel it in my stomach...
'...much like I did after I had spent a few days on the old king's ship as a boy. I wasn't the only passenger on that vessel.'
'The king was also bringing home a woman, Catia, believed to be the most beautiful female from his enemy's conquered land.'
'This woman was a gift from his foes—a prize offered to him as the leader of the winning side. She was to be the old king's new bride.'
Is she not the most enchanting creature you have ever beheld?
She is lovely to look at, yes. But then, so are many vipers, Father! And, I wouldn't be so quick to take one of those into my home either!
My dear, please! She is to be my bride and your new mother! At least try to get to know her!
And what are you handsome men conspiring about?

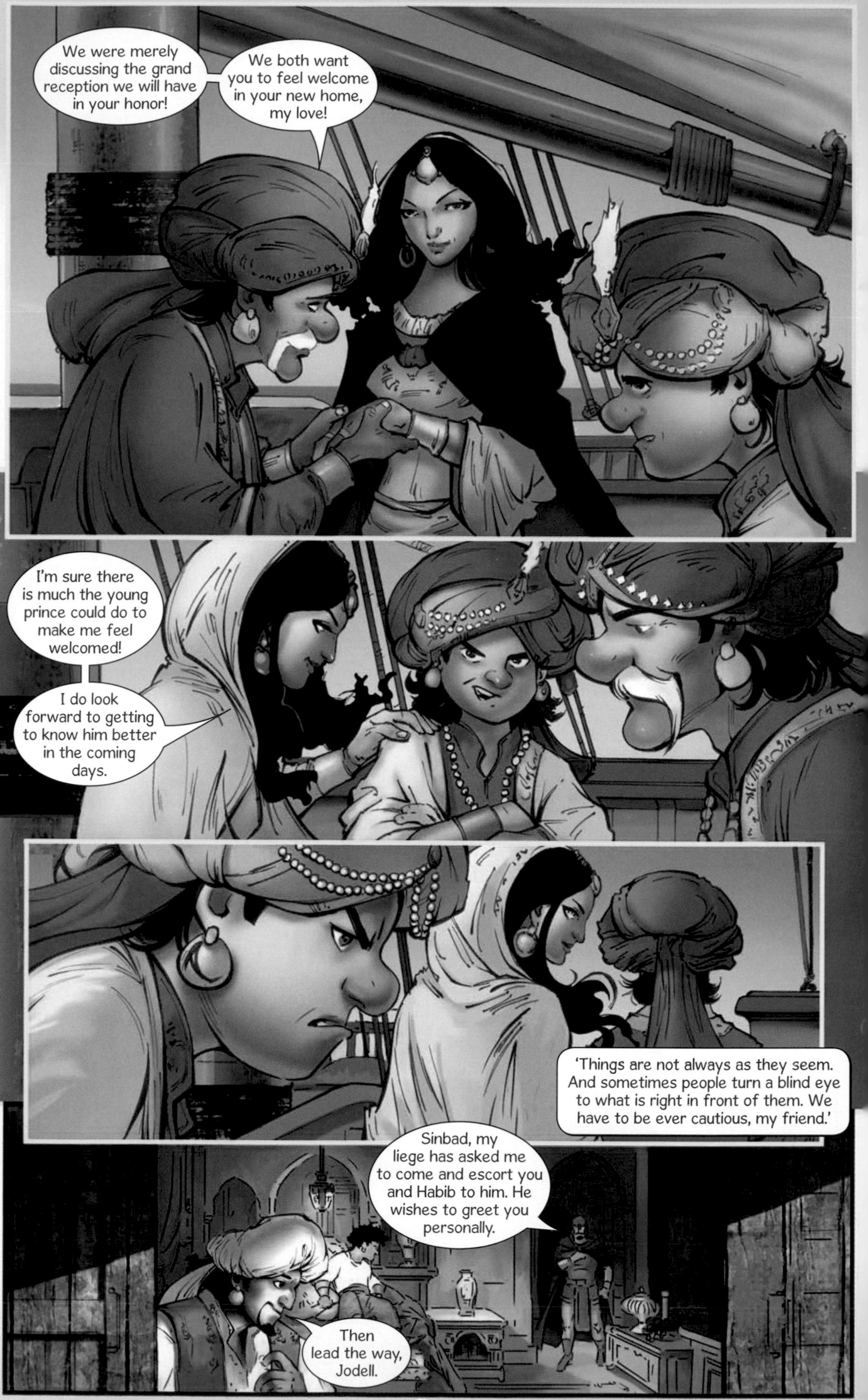

We were merely discussing the grand reception we will have in your honor!
We both want you to feel welcome in your new home, my love!
I'm sure there is much the young prince could do to make me feel welcomed!
I do look forward to getting to know him better in the coming days.
'Things are not always as they seem. And sometimes people turn a blind eye to what is right in front of them. We have to be ever cautious, my friend.'
Sinbad, my liege has asked me to come and escort you and Habib to him. He wishes to greet you personally.
Then lead the way, Jodell.

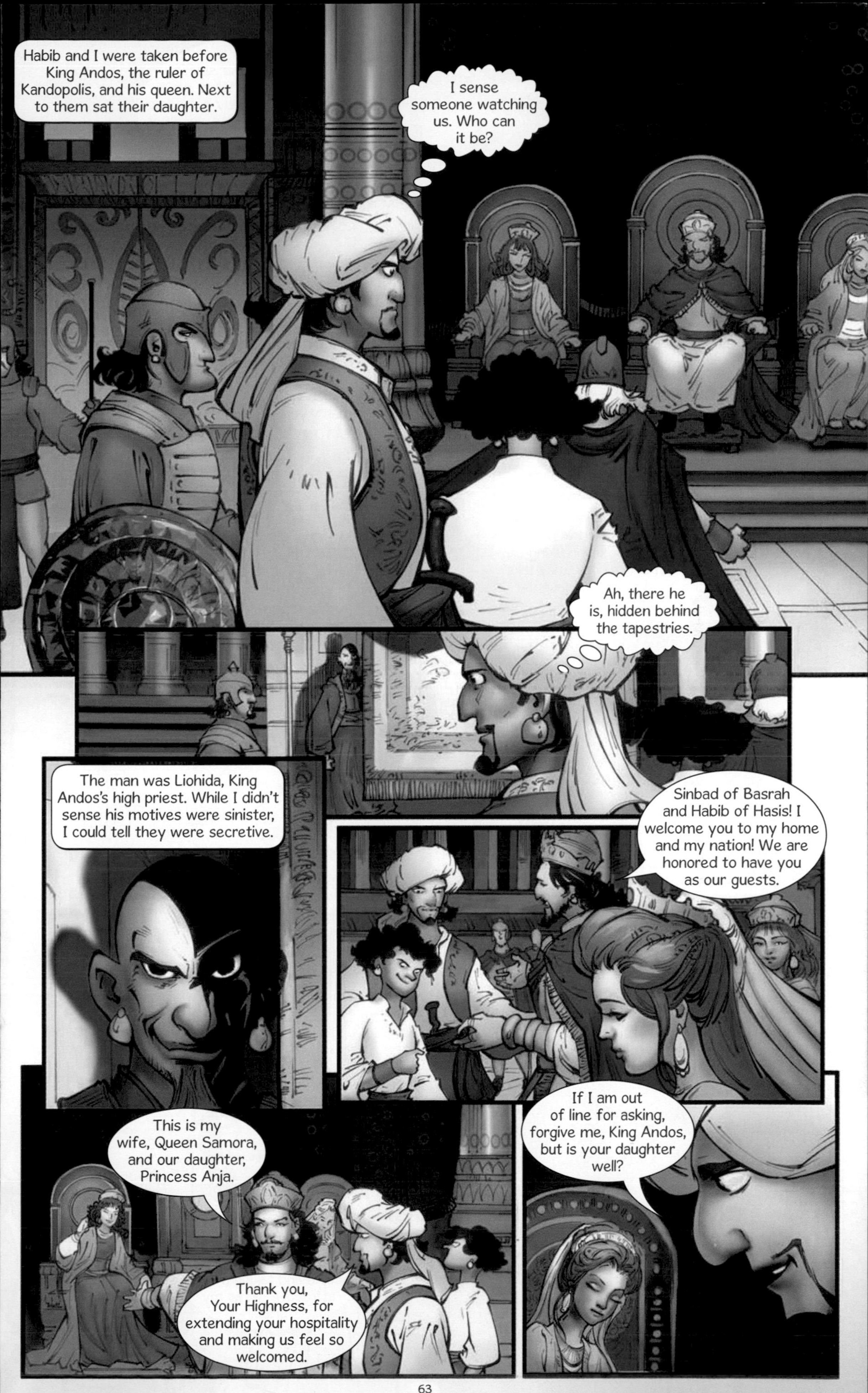

Habib and I were taken before King Andos, the ruler of Kandopolis, and his queen. Next to them sat their daughter.
I sense someone watching us. Who can it be?
Ah, there he is, hidden behind the tapestries.
The man was Liohida, King Andos's high priest. While I didn't sense his motives were sinister, I could tell they were secretive.
Sinbad of Basrah and Habib of Hasis! I welcome you to my home and my nation! We are honored to have you as our guests.
This is my wife, Queen Samora, and our daughter, Princess Anja.
Thank you, Your Highness, for extending your hospitality and making us feel so welcomed.
If I am out of line for asking, forgive me, King Andos, but is your daughter well?

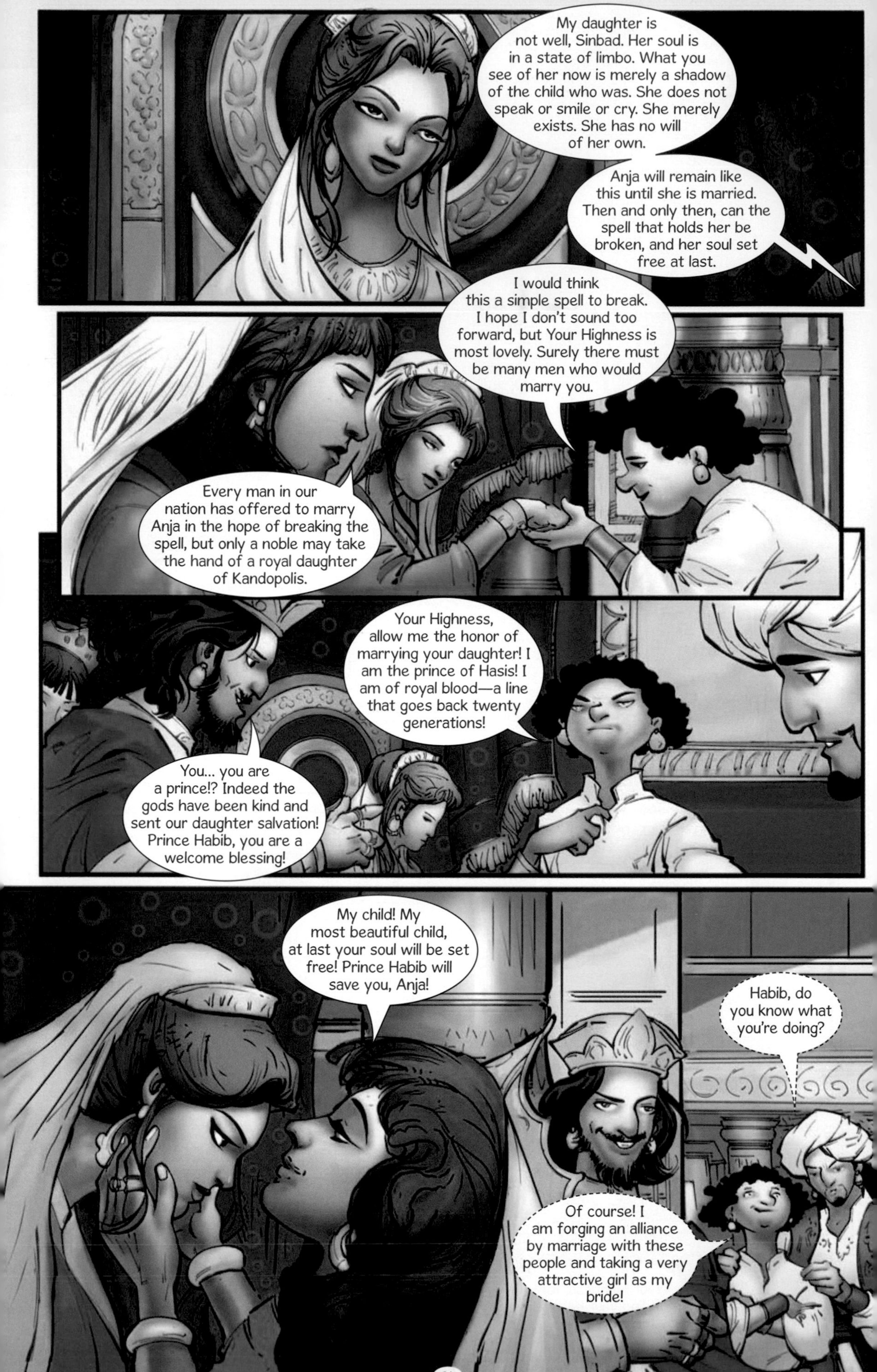
My daughter is not well, Sinbad. Her soul is in a state of limbo. What you see of her now is merely a shadow of the child who was. She does not speak or smile or cry. She merely exists. She has no will of her own.
Anja will remain like this until she is married. Then and only then, can the spell that holds her be broken, and her soul set free at last.
I would think this a simple spell to break. I hope I don't sound too forward, but Your Highness is most lovely. Surely there must be many men who would marry you.
Every man in our nation has offered to marry Anja in the hope of breaking the spell, but only a noble may take the hand of a royal daughter of Kandopolis.
Your Highness, allow me the honor of marrying your daughter! I am the prince of Hasis! I am of royal blood—a line that goes back twenty generations!
You... you are a prince!? Indeed the gods have been kind and sent our daughter salvation! Prince Habib, you are a welcome blessing!
My child! My most beautiful child, at last your soul will be set free! Prince Habib will save you, Anja!
Habib, do you know what you're doing?
Of course! I am forging an alliance by marriage with these people and taking a very attractive girl as my bride!

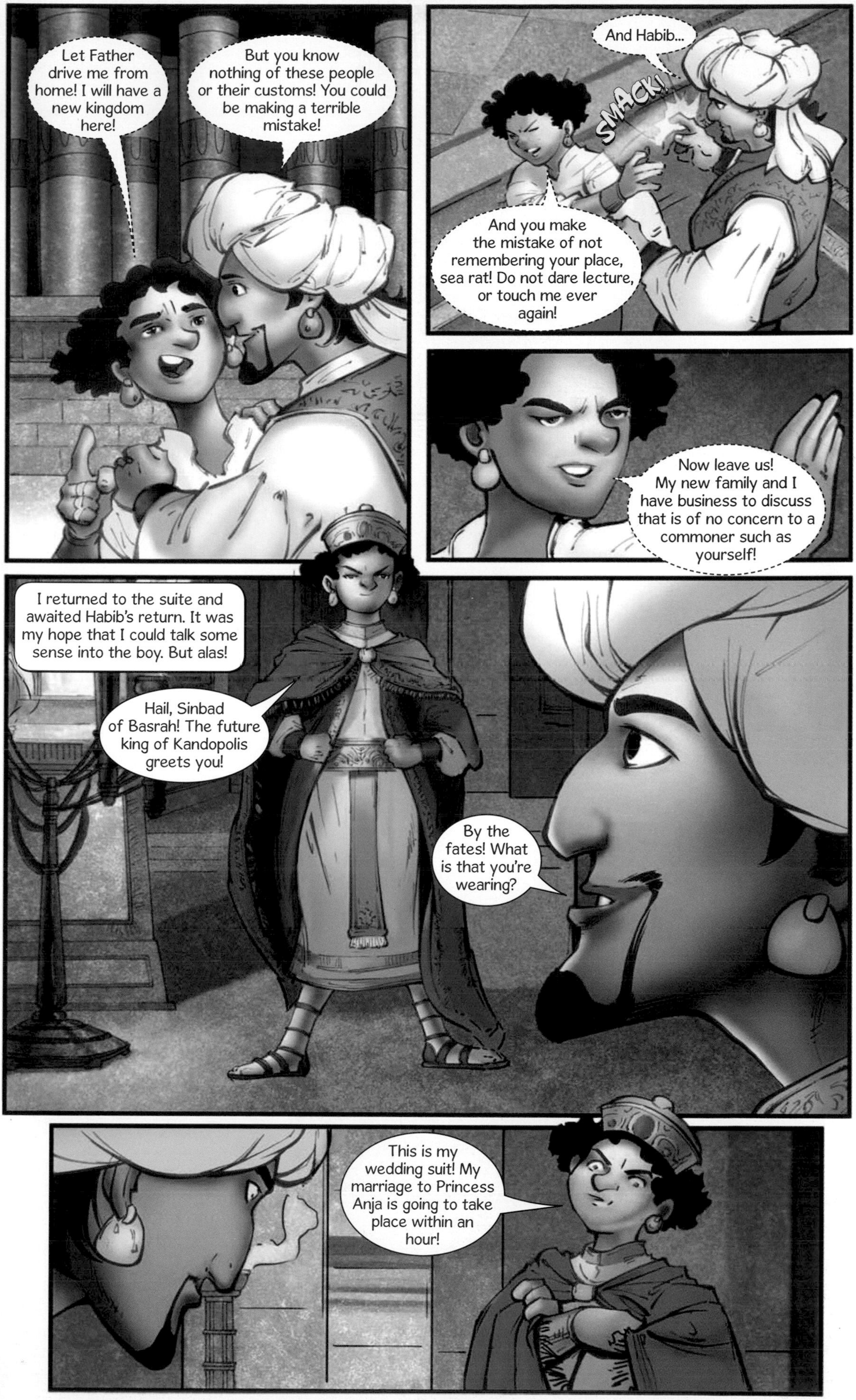
Let Father drive me from home! I will have a new kingdom here!
But you know nothing of these people or their customs! You could be making a terrible mistake!
And Habib...
SMACK!
And you make the mistake of not remembering your place, sea rat! Do not dare lecture, or touch me ever again!
Now leave us! My new family and I have business to discuss that is of no concern to a commoner such as yourself!
I returned to the suite and awaited Habib's return. It was my hope that I could talk some sense into the boy. But alas!
Hail, Sinbad of Basrah! The future king of Kandopolis greets you!
By the fates! What is that you're wearing?
This is my wedding suit! My marriage to Princess Anja is going to take place within an hour!

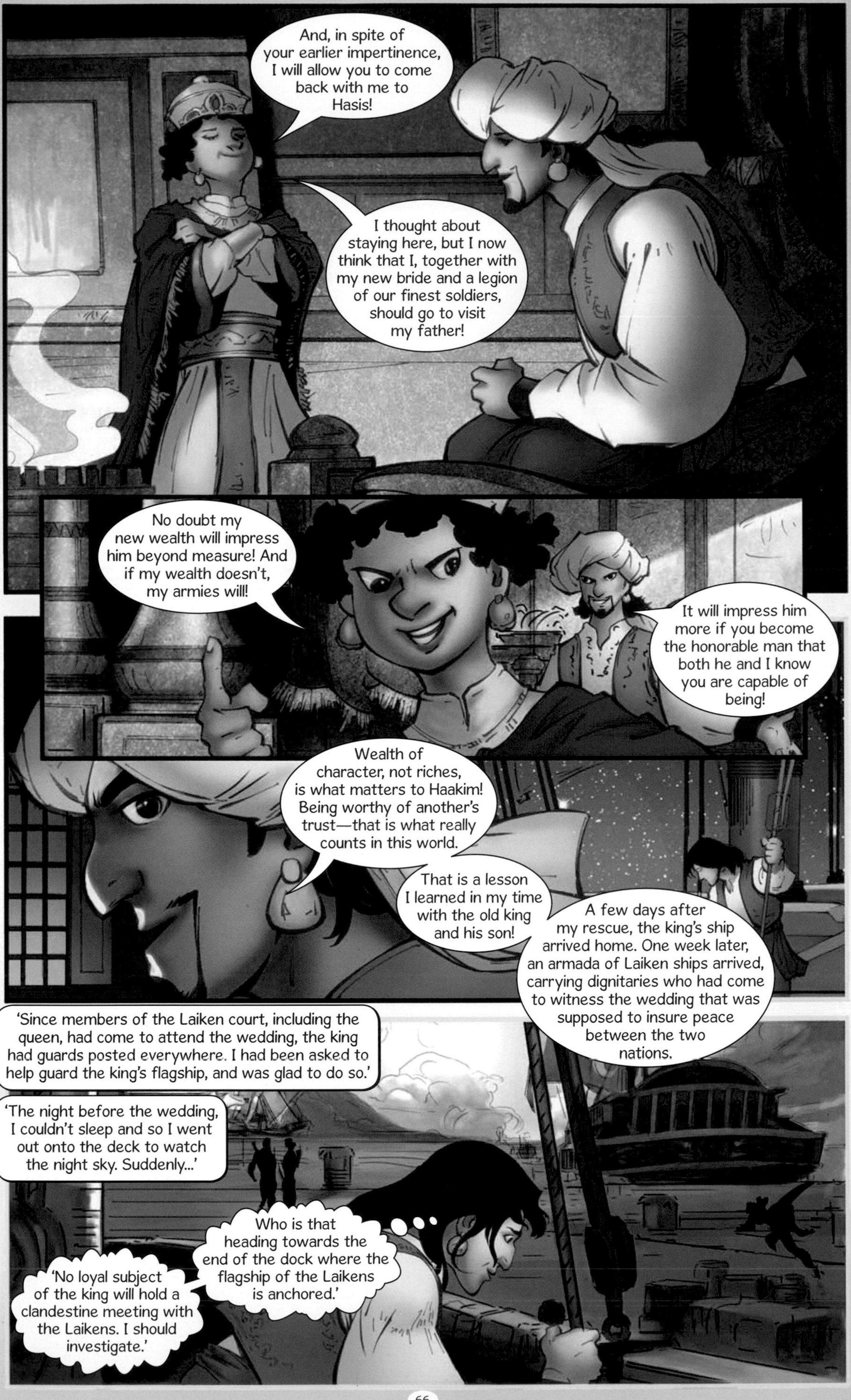

And, in spite of your earlier impertinence, I will allow you to come back with me to Hasis!
I thought about staying here, but I now think that I, together with my new bride and a legion of our finest soldiers, should go to visit my father!
No doubt my new wealth will impress him beyond measure! And if my wealth doesn't, my armies will!
It will impress him more if you become the honorable man that both he and I know you are capable of being!
Wealth of character, not riches, is what matters to Haakim! Being worthy of another's trust—that is what really counts in this world.
That is a lesson I learned in my time with the old king and his son!
A few days after my rescue, the king's ship arrived home. One week later, an armada of Laiken ships arrived, carrying dignitaries who had come to witness the wedding that was supposed to insure peace between the two nations.
'Since members of the Laiken court, including the queen, had come to attend the wedding, the king had guards posted everywhere. I had been asked to help guard the king's flagship, and was glad to do so.'
'The night before the wedding, I couldn't sleep and so I went out onto the deck to watch the night sky. Suddenly...'
Who is that heading towards the end of the dock where the flagship of the Laikens is anchored.'
'No loyal subject of the king will hold a clandestine meeting with the Laikens. I should investigate.'

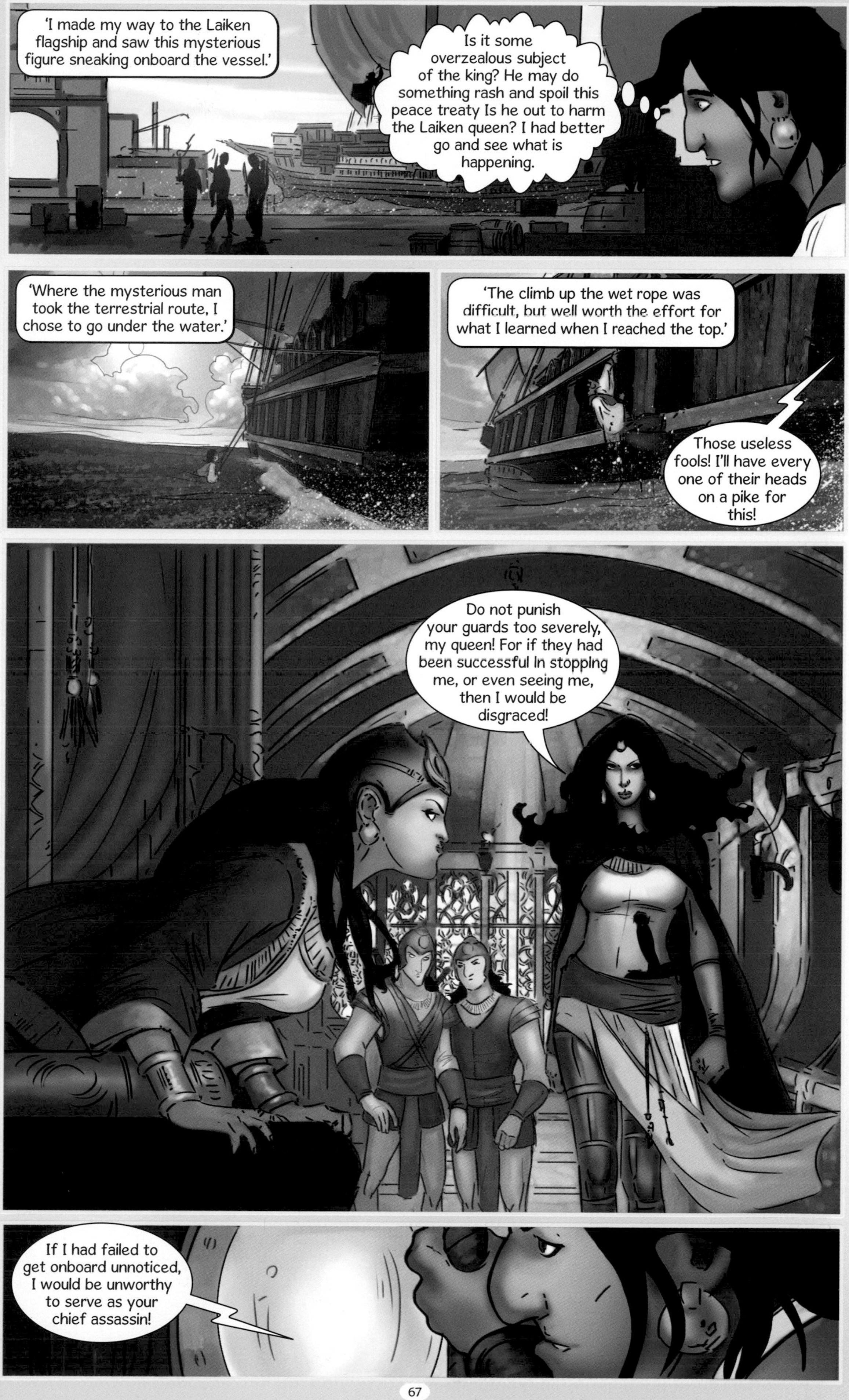
'I made my way to the Laiken flagship and saw this mysterious figure sneaking onboard the vessel.'
Is it some overzealous subject of the king? He may do something rash and spoil this peace treaty Is he out to harm the Laiken queen? I had better go and see what is happening.
'Where the mysterious man took the terrestrial route, I chose to go under the water.'
'The climb up the wet rope was difficult, but well worth the effort for what I learned when I reached the top.'
Those useless fools! I'll have every one of their heads on a pike for this!
Do not punish your guards too severely, my queen! For if they had been successful In stopping me, or even seeing me, then I would be disgraced!
If I had failed to get onboard unnoticed, I would be unworthy to serve as your chief assassin!

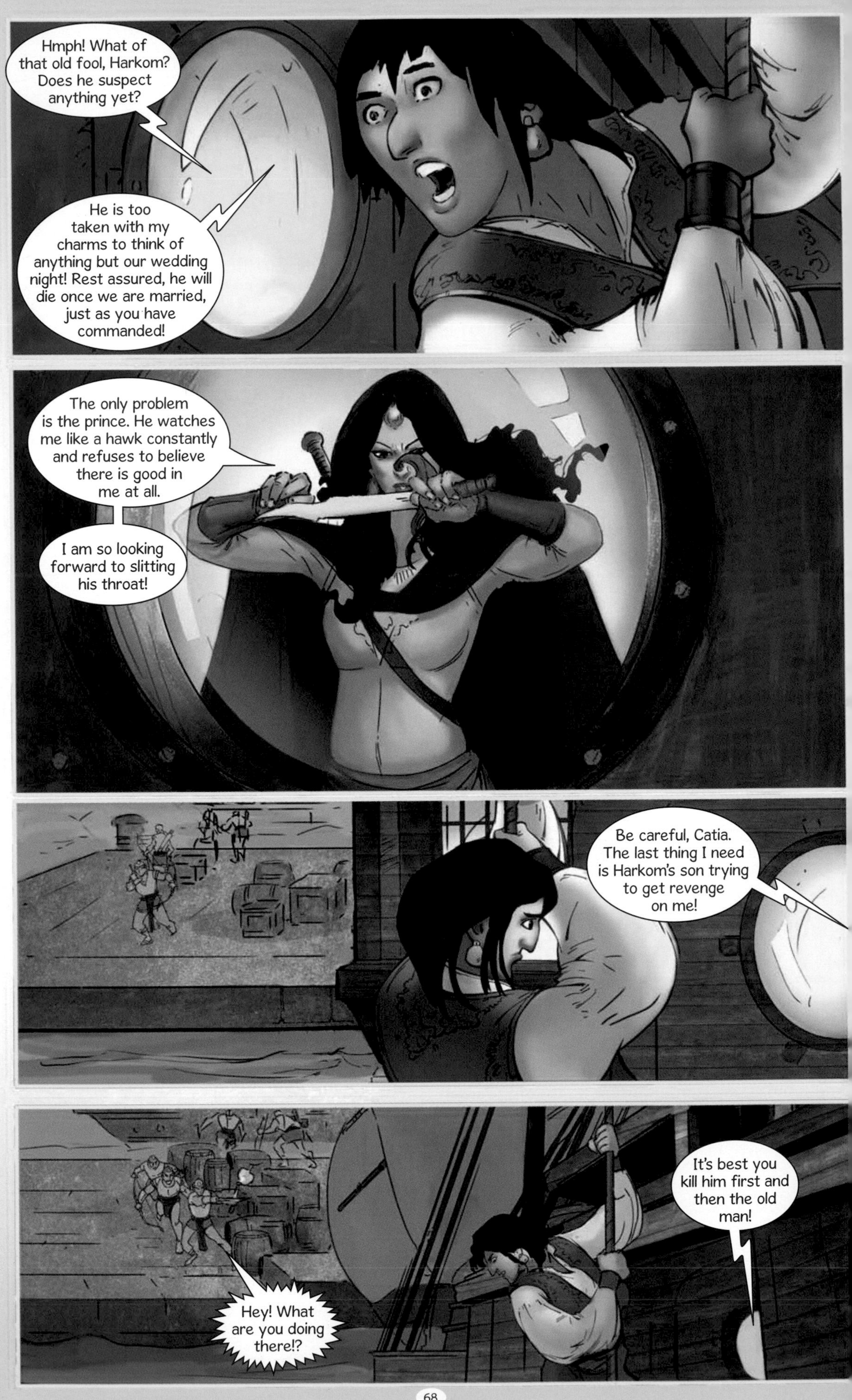
Hmph! What of that old fool, Harkom? Does he suspect anything yet?
He is too taken with my charms to think of anything but our wedding night! Rest assured, he will die once we are married, just as you have commanded!
The only problem is the prince. He watches me like a hawk constantly and refuses to believe there is good in me at all.
I am so looking forward to slitting his throat!
Be careful, Catia. The last thing I need is Harkom's son trying to get revenge on me!
It's best you kill him first and then the old man!
Hey! What are you doing there!?

KA-SPLASH!

Get him, you fools! He mustn't be allowed to escape!

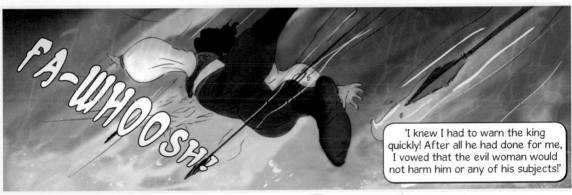

FA-WHOOSH!

'I knew I had to warn the king quickly! After all he had done for me, I vowed that the evil woman would not harm him or any of his subjects!'

What is all the commotion outside!? What is going on!?

My... my queen... we think one of King Harkom's spies had come onboard! He was right outside your window!

Get out! Get out of here right now and find that dog! Every second he lives is a threat to me!

'The order was, however indirectly, addressed to Catia, who was always willing to spill blood for her queen. She took off without a moment's hesitation, to kill the king and the young prince.'

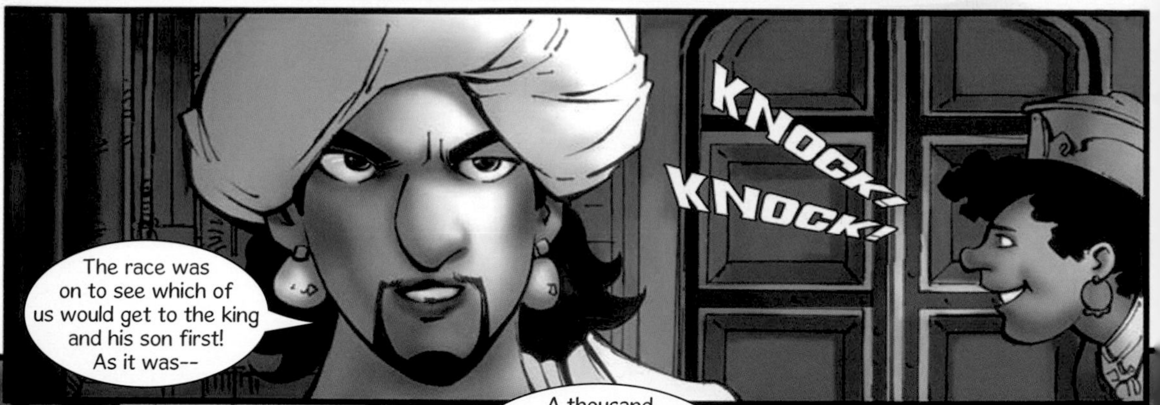
KNOCK! KNOCK!
The race was on to see which of us would get to the king and his son first! As it was--

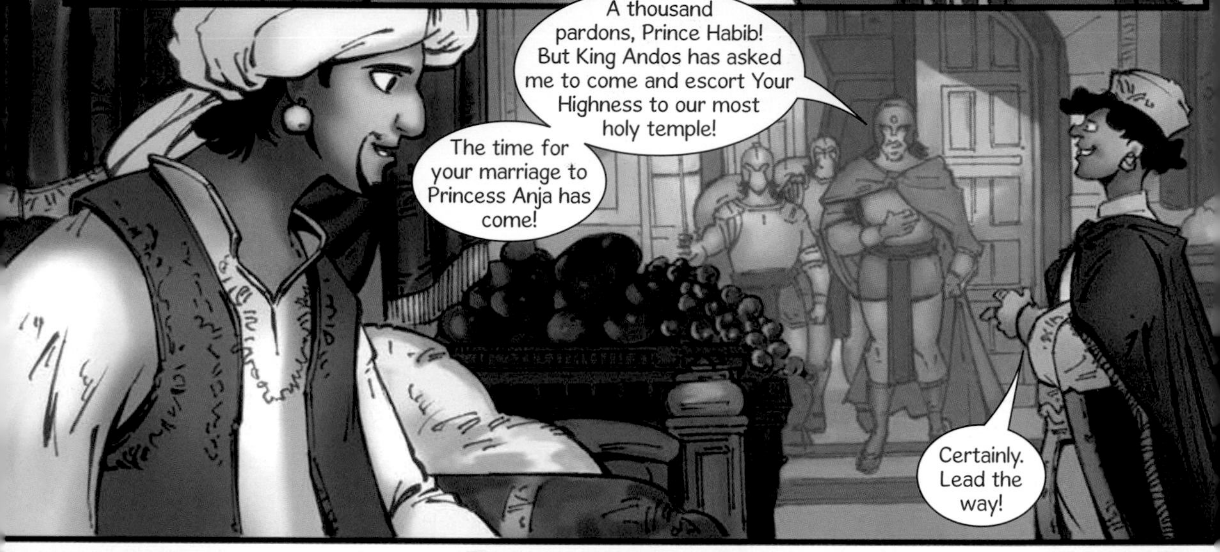
A thousand pardons, Prince Habib! But King Andos has asked me to come and escort Your Highness to our most holy temple!
The time for your marriage to Princess Anja has come!
Certainly. Lead the way!

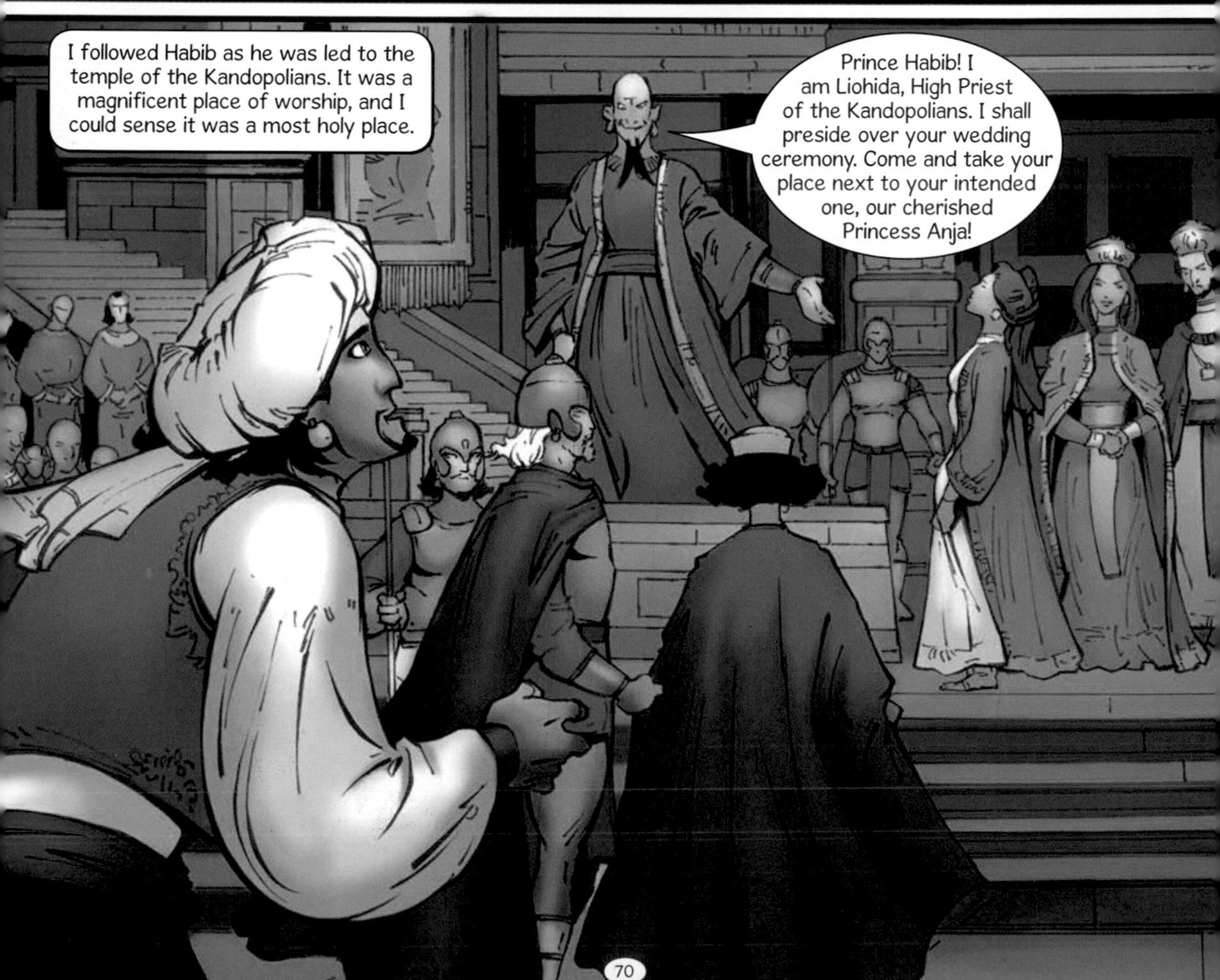
I followed Habib as he was led to the temple of the Kandopolians. It was a magnificent place of worship, and I could sense it was a most holy place.
Prince Habib! I am Liohida, High Priest of the Kandopolians. I shall preside over your wedding ceremony. Come and take your place next to your intended one, our cherished Princess Anja!

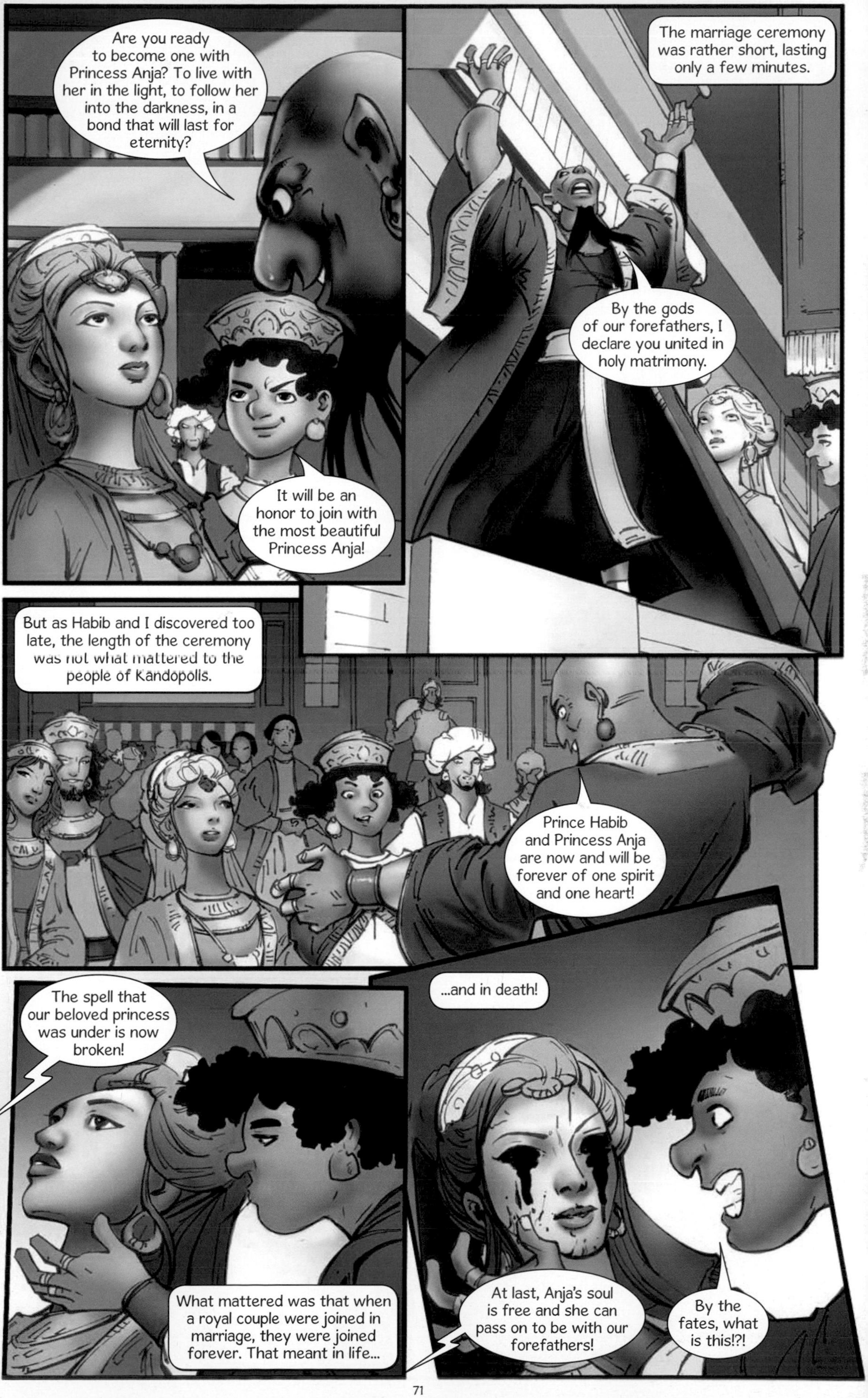

Are you ready to become one with Princess Anja? To live with her in the light, to follow her into the darkness, in a bond that will last for eternity?
It will be an honor to join with the most beautiful Princess Anja!
The marriage ceremony was rather short, lasting only a few minutes.
By the gods of our forefathers, I declare you united in holy matrimony.
But as Habib and I discovered too late, the length of the ceremony was not what mattered to the people of Kandopolis.
Prince Habib and Princess Anja are now and will be forever of one spirit and one heart!
The spell that our beloved princess was under is now broken!
What mattered was that when a royal couple were joined in marriage, they were joined forever. That meant in life...
...and in death!
At last, Anja's soul is free and she can pass on to be with our forefathers!
By the fates, what is this!?!

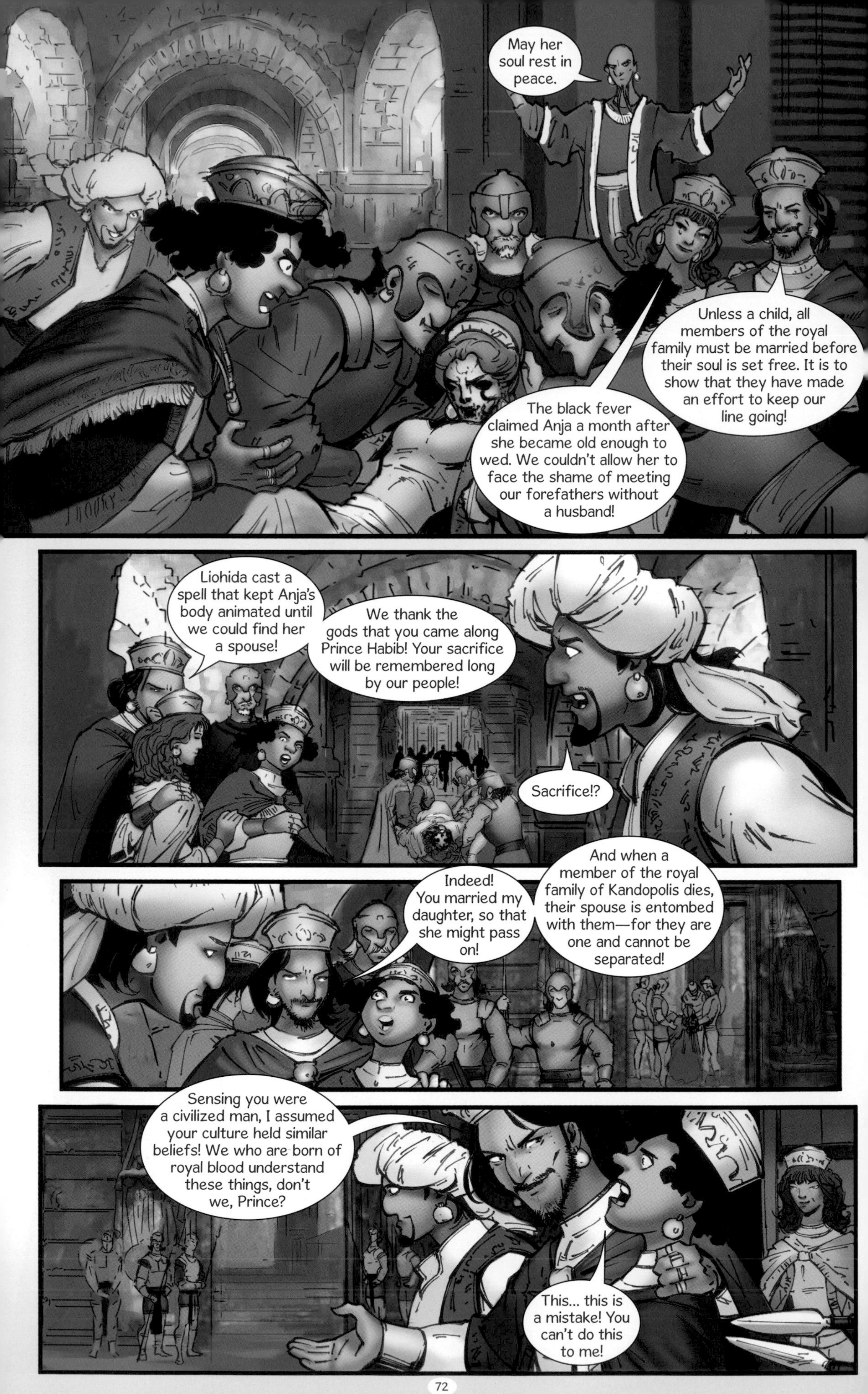
May her soul rest in peace.
The black fever claimed Anja a month after she became old enough to wed. We couldn't allow her to face the shame of meeting our forefathers without a husband!
Unless a child, all members of the royal family must be married before their soul is set free. It is to show that they have made an effort to keep our line going!
Liohida cast a spell that kept Anja's body animated until we could find her a spouse!
We thank the gods that you came along Prince Habib! Your sacrifice will be remembered long by our people!
Sacrifice!?
Indeed! You married my daughter, so that she might pass on!
And when a member of the royal family of Kandopolis dies, their spouse is entombed with them—for they are one and cannot be separated!
Sensing you were a civilized man, I assumed your culture held similar beliefs! We who are born of royal blood understand these things, don't we, Prince?
This... this is a mistake! You can't do this to me!

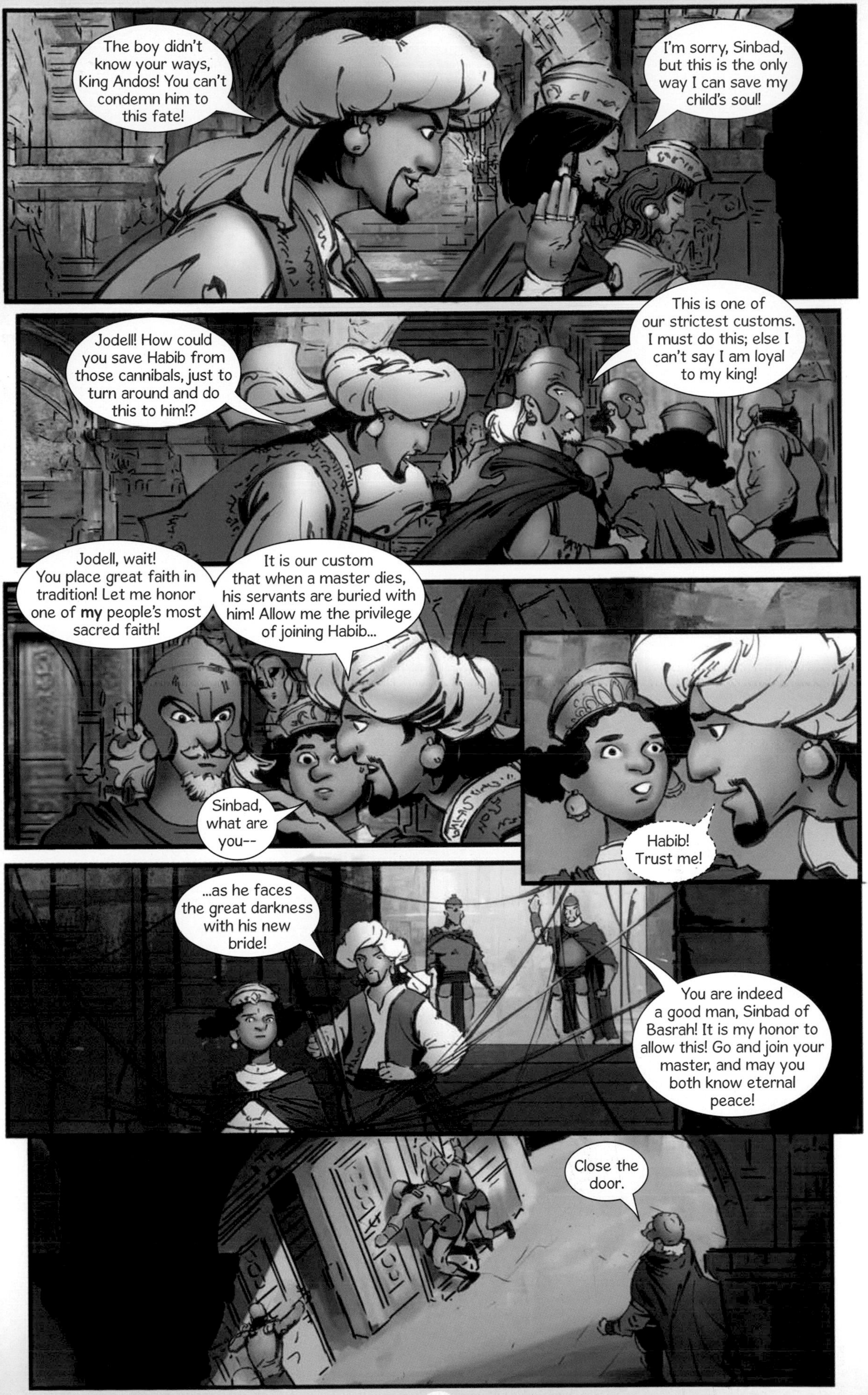
The boy didn't know your ways, King Andos! You can't condemn him to this fate!
I'm sorry, Sinbad, but this is the only way I can save my child's soul!
Jodell! How could you save Habib from those cannibals, just to turn around and do this to him!?
This is one of our strictest customs. I must do this; else I can't say I am loyal to my king!
Jodell, wait! You place great faith in tradition! Let me honor one of **my** people's most sacred faith!
It is our custom that when a master dies, his servants are buried with him! Allow me the privilege of joining Habib...
Sinbad, what are you--
Habib! Trust me!
...as he faces the great darkness with his new bride!
You are indeed a good man, Sinbad of Basrah! It is my honor to allow this! Go and join your master, and may you both know eternal peace!
Close the door.

You have a plan to get out of here, right? Please tell me you have a plan!

I could not just allow them to entomb you alive. We will have to figure a way out.

Look at those bones, Habib! They have been picked clean. This isn't just natural decay.

Something devoured these people!

And if something got in here to feed, that means there is a way out! Come on! We're going to explore these tunnels!

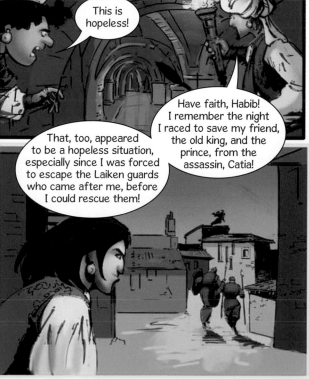

This is hopeless!

Have faith, Habib! I remember the night I raced to save my friend, the old king, and the prince, from the assassin, Catia!

That, too, appeared to be a hopeless situation, especially since I was forced to escape the Laiken guards who came after me, before I could rescue them!

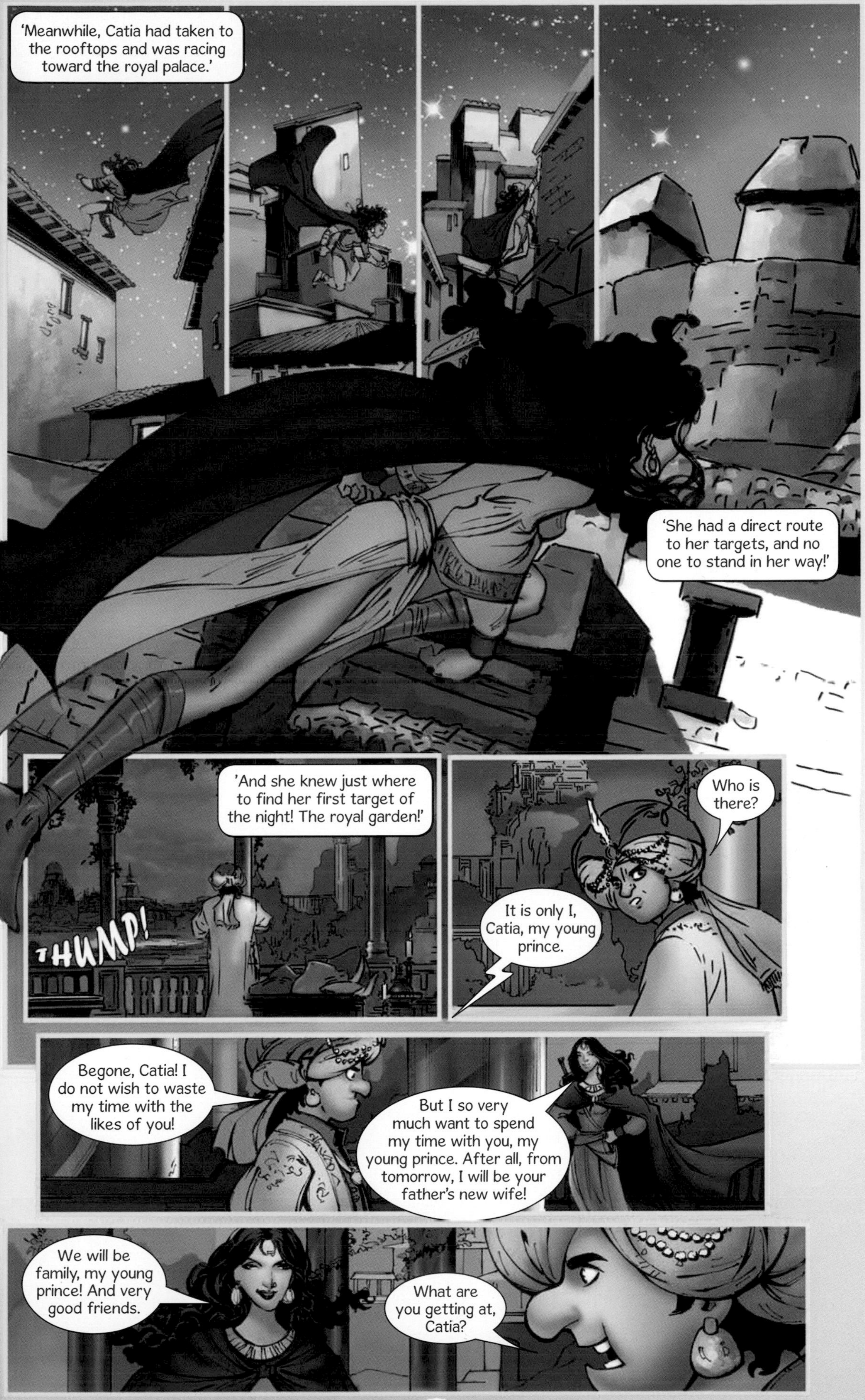

'Meanwhile, Catia had taken to the rooftops and was racing toward the royal palace.'
'She had a direct route to her targets, and no one to stand in her way!'
'And she knew just where to find her first target of the night! The royal garden!'
THUMP!
Who is there?
It is only I, Catia, my young prince.
Begone, Catia! I do not wish to waste my time with the likes of you!
But I so very much want to spend my time with you, my young prince. After all, from tomorrow, I will be your father's new wife!
We will be family, my young prince! And very good friends.
What are you getting at, Catia?

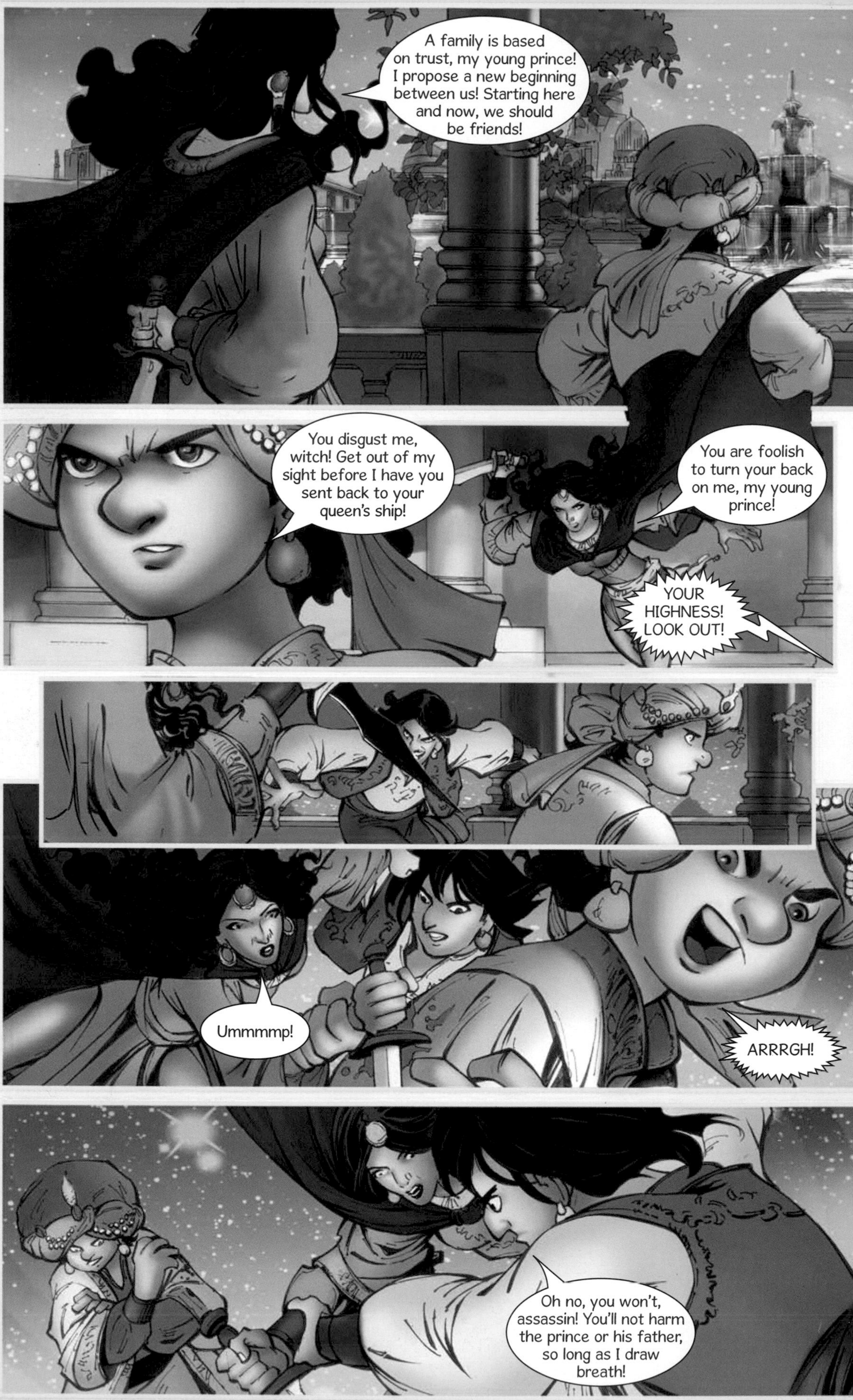
A family is based on trust, my young prince! I propose a new beginning between us! Starting here and now, we should be friends!
You disgust me, witch! Get out of my sight before I have you sent back to your queen's ship!
You are foolish to turn your back on me, my young prince!
YOUR HIGHNESS! LOOK OUT!
Ummmmp!
ARRRGH!
Oh no, you won't, assassin! You'll not harm the prince or his father, so long as I draw breath!

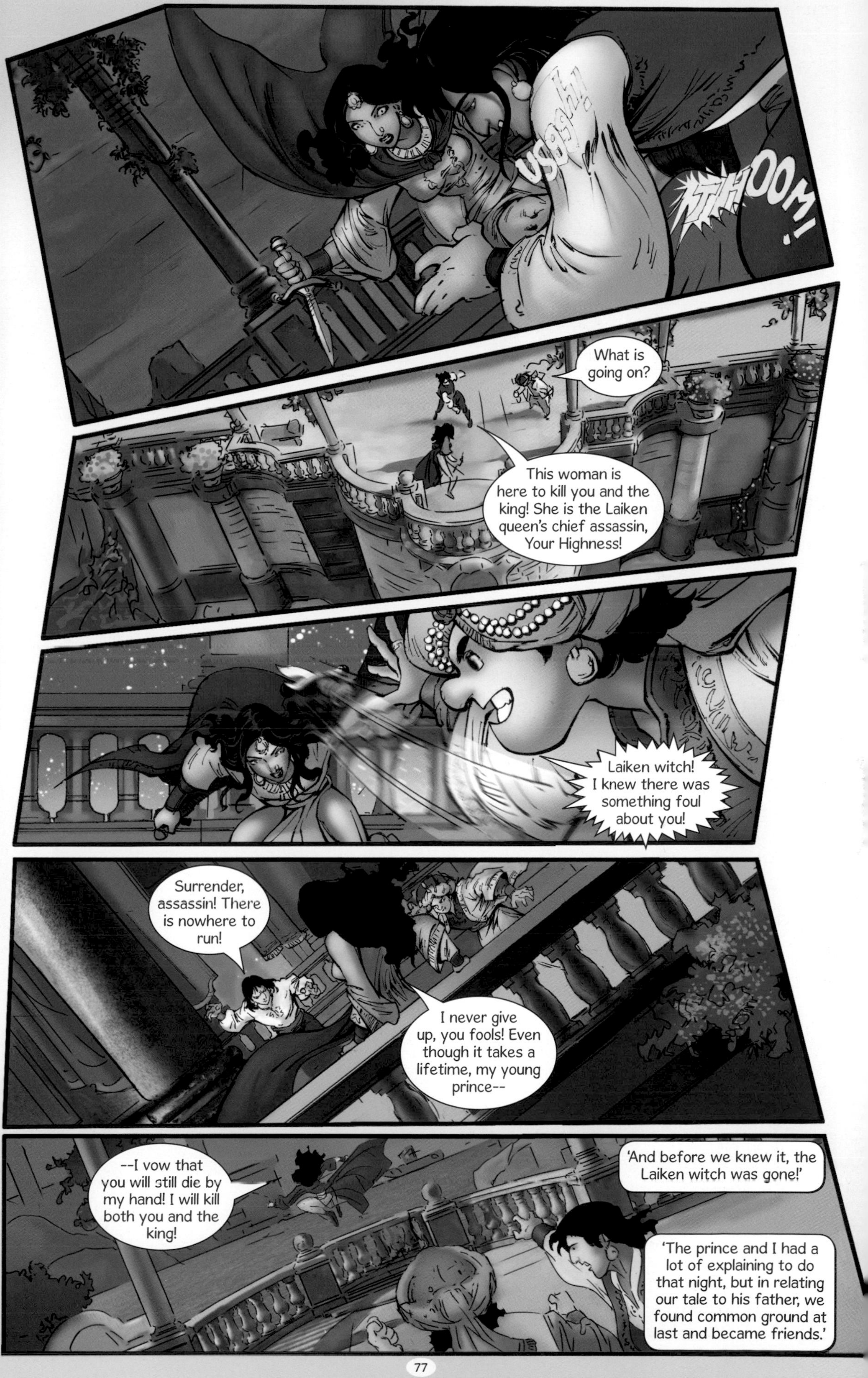
USSSHH!!
KTHOOM!
What is going on?
This woman is here to kill you and the king! She is the Laiken queen's chief assassin, Your Highness!
Laiken witch! I knew there was something foul about you!
Surrender, assassin! There is nowhere to run!
I never give up, you fools! Even though it takes a lifetime, my young prince--
--I vow that you will still die by my hand! I will kill both you and the king!
'And before we knew it, the Laiken witch was gone!'
'The prince and I had a lot of explaining to do that night, but in relating our tale to his father, we found common ground at last and became friends.'

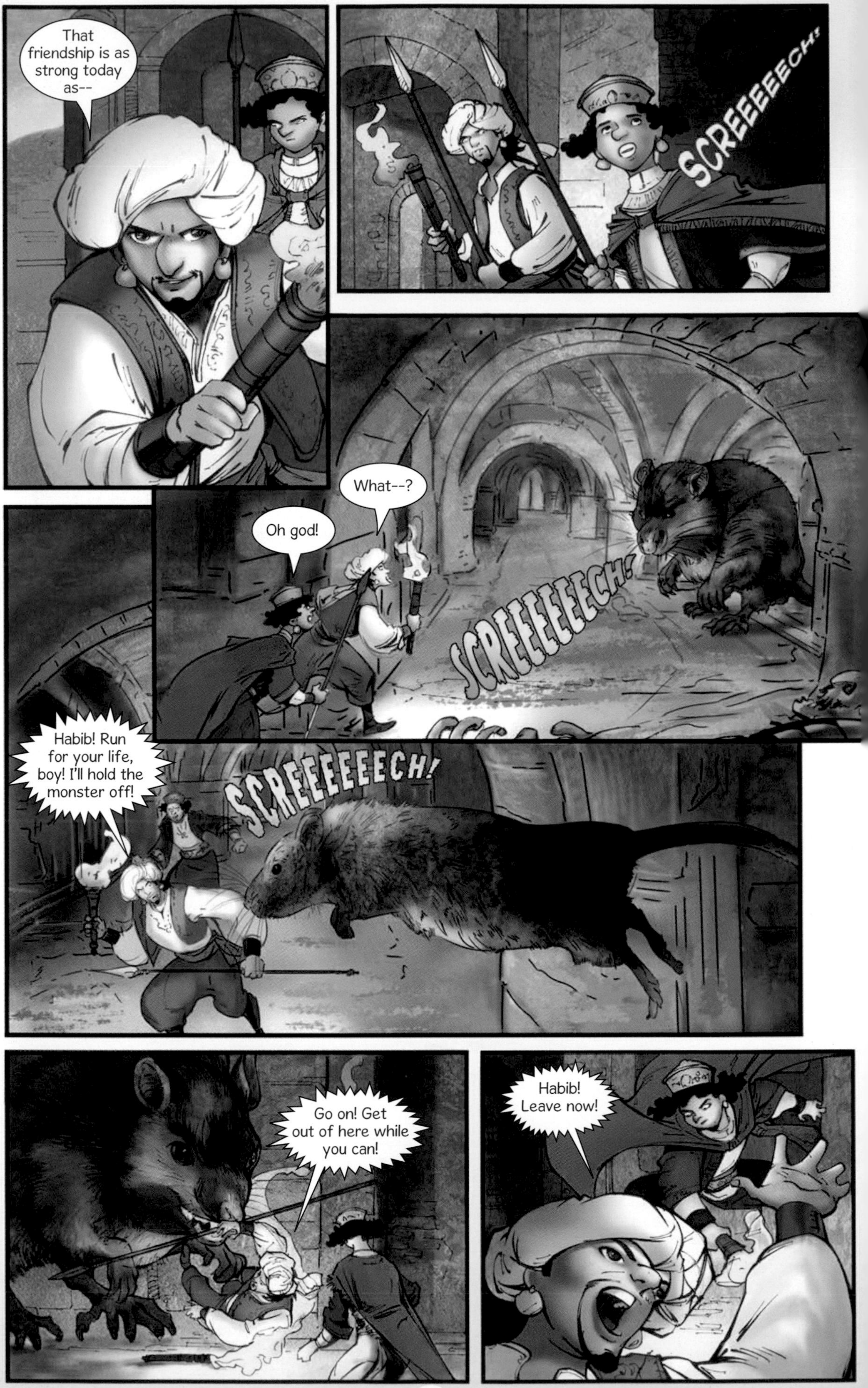
That friendship is as strong today as--
SCREEEEEECH!
What--?
Oh god!
SCREEEEEEECH!
Habib! Run for your life, boy! I'll hold the monster off!
SCREEEEEECH!
Go on! Get out of here while you can!
Habib! Leave now!

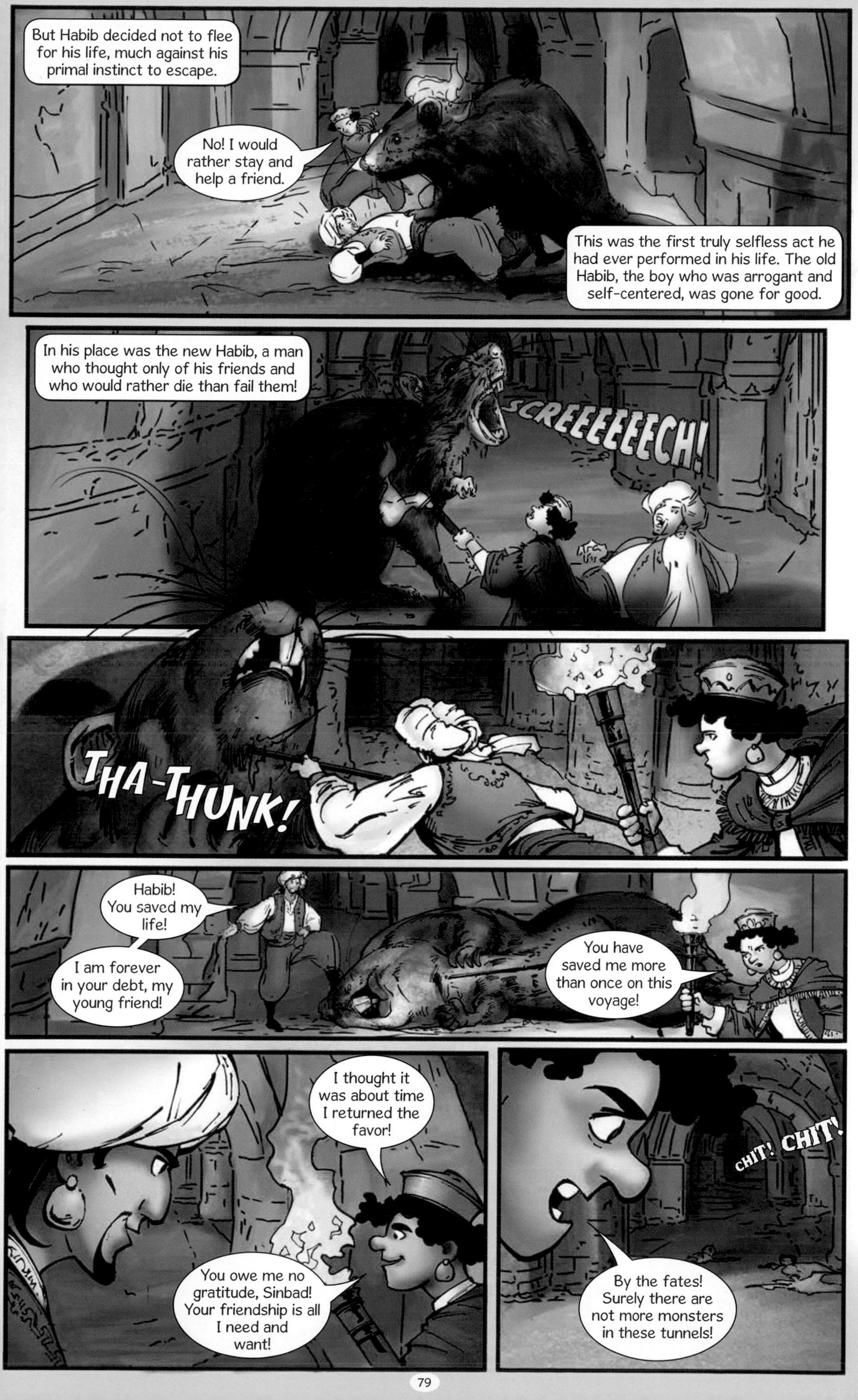

But Habib decided not to flee for his life, much against his primal instinct to escape.
No! I would rather stay and help a friend.
This was the first truly selfless act he had ever performed in his life. The old Habib, the boy who was arrogant and self-centered, was gone for good.
In his place was the new Habib, a man who thought only of his friends and who would rather die than fail them!
SCREEEEEEECH!
THA-THUNK!
Habib! You saved my life!
I am forever in your debt, my young friend!
You have saved me more than once on this voyage!
I thought it was about time I returned the favor!
You owe me no gratitude, Sinbad! Your friendship is all I need and want!
CHIT! CHIT!
By the fates! Surely there are not more monsters in these tunnels!

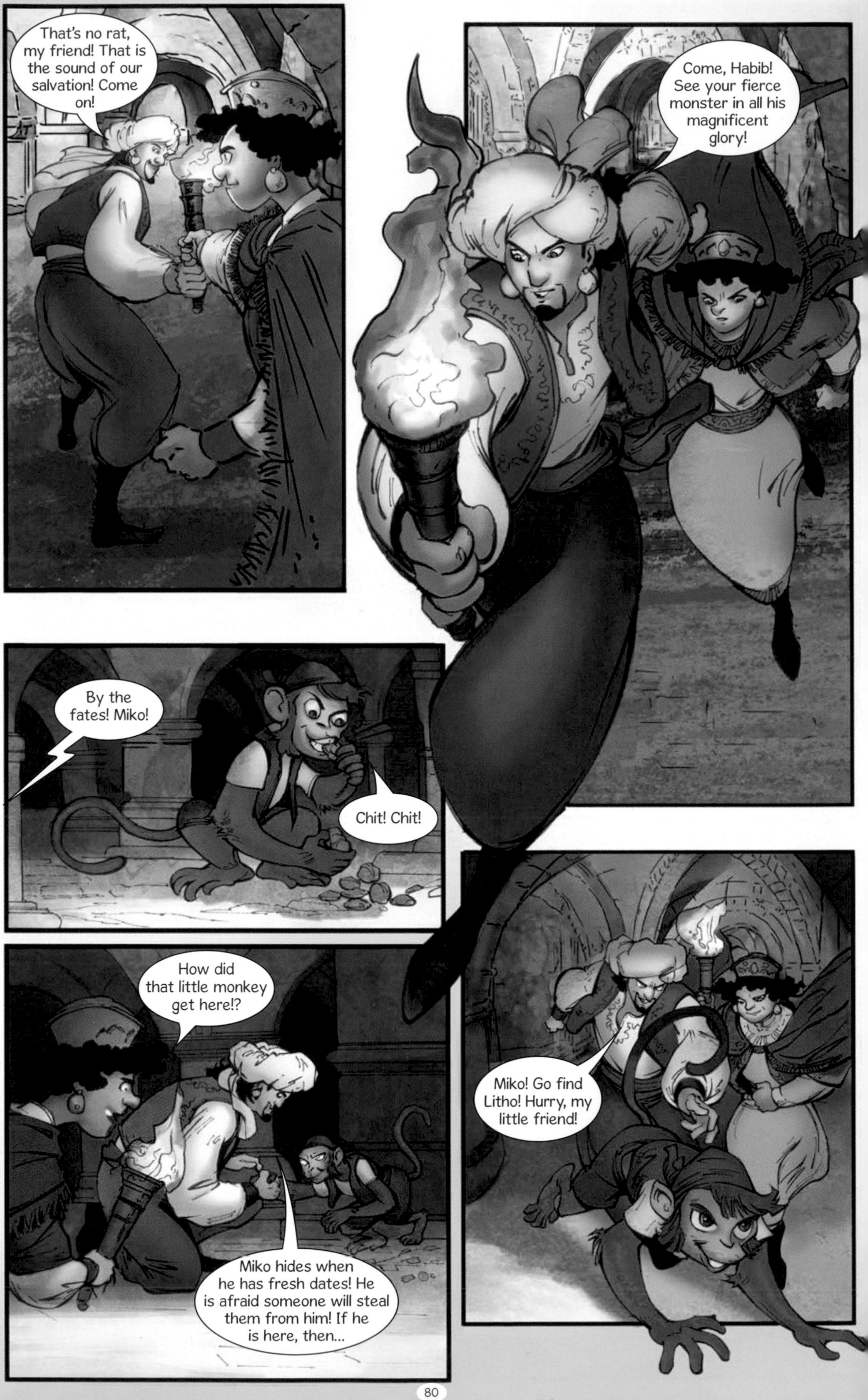
That's no rat, my friend! That is the sound of our salvation! Come on!
Come, Habib! See your fierce monster in all his magnificent glory!
By the fates! Miko!
Chit! Chit!
How did that little monkey get here!?
Miko hides when he has fresh dates! He is afraid someone will steal them from him! If he is here, then...
Miko! Go find Litho! Hurry, my little friend!

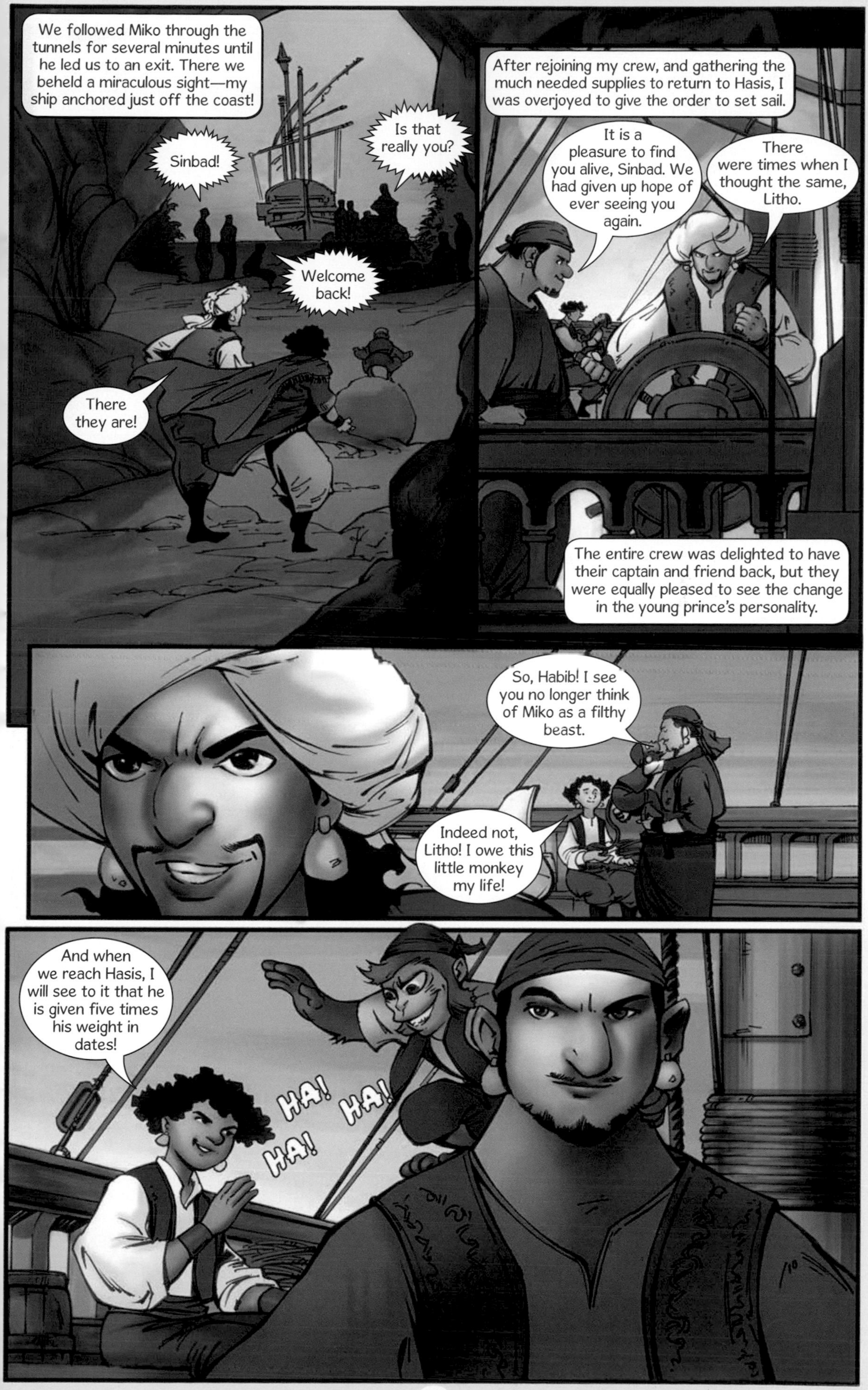
We followed Miko through the tunnels for several minutes until he led us to an exit. There we beheld a miraculous sight—my ship anchored just off the coast!
Sinbad!
Is that really you?
Welcome back!
There they are!
After rejoining my crew, and gathering the much needed supplies to return to Hasis, I was overjoyed to give the order to set sail.
It is a pleasure to find you alive, Sinbad. We had given up hope of ever seeing you again.
There were times when I thought the same, Litho.
The entire crew was delighted to have their captain and friend back, but they were equally pleased to see the change in the young prince's personality.
So, Habib! I see you no longer think of Miko as a filthy beast.
Indeed not, Litho! I owe this little monkey my life!
And when we reach Hasis, I will see to it that he is given five times his weight in dates!
HA! HA! HA!

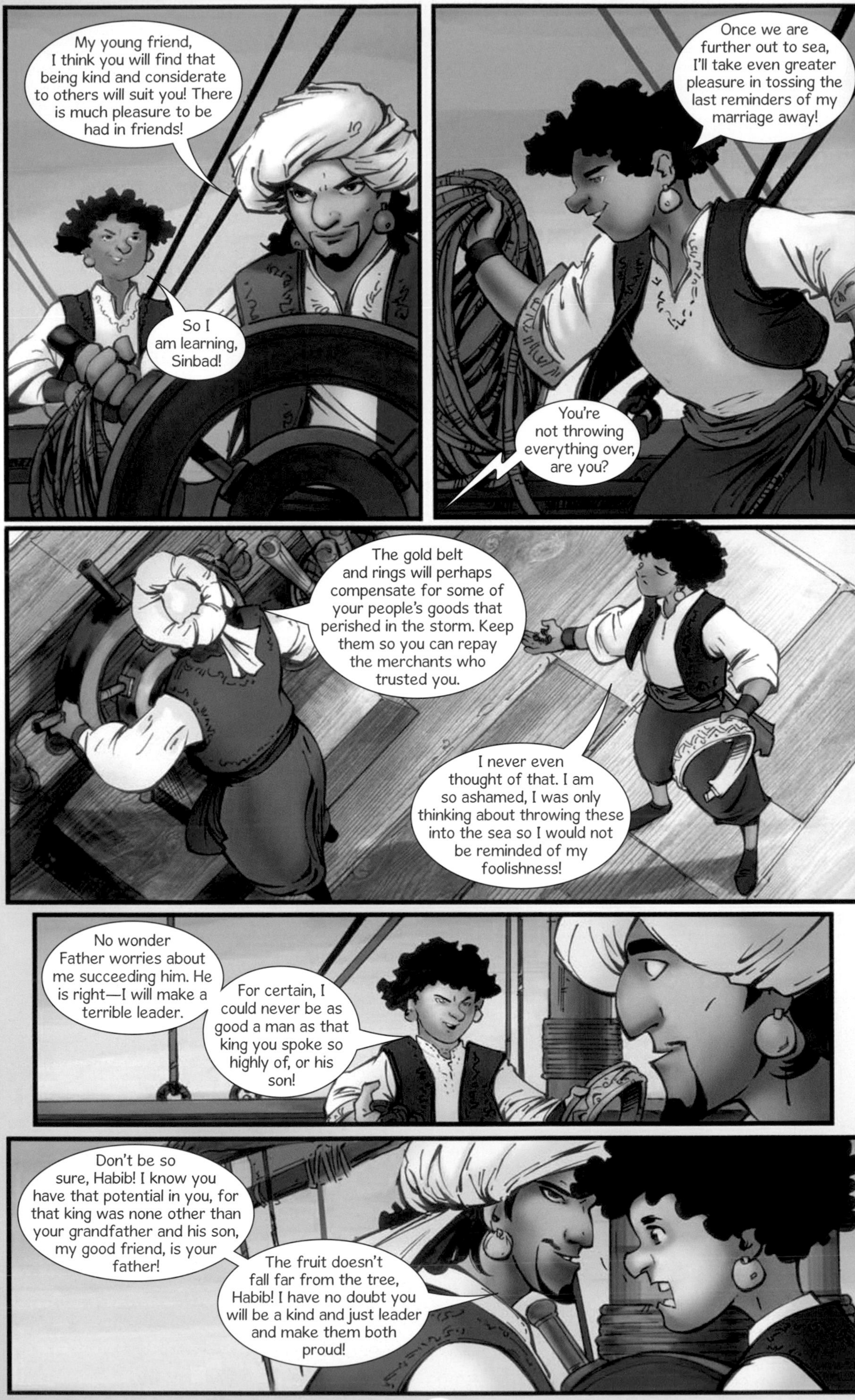
My young friend, I think you will find that being kind and considerate to others will suit you! There is much pleasure to be had in friends!
So I am learning, Sinbad!
Once we are further out to sea, I'll take even greater pleasure in tossing the last reminders of my marriage away!
You're not throwing everything over, are you?
The gold belt and rings will perhaps compensate for some of your people's goods that perished in the storm. Keep them so you can repay the merchants who trusted you.
I never even thought of that. I am so ashamed, I was only thinking about throwing these into the sea so I would not be reminded of my foolishness!
No wonder Father worries about me succeeding him. He is right—I will make a terrible leader.
For certain, I could never be as good a man as that king you spoke so highly of, or his son!
Don't be so sure, Habib! I know you have that potential in you, for that king was none other than your grandfather and his son, my good friend, is your father!
The fruit doesn't fall far from the tree, Habib! I have no doubt you will be a kind and just leader and make them both proud!

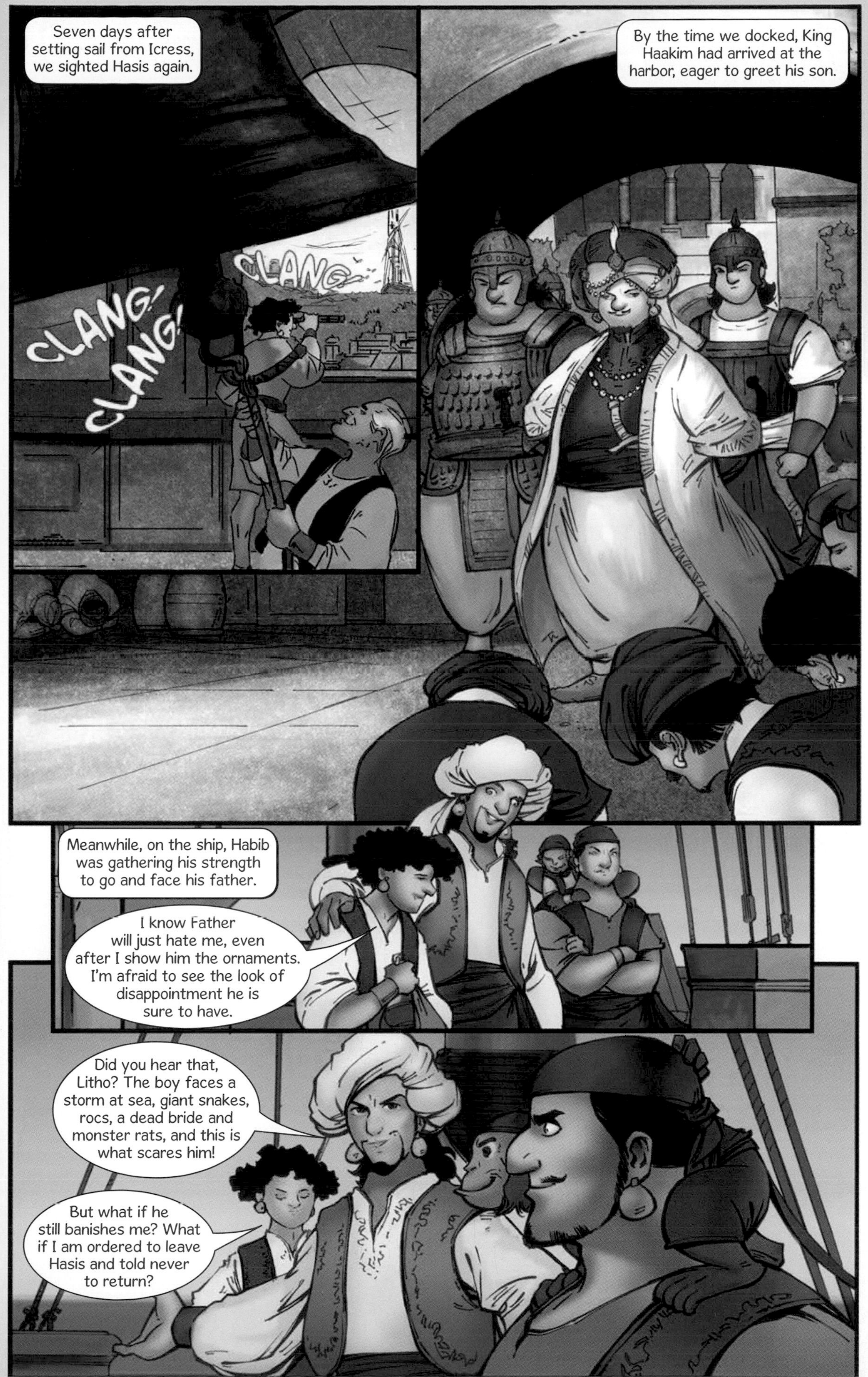
Seven days after setting sail from Icress, we sighted Hasis again.
CLANG!
CLANG!
CLANG!
CLANG!
By the time we docked, King Haakim had arrived at the harbor, eager to greet his son.
Meanwhile, on the ship, Habib was gathering his strength to go and face his father.
I know Father will just hate me, even after I show him the ornaments. I'm afraid to see the look of disappointment he is sure to have.
Did you hear that, Litho? The boy faces a storm at sea, giant snakes, rocs, a dead bride and monster rats, and this is what scares him!
But what if he still banishes me? What if I am ordered to leave Hasis and told never to return?

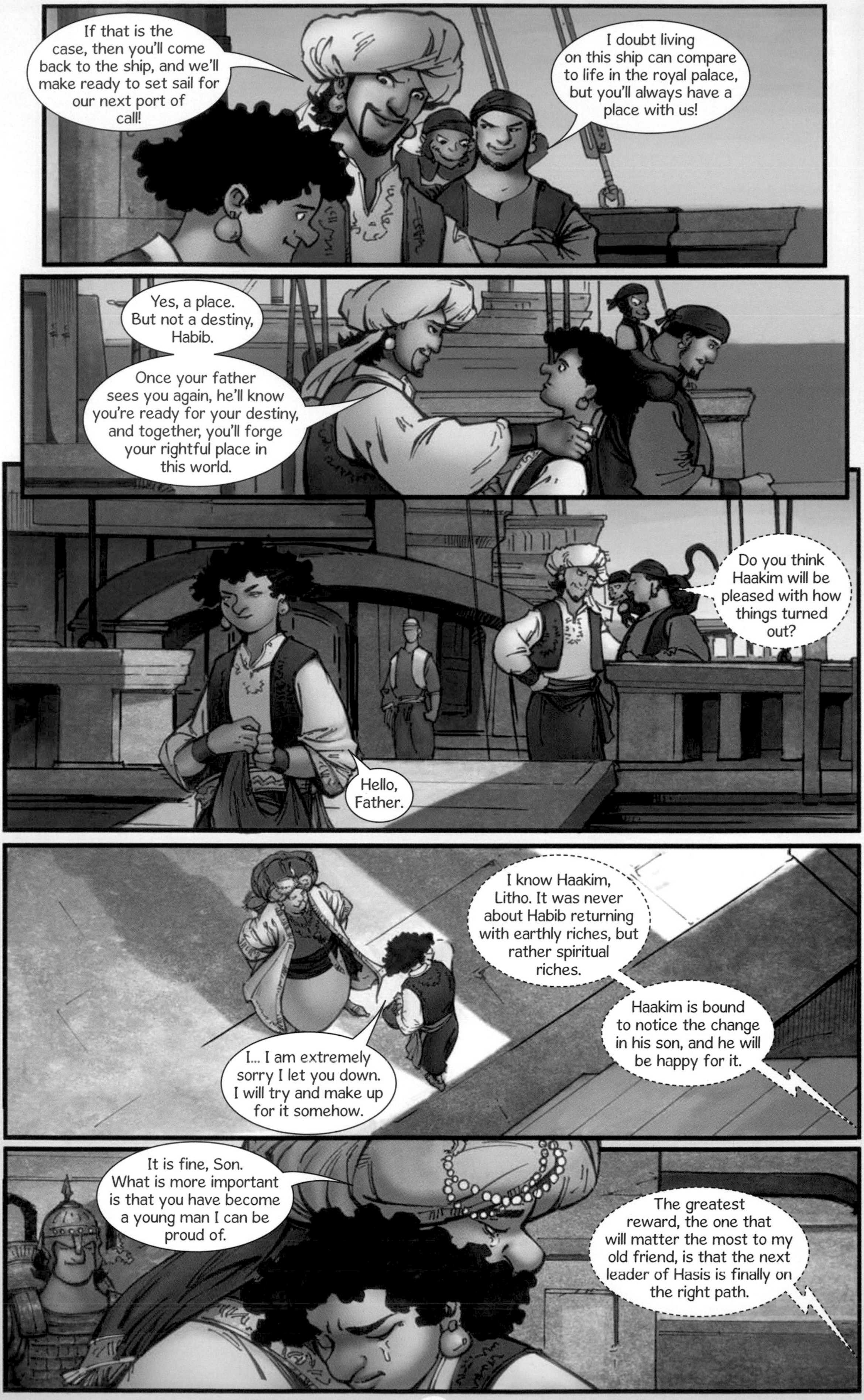
If that is the case, then you'll come back to the ship, and we'll make ready to set sail for our next port of call!
I doubt living on this ship can compare to life in the royal palace, but you'll always have a place with us!
Yes, a place. But not a destiny, Habib.
Once your father sees you again, he'll know you're ready for your destiny, and together, you'll forge your rightful place in this world.
Do you think Haakim will be pleased with how things turned out?
Hello, Father.
I know Haakim, Litho. It was never about Habib returning with earthly riches, but rather spiritual riches.
Haakim is bound to notice the change in his son, and he will be happy for it.
I... I am extremely sorry I let you down. I will try and make up for it somehow.
It is fine, Son. What is more important is that you have become a young man I can be proud of.
The greatest reward, the one that will matter the most to my old friend, is that the next leader of Hasis is finally on the right path.

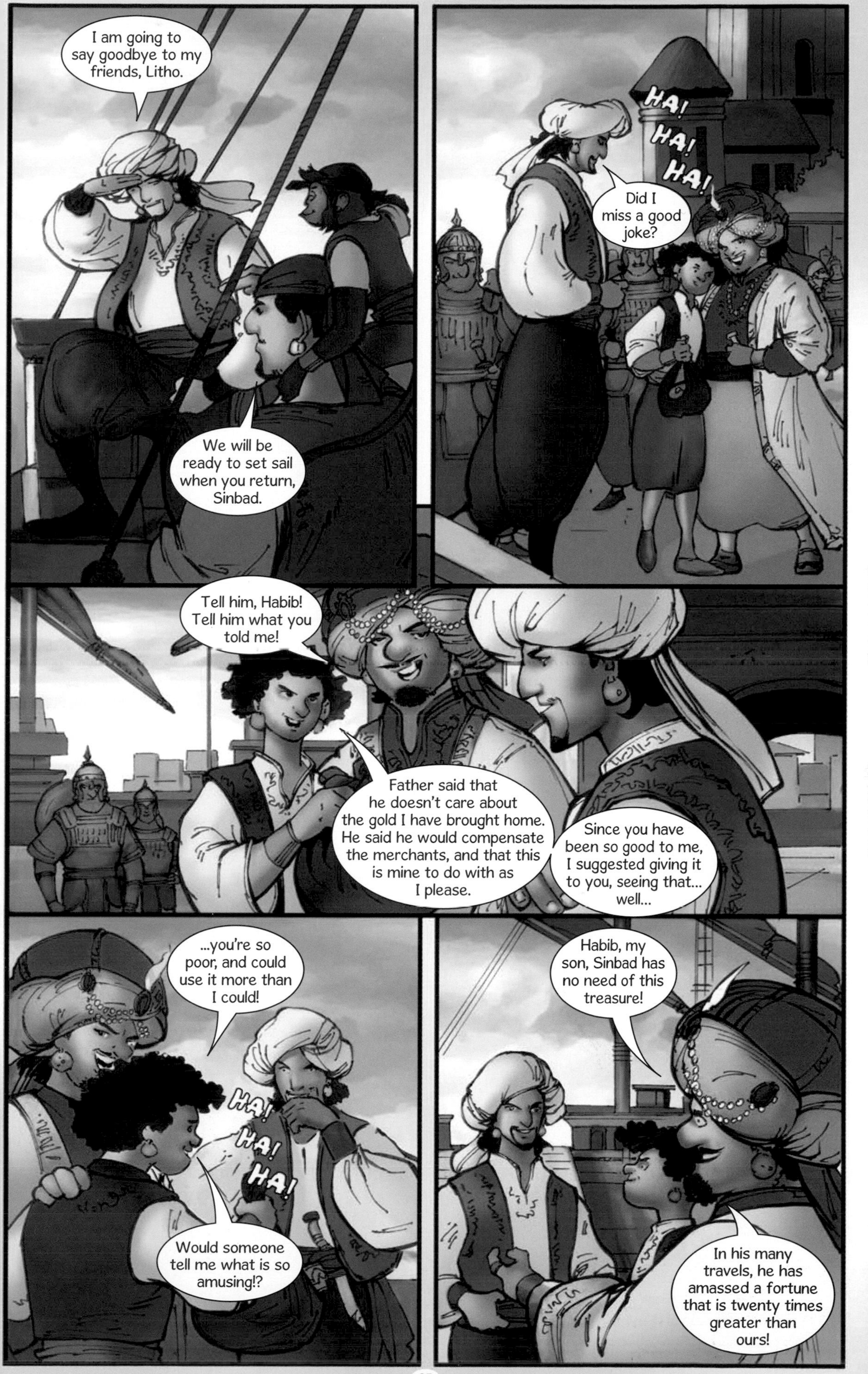
I am going to say goodbye to my friends, Litho.
We will be ready to set sail when you return, Sinbad.
HA! HA! HA!
Did I miss a good joke?
Tell him, Habib! Tell him what you told me!
Father said that he doesn't care about the gold I have brought home. He said he would compensate the merchants, and that this is mine to do with as I please.
Since you have been so good to me, I suggested giving it to you, seeing that... well...
...you're so poor, and could use it more than I could!
HA! HA! HA!
Would someone tell me what is so amusing!?
Habib, my son, Sinbad has no need of this treasure!
In his many travels, he has amassed a fortune that is twenty times greater than ours!

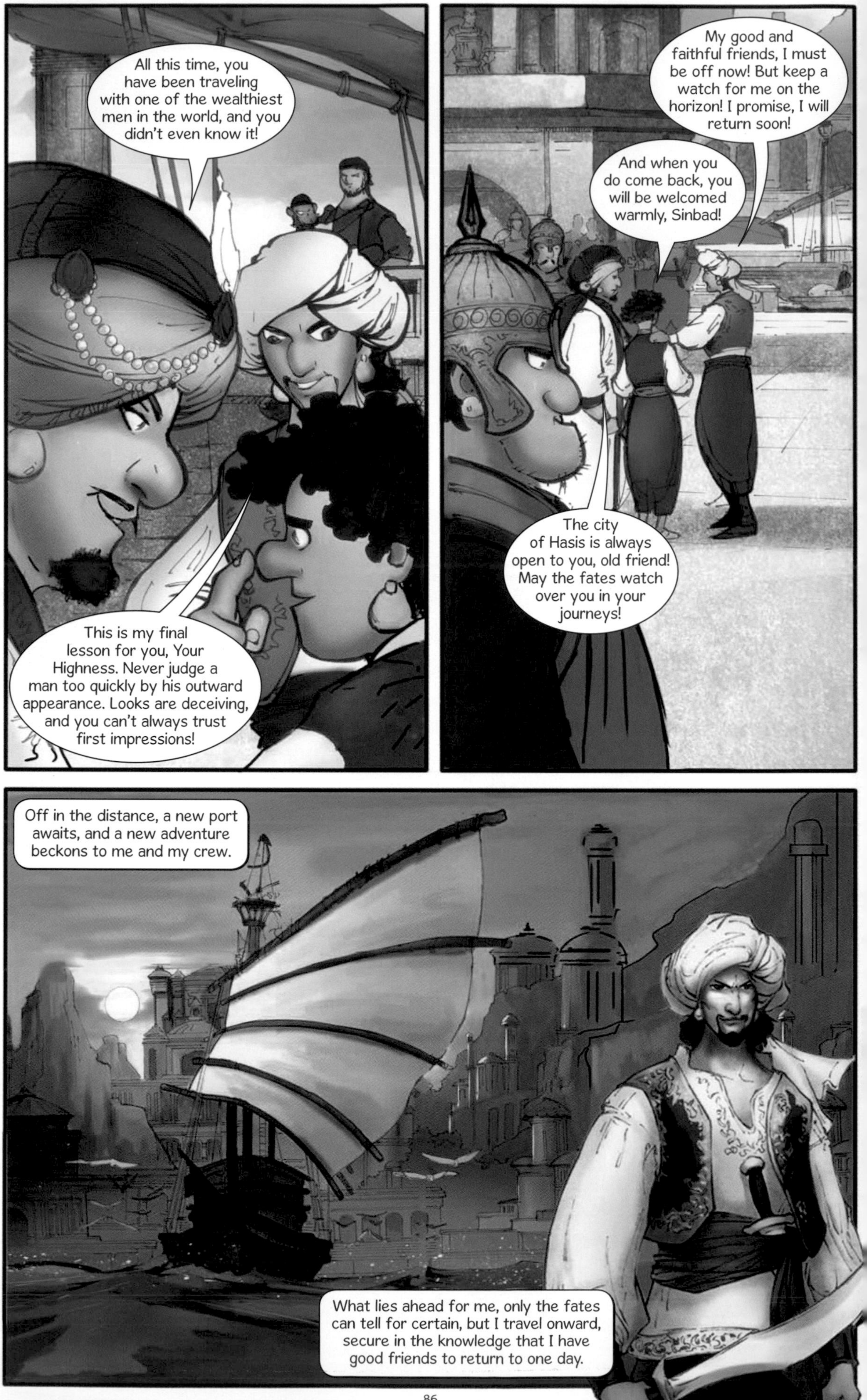
All this time, you have been traveling with one of the wealthiest men in the world, and you didn't even know it!
This is my final lesson for you, Your Highness. Never judge a man too quickly by his outward appearance. Looks are deceiving, and you can't always trust first impressions!
My good and faithful friends, I must be off now! But keep a watch for me on the horizon! I promise, I will return soon!
And when you do come back, you will be welcomed warmly, Sinbad!
The city of Hasis is always open to you, old friend! May the fates watch over you in your journeys!
Off in the distance, a new port awaits, and a new adventure beckons to me and my crew.
What lies ahead for me, only the fates can tell for certain, but I travel onward, secure in the knowledge that I have good friends to return to one day.

TAKE TO THE SEAS!

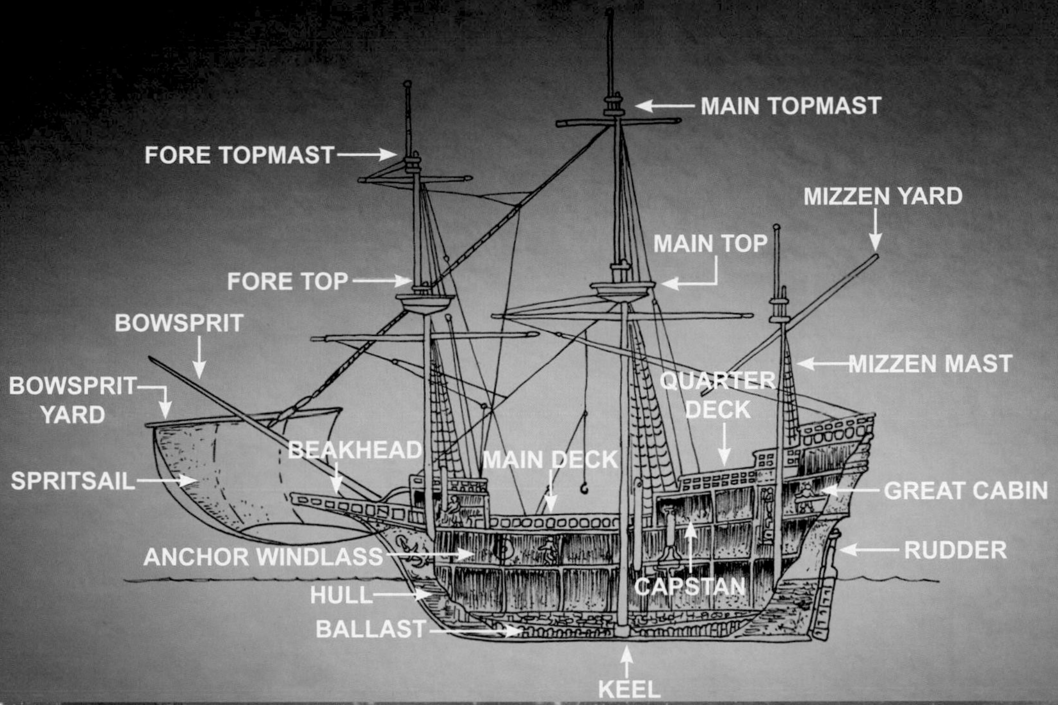
MAIN TOPMAST
FORE TOPMAST
MIZZEN YARD
MAIN TOP
FORE TOP
BOWSPRIT
MIZZEN MAST
BOWSPRIT YARD
QUARTER DECK
BEAKHEAD
MAIN DECK
SPRITSAIL
GREAT CABIN
RUDDER
ANCHOR WINDLASS
CAPSTAN
HULL
BALLAST
KEEL

Sinbad would be lost, quite literally, without his sextant! Every ship needs a navigator, and with this easy to make sextant, you will soon be able to plot your position all across the ocean!

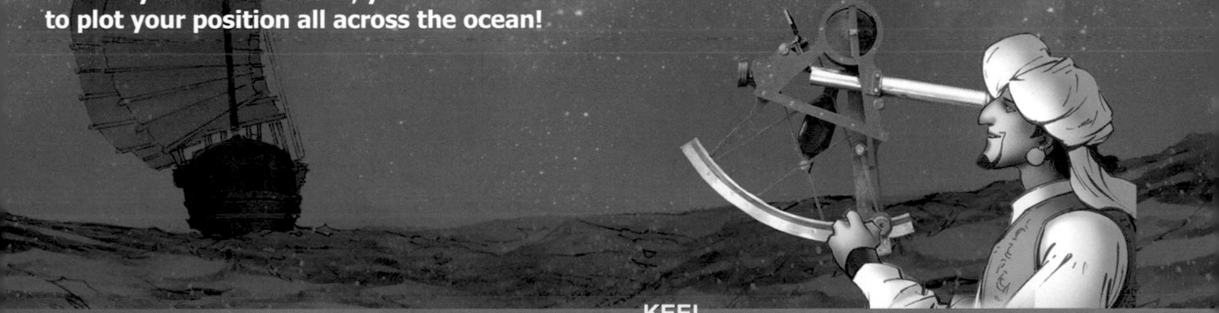

KEEL

What is a sextant?

A sextant is a tool that navigators found invaluable in olden days. They used it to measure the angles between the stars, and then find their point of latitude on the map. That way, the sailors knew where they were even though all they could see around them was the ocean!

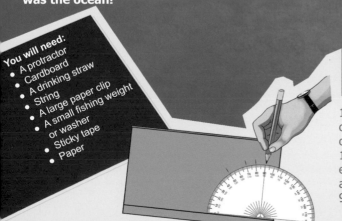

You will need:

- A protractor
- Cardboard
- A drinking straw
- String
- A large paper clip
- A small fishing weight or washer
- Sticky tape
- Paper

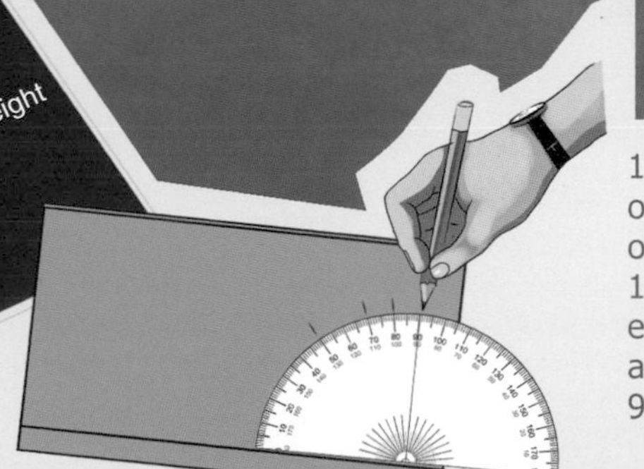

1. Lay your protractor down on your sheet of card and mark the points from 0º to 90º on the card. Label the degrees in units of 10, and then add smaller marks between each line to signify units of 5. Now punch a hole through the place where the 0º and 90º lines meet.

2. Thread your string through the hole in your card. Tie one end of the string to your paper clip to stop it slipping back out of the hole. Tie the other end to your small fishing weight or washer. Now tape your drinking straw along the top of your sheet of card.

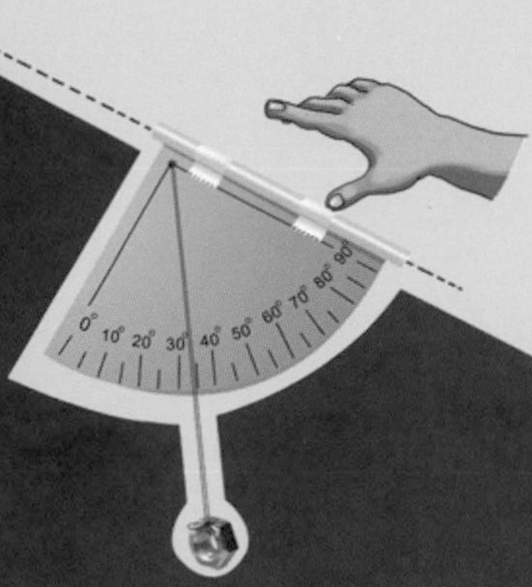
0° 10° 20° 30° 40° 50° 60° 70° 80° 90°

Top Navigator's Tip!

If you poke a small square of paper through the end of your straw, this will help to cut out any unwanted light while you use your sextant!

What is Latitude?

All good maps have lines of latitude and longitude on them to help you find out exactly where a place is. The lines of latitude run horizontally across the map, and each line of latitude has a number. Lines of latitude begin at the equator which is numbered 0°. The numbers get higher the further you get from the equator. The North Pole is 90° north, and the South Pole is 90° south.

Using My Sextant

If you live in a place that is north of the equator, then you are in the northern hemisphere, and to use your sextant you will need to locate Polaris, the Northern Star, in the evening sky.

How to Find The Northern Star

Finding the Northern Star can be tricky at first, but after some practice you'll find it gets easier and easier to find. First, you need to start somewhere away from bright lights (bright lights make it harder to spot the stars), with a clear view of the northern horizon. Now you need to look for the Big Dipper constellation of stars. The Big Dipper looks a little bit like a frying pan with a handle seen from the side. In front of the dipper you will see two bright stars. These are the farthest away from the handle, and are called the Pointer Stars. Now, guess the distance between those two stars, count five of them up away from the end of the Big Dipper, and you'll find Polaris, the Northern Star. The Northern Star is also the last star in the handle of the Little Dipper!

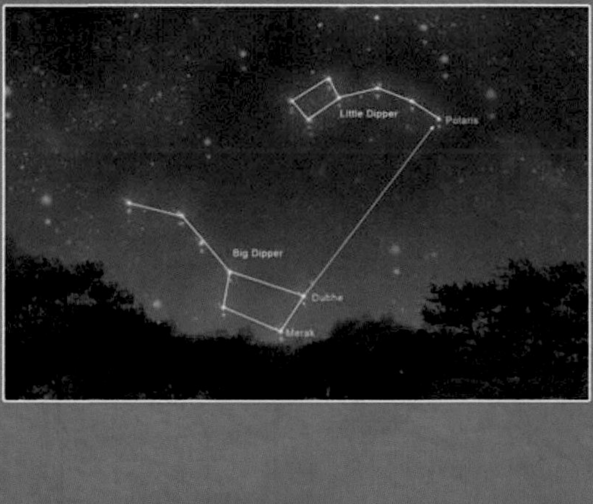
Little Dipper
Polaris
Big Dipper
Dubhe
Merak

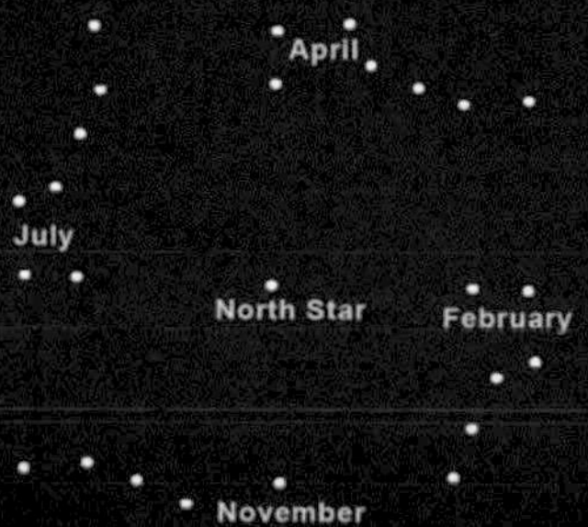
April
July
North Star
February
November

Rotating Stars!

The position of the Big Dipper around the Northern Star changes depending on the time of night, and of the year, because the stars rotate in the sky. This chart shows you the position of the Big Dipper in the early evening, at different times of year.

Time To Use Your Sextant!

Now that you have spotted the Northern Star, find it through the straw on your sextant. The weighted string will point down toward the degree of latitude, telling you your position on the map!

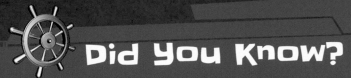

Did You Know?

The State of Alaska's flag shows the eight stars of the Big Dipper and Polaris!

Navigating in the South

If you live south of the equator, then you are in the southern hemisphere. You will need to use the Southern Cross constellation to help you find due South. This is a small constellation of four bright stars, in the shape of a cross, with two bright 'pointer stars' nearby, pointing toward them.

Finding The Southern Cross

On a clear evening, as soon as night falls, face south, and look up into the sky. You will see two very bright stars, quite near the horizon, more or less on top of the other. These are the 'pointer stars'. Imagine a line going up, and you will soon come to the cross. When you have found the Southern Cross, draw an imaginary line down from its brightest star for four and a half times the length of the cross. Now drop a line straight down to the horizon, and you've found due south!

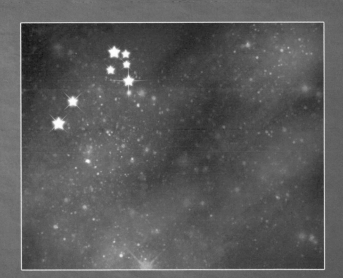

Remember: Finding either the Northern Star or the Southern Cross isn't as easy as finding the moon. It will take patience and practice, but after a short while, you'll find it gets easier and easier!

 Happy navigating, Captain!

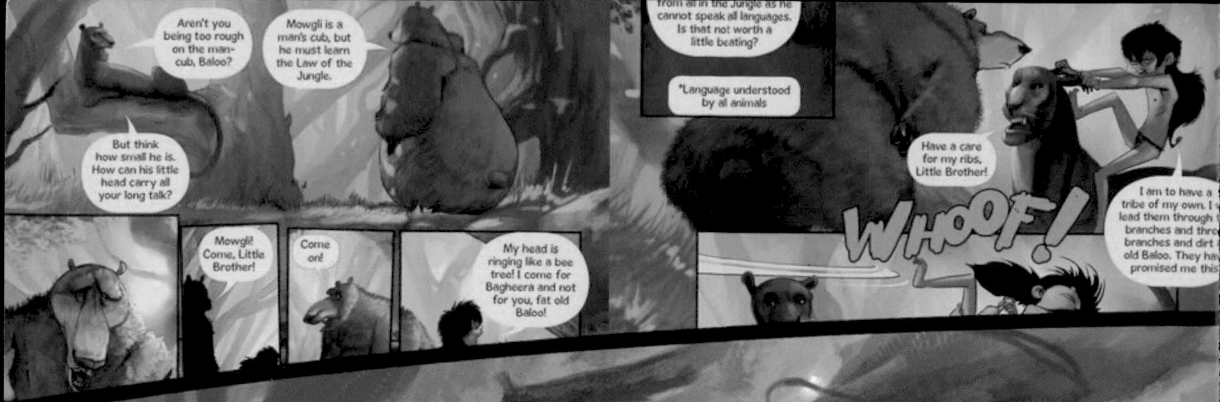

Aren't you being too rough on the man-cub, Baloo?
Mowgli is a man's cub, but he must learn the Law of the Jungle.
But think how small he is. How can his little head carry all your long talk?
cannot speak all languages. Is that not worth a little beating?
*Language understood by all animals
Have a care for my ribs, Little Brother!
WHOOF!
Mowgli! Come, Little Brother!
Come on!
My head is ringing like a bee tree! I come for Bagheera and not for you, fat old Baloo!

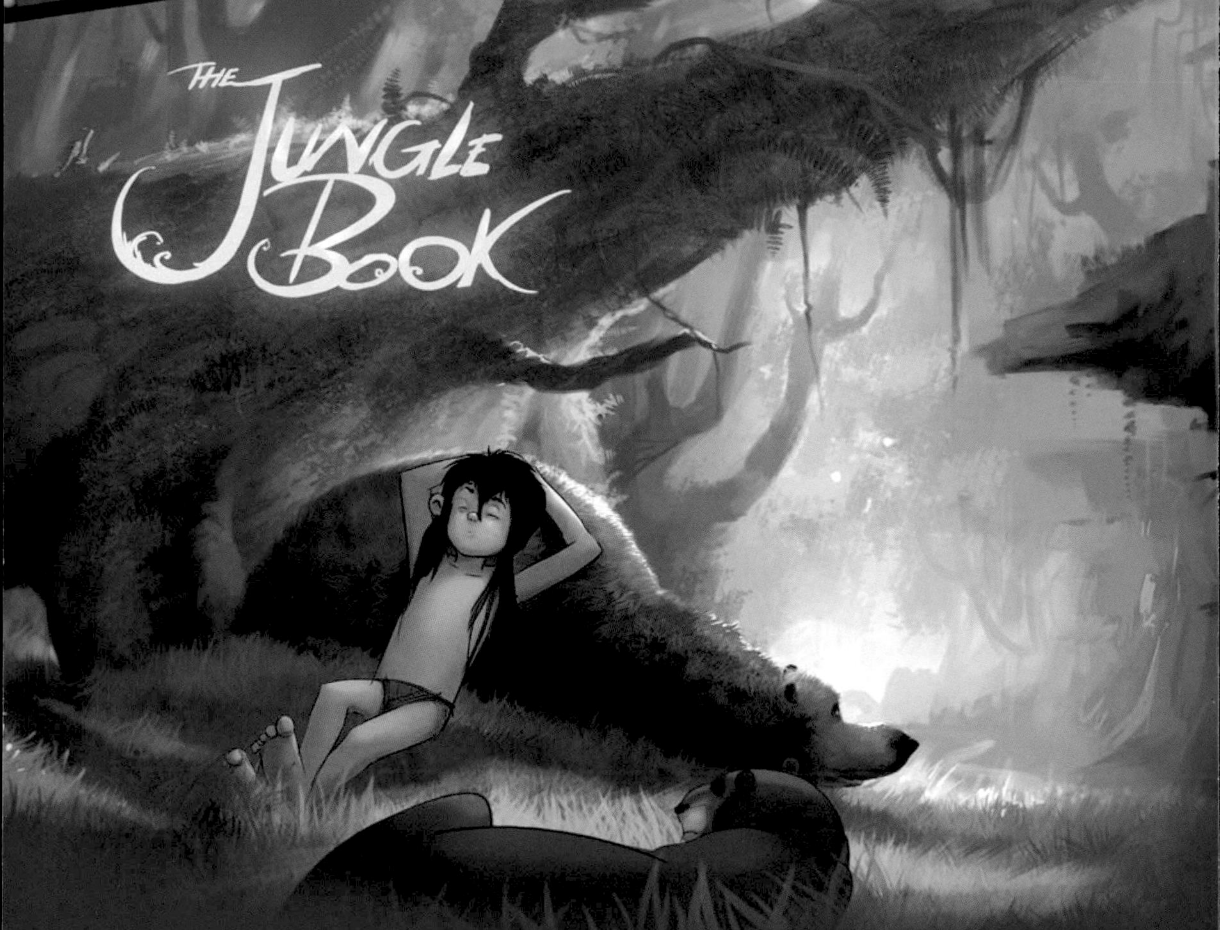

The Jungle Book

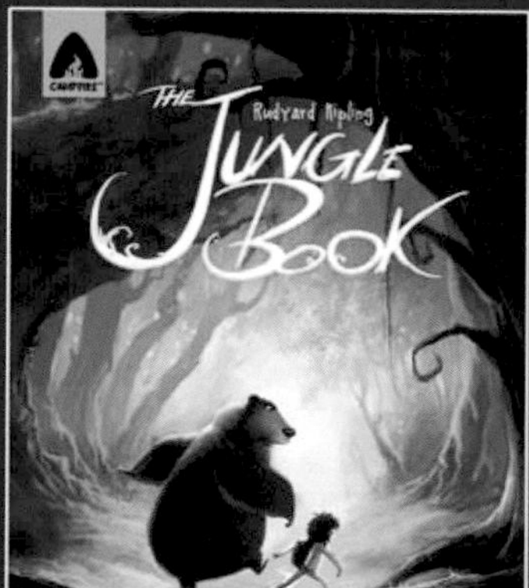

Rudyard Kipling
The Jungle Book
Adapted by Dan Johnson Illustrated by Amit Tayal

The adventure of a lifetime begins on the night a man-cub escapes certain doom at the hands of the tiger Shere Khan. In defiance of the tiger, the boy, Mowgli, is taken in by the Seeonee Wolf Pack and made a member.

Mowgli comes of age in the jungle and is taught how to survive by Bagheera, the black panther; Baloo, the brown bear; and Kaa, the python.

Always lurking nearby, though, is Shere Khan, who is determined that Mowgli will be his prey. But the hunter soon becomes the hunted when the boy and the tiger square off in an epic struggle in which only one will survive.

But greater than his fight with Shere Khan is the conflict Mowgli faces as he tries to find a place among wolves and humans—neither of whom truly accept him as one of their own.

Written by Rudyard Kipling

Illustrated by Amit Tayal

www.campfire.co.in

Ancient Egypt. In the time of pyramids and pharaohs...

A beautiful young princess has arrived at the grand capital of Memphis—home to the legendary pharaoh Rhampsinitus. She has journeyed from the western lands, apparently in search of a husband. While meeting her suitors, the princess becomes privy to a secret tale.

It is a story of desperation, thievery, and murder. But it is also a story of family, sacrifice, and love. As this tale is laid bare before her, the princess learns of three impossible feats of brotherhood, ingenuity, and the boldness of a man who would thwart the will of a pharaoh.

Packed with action, intrigue, and romance, this is the story of one of the greatest thieves of the ancient world—the 'Treasure Thief' who went on to become the 'Treasured Thief'!

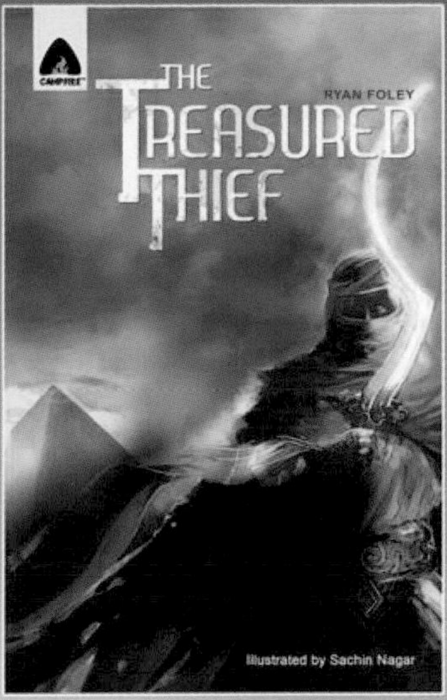
CAMPFIRE
THE TREASURED THIEF
RYAN FOLEY
Illustrated by Sachin Nagar

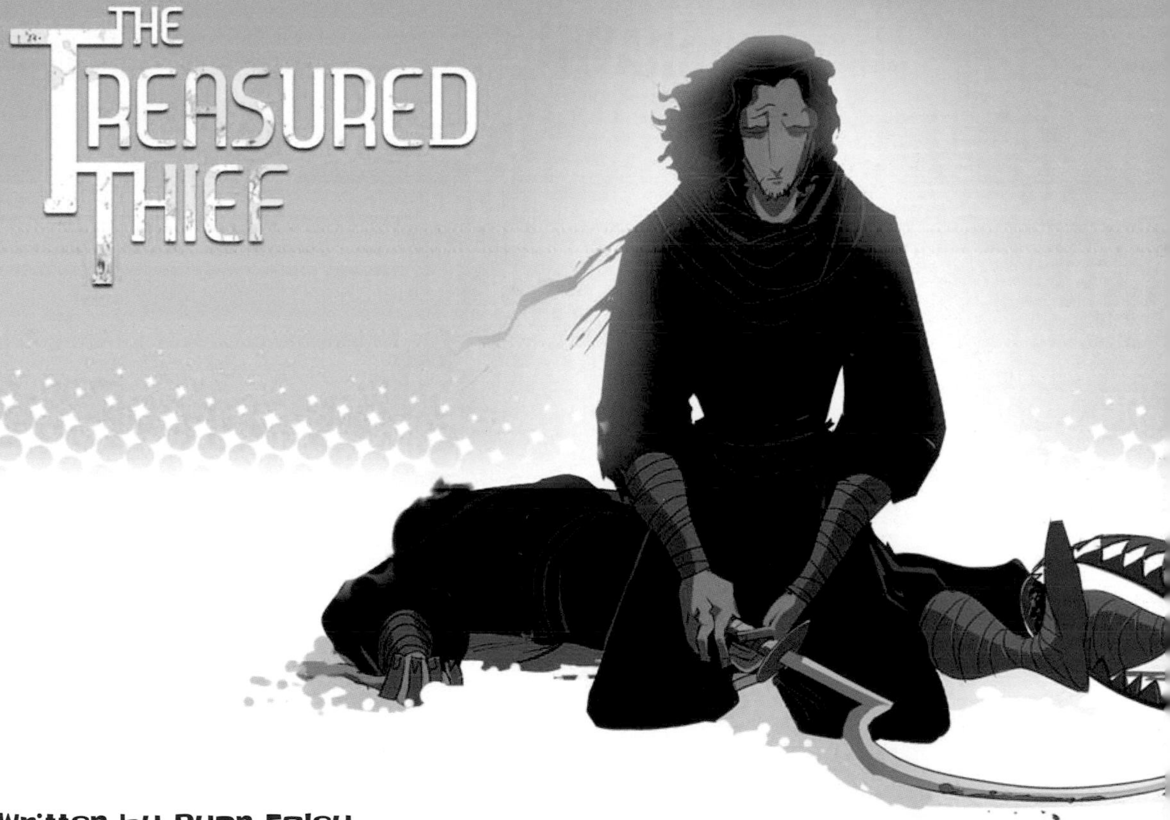
THE TREASURED THIEF

Written by Ryan Foley

Illustrated by Sachin Nagar

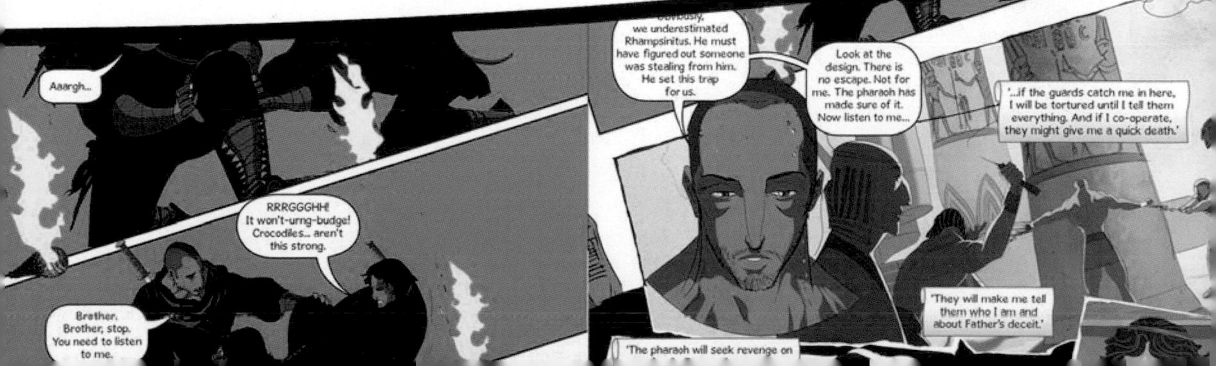
Aaargh...
RRRGGGHH! It won't-urng-budge! Crocodiles... aren't this strong.
Brother. Brother, stop. You need to listen to me.
we underestimated Rhampsinitus. He must have figured out someone was stealing from him. He set this trap for us.
Look at the design. There is no escape. Not for me. The pharaoh has made sure of it. Now listen to me...
'...if the guards catch me in here, I will be tortured until I tell them everything. And if I co-operate, they might give me a quick death.'
'They will make me tell them who I am and about Father's deceit.'
'The pharaoh will seek revenge on

You may also like to read other titles from our **ORIGINALS SERIES**

Sidney Williams
Mark Jones
THE DUSK SOCIETY

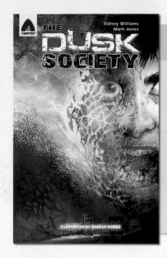

THE DUSK SOCIETY

In the hands of the newest recruits of The Dusk Society lies the fate of the world. Under the leadership of an evil man named Pierceblood, a whole host of terrifying monsters, including Count Dracula and Doctor Frankenstein, are getting ready to destroy the world. A secret organization created after World War I, The Dusk Society has to ensure that ancient, magical weapons do not fall into the wrong hands. Will they be able to stop Pierceblood's evil plan and save the world?

ALI BABA AND THE FORTY THIEVES RELOADED

In the reloaded version of the story of Ali Baba and the Forty Thieves, the world of Arabian Nights gives way to modern day Mumbai—the men wear suits and carry guns; their chosen steed has wheels instead of legs. An honest and hardworking auto rickshaw driver, Ali Baba's life is far from perfect. A chaotic sequence of events leads him, and a gang of forty thieves, on a merry chase through the suburbs of a modern metropolis. See how the turn of events, a few good friends, and presence of mind delivers Ali Baba from the most impossible of situations.

Ali Baba and the Forty Thieves
RELOADED
AMIT TAYAL

LEWIS HELFAND
PHOTOBOOTH
Illustrated by
SACHIN NAGAR

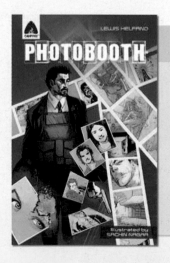

PHOTO BOOTH

A deadly drug is about to flood the streets of New York City. The police has no leads on who is producing the drug, or where it is coming from. As far as Praveer Rajani, a ruthless Interpol agent, is concerned, the only way to prevent countless deaths lies in a handful of mysterious photographs. In the photographs, Praveer can see images of places that he has never known, and people he has long forgotten. But the photographs hold much more than clues to find the culprits —they carry the answers to the mystery of his own life!